The Evil League

A Kayne Sorenson Mystery

Thomas Paul Severino

Thomas Paul Severino

The Evil League

A Kayne Sorenson Mystery

Thomas Paul Severino

Copyright 2020

Pollywog Pond Communications, Ft. Lauderdale

tomseverino.com

tomseverino100@gmail.com

ISBN: 978-1-7343753-9-8

Cover: "The Zodiacal Light" from Travelot Astronomical Drawings by E.L. Travelot (The Smithsonian Collection)

The Evil League

Also by Thomas Paul Severino

The Kayne Sorenson Mysteries: The Quartet of Blood

Seed Blood

Tribal Blood

Stage Blood

Ancient Blood

The Kayne Sorenson Mysteries: The Quartet of Evil

The Evil Genius

The Shadow of Evil

The Pearl of Great Evil

The Evil League

The Kayne Sorenson Mysteries: The New Adventures

The Crystal Orb

The Flower of Gold

The Amazing Adventures of Rebecca Quinto

The Frozen Diva

The Lost Museum

The Last Maya

Thomas Paul Severino

In the beginning, God created the heavens and the earth, and the earth was waste and void. And the darkness was on the face of the deep.

– Genesis 1.1

Then tell me, O Critias, how will a man choose the ruler that shall rule over him? Will he not choose a man who has first established order in himself, knowing that any decision that has its spring from anger or pride or vanity can be multiplied a thousandfold in its effects upon the citizens? – Plato, The Republic

Thomas Paul Severino

The Evil League

For Keith

Thomas Paul Severino

Dramatis Personae

For Sorenson and Sechi Consulting Detectives, Inc.

- Kayne J. Sorenson, Ph.D., Professor of Psycho-Criminology; Partner, Sorenson and Sechi, Consulting Detectives, Inc.; Sagittarius

- Nichola M. Sechi, Partner, Sorenson and Sechi, Consulting Detectives, Inc.; Cancer
- The Honorable Kristof (The Kris) Saxe-Coburg Gotha-Koháry Sorenson, Student, University of San Francisco; Aries
- Jessamyn R. Trasker, Housekeeper; Taurus
- Andi S. Rodriguez, Administrative Assistant, Sorenson and Sechi, Consulting Detectives, Inc.; Gemini
- Rebecca S. Quinto, President and CEO, The Frischer Museum of Fine Arts, Ft. Lauderdale; Cancer
- Mark C. Gadarn, Journalist, CBN, Inc.; Ophiuchus
- Jiro (Jack) Ishida, Sensei; The Year of the Dragon
- Scott P. Iverson, Director of Technology, Aerie Enterprises, Inc.; Capricorn
- Mitchell L. Sorenson, MD, President and CEO, Aerie Enterprises, Inc.; Aquarius
- Thomas M. (Kick) Sorenson, Jr, Vice President of Operations, Aerie Enterprises, Inc.; Sagittarius
- Priyanka I. Ngwogu, Ph.D., Professor of Astrophysics, University of California, Berkeley; Obatalá,
- Eric N. Sorenson, Sagittarius
- Austin R. McDaniel, Head Soccer Coach, University of San Francisco; Pisces
- Jesse L. Okeyo, Soccer Team Captain, University of San Francisco; Baobab
- Raul Dos Santos, Virgo
- Matthew A. Crowley, RN; Virgo
- Chouko, an Akita; Gemini
- Alice, an Australian Border Collie; Unknown

Law Enforcement

- Rosario S. Martell, Contra Costa County Detective Inspector; Scorpio
- Timothy B. Leonard, Contra Costa County Medical Examiner; Gemini
- Ruben D. Martell, San Mateo County Detective Inspector; Libra
- Captain Martin Simmons, SFPD; Aquarius

Blackhawk Navy Air Warfare Center

- Petty Officer 3rd Class Brian D. LaCroix, USN; Sagittarius
- Captain Michael P. Clarke-Mills, USN, Director of Blackhawk; Leo
- Chief Petty Officer Jacob (Jake) Davies, Director of Security, Blackhawk; Aries
- Martina G. Howard, Ph.D., Director of Research, Blackhawk; Virgo
- Seaman Derek Sanders, USN, Security Guard, Blackhawk, Taurus

Ballet Purgatorio

- Maria L. Berman, Artistic Director; Gemini
- Robert T. Amenti, MFA, Choreographer and Danseur; Pisces
- Artem D. Eglievsky, Danseur Extraordinaire; Leo
- Ashraf Sah, Board Chair; Capricorn
- John Shepherd Marsden, Honorary Board President; Ophiuchus
- Olivia Ortiz Leon, Company Regisseur; Libra
- Antonia K. Ivanova, Prima Ballerina Assoluta; Aries
- Phobe Garcia-Dolan, Ballerina; Scorpio
- Michael Lee, Musical Director; Virgo
- Raymond E. Sandell, Danseur; Cancer

Estiatório Darius Sastre

- Darius P. Sastre, Restauranteur; Taurus
- Spiros Papatonis, *Maître d'*; Ophiuchus
- Giannis Papatonis, Bartender; Libra

Tea House of the Autumn Moon

- Max Chang, Proprietor; The Year of the Dog
- Constance Xing Zhen, Ph.D., Professor of Fine Arts, The University of San Francisco; The Year of the Ox
- Wan Guchan; Security Guard, The San Francisco Historical Society; The Year of the Monkey

And

- Gretchen Rockland, Ph.D.
- Jasmine Elizabeth Stokes, Ph.D.
- Wade Bronson, Ph.D.
- Melchior Aaron Chandler, Ph.D.
- Esmail Faiz Haqqani
- Diana Culvert Sans
- Kalisto Serian
- Gantulga Nergūl

Thomas Paul Severino

Prologue: Quench
Tassajara, California

The woman in the towel kissed the back of the head of the naked man, who was sound asleep. His body had kicked free of the covers. Fresh from the shower, she picked up his underwear and pieces of his uniform, dropping them on the bench at the foot of the bed. She continued to tiptoe around the room, searching for her jeans and a specific, very nerdy science t-shirt. He had bought it for her when they spent the weekend in the Napa Valley. That trip was soon after they met, and they had rarely left the room.

It was her favorite. White with a black protest fist gripping a red microscope, the shirt's logo read "Act in Defiance, Embrace Science! Resist Ignorance." She pulled it over her head and stepped into her briefs and jeans. Gathering her hair into a banded ponytail, she added half-socks and running shoes to her ensemble. Finally, she included a dash of beauty by knotting a silk scarf around her neck.

Light makeup in the car...

As she reached behind the door to grab her lab coat, the petite scientist looked back at the face-down, sleeping man beauty -- broad back, substantial shoulders, strong arms, 'dat ass,' and those incredible legs spread out on three-quarters of her bed. His military buzz was just a whisper of fuzz on a handsome head partially buried in the pillow.

Hot Navy guy, six years her junior – sexual stamina for days, oh, hell, yes... and a sweet guy, also. "The *Physikoi* Babes," as she called her gal pal colleagues, were all so jealous, and the family in Milwaukee – well, not quite ready for Petty Officer 3rd Class Brian Daniel LaCroix.

As she passed through the kitchen, Gretchen Rockland, Ph.D., opened the refrigerator for her lunch. An apple and a bagel wrapped in plastic found their way into a coat pocket as she grabbed a to-go cup of automatically brewed coffee from the counter. The perky academic stepped into the crisp Sierra Nevada mountain air, heading for her car. As she crossed the parking lot, the night was full of the serene sounds of the wilderness community: a cricket's chirp, an owl's cry, and a coyote's howl. Out over the foothills, a thunderstorm sent forks of lightning onto the dark crests of the steep escarpment.

I should make it to the Center before the rain. Easy.

The Blackhawk Navy Air Warfare Center sat in its own valley among the rolling foothills of California's Mt. Diablo. Rocket propellant analysis was the priority project. The government hired chemists and engineers from universities worldwide to test the military's rocket fuel. Researchers could adjust their schedules according to the equipment's availability and often worked long hours into the night.

***

"I am so sorry."

"*Perdona, Señorita.*"

"Whoa. There you go. Steady on. I think you dropped these."

Gretchen bent to help the woman to her feet and retrieve the fallen cleaning items. The maintenance worker swayed a bit on the way up and steadied herself with a close clutch. The woman apologized again for the collision. Gretchen held the door as the cleaning woman maneuvered her work cart into the extensive research lab. She followed the staffer in and made for the NMR area. Punching the access code into the door's keypad, the scientist went inside. A motion detector lit up the smaller room.

Gretchen Rockland placed her bagel and apple on the desk next to the laminated sign that announced: "Absolutely No Food in the Lab." After shaking the mouse, she logged in and set up the program.

"Wake up, Ms. Brückner. We have work to do."

***

Why was this woman dead? It made no sense.

The night security guard had called the police, and they were on their way. He looked at the woman sprawled out on the floor of the lab. She was dressed casually, wearing a white lab coat. Three file folders spilled next to the body, and the contents of one of the big pockets, the one she had not landed on, were scattered close by.

The Navy security guard thought perhaps it was a sudden heart or brain malfunction, one of those dead-before-they-hit-the-ground things. There were no other researchers in the lab complex. He remembered there were few cars in the parking lot and that they had glistened with the unexpected night shower. It was 3 AM.

Through the large inside windows, he could see a cleaning woman move her cart, mop, and pail out into the hallway. She was making for the exit, and it looked like she was done. Other maintenance folks walked through the outer corridor, entering and exiting offices and lab facilities.

Dropping to one knee, the guard placed two fingers on the side of the woman's neck on the floor. No pulse. He was careful not to disturb anything while awaiting the officer in charge of night security and the police.

Probably should not have touched her.

As he scanned the inner research lab, he noticed one of the monitors blinking a red warning message that took up the entire screen. A flashing light from the monster machine in the center of the room created a red and yellow spinning halo.

Three days on the job, and Seaman Derek Sanders had come up with a corpse.

Thomas Paul Severino

Chapter One: Calling in the Night

Morgan Territory Regional Preserve, Livermore, California

Nick Sechi's Journal

"Damn, Kayne, please answer it. Say you're me, Boss."

I turned face down and snuggled under the covers in an attempt to get back to sleep. The ground was hard, but the bedroll was warm and soft.

"Huh? Oh, sorry, my love. It's Rosario. Hope nothing's… Hey Rosie, lass, What's going… Yes, this is Kayne. Nick is too sleepy… ah, we are planning to stay at the campsite for a few more days … What's that?"

He listened a bit to the county police detective.

"Right. OK, we are on our way. Please keep the site uncontaminated. Thank you."

I felt his firm hand on my back.

"Let's go, my love. The game is on."

***

Kayne drove through the campsite and headed southwest out of the park. The road continued around the mountains and then cut back due west to the Navy facility deep in the valley. It was just after three am, and there was not a car on the highway. The headlights of our rented Subaru Forrester cut through the darkness and climbed up the canyon walls.

I popped a cold caffeine triple-shot drink from our gear and handed Kayne an ashwagandha supplement drink for energy. Our nephew, Kris, put us on to this medicinal herb from India. He was all about natural fitness. I called it "The Green Shit."

"You doing OK, Boss?"

"Wide awake, my love. No worries. That storm that blew through seems to be heading off to the east."

Our evening of relaxation was so fantastic. After a day of hiking in the park, we made a campfire supper and did things in the firelight that would have frightened the bears away.

When the storm broke, we took our lovemaking into the pup tent. The pyrotechnics and the booming outside were almost matched by the sparks and the gasping we were generating inside. At one point, I remember a restart of the very energetic and passionate coupling in the warm night rain. My husband is an accomplished lover, and our sensual variations are well-coordinated. We have great chemistry.

The country vacation to the northeast of our home in San Francisco came at the end of a case of international intrigue and thrilling adventure. We spent the better part of two weeks wandering from the Napa Valley over to the Sierra Nevadas, hiking, kayaking, dining, and making love, mainly in the great outdoors.

I looked over at my Bossman. Damn, I was still hot for teacher. We were about the same size at 6'2" and 198 pounds of lean muscle. He is dark-haired and wears it savage-long. An Australian import, he has one of the keenest minds in the field of criminology.

I was a buff, ginger Bronx Boy, the only male in a big and very dramatic Italian American Family. Both of us liked martial arts, and he was the better of the two of us -- a lot better, for he kicked my ass, to be truthful. Not bad for a professor of psycho-criminology and his husband, a former member of law enforcement.

We joined forces to consult on crime-fighting about two years ago to form Sorenson Sechi Consulting Detectives, Inc. Our work involved cases large and small at home and abroad. I was the chronicler, publishing our adventure blog, The Kayne Sorenson Mysteries, which had just over a hundred thousand followers.

Oh, yeah – I forgot. Kayne is a triplet with one older brother.

"One in a million births are spontaneous triplets, Nick. Eric, Kick, and I are all gay. The odds are off the charts. We made biological history, my love."

"Also, Mitch. That sexy dude is as gay as Uncle Brother Boy."

We said the next line from the film "Sordid Lives" in unison and laughed.

"Nobody's that gay."

"Mitch is adopted, remember. So different DNA."

"Ace must have been crazy for one straight son among you four -- like he was running a gay bathhouse, for heaven's sake."

"As accepting as he is, I think Da would like this new child to be straight. Would make for more diversity in the Sorenson clan."

He chuckled at the thought of his father and his new wife in the Outback, expecting a new arrival. The former Aussie Marine was an alpha dog of the rough, robust, and ballsy kind.

Ace's triplet sons also had another commonality. Each had a variation of a chronic brain disorder.

"Nothing wrong with my brain, my love. I am a mutant with superior intellectual powers."

Kayne has Attention-Deficit/Hyperactivity Disorder. His thought processes went in many directions at once. He could think on many levels ("Hey, look, a bright shiny object"). He was able to bring it all under control and stay focused by using determination and sometimes meditation.

Kayne's brother, Kick, had Bipolar II Disorder, for which he reluctantly took medication. Mitch, his husband and brother, was the force behind keeping "The Hot Mess" in line and on his meds. Without them, the superb athlete had physical and emotional highs and lows.

Aversion to taking medicine was also a characteristic of the third "trip," Eric, Kris' father. He needed to take regular doses of antipsychotic medications to control his schizophrenia. When he was on the proper drugs, reality made sense.

"There's the turn-off, Boss."

It started to rain again as we took the service road through Tassajara's town center and into some rolling hills. A highway marked "private" took us to the guardhouse for the Blackhawk Navy Air Warfare Center.

Checking our IDs, the young guard gave us directions.

"You can't miss the lab complex, Dr. Sorenson. Look for the ambulance and State Trooper vehicles. They will have their lights on."

Chapter Two: Quench

Blackhawk Navy Air Warfare Center, Blackhawk, California

Nick Sechi's Journal

"Dr. Rockland was, unfortunately, murdered. Has her family been notified of her death? Please keep your law enforcement officers back for just a few more minutes. While my conclusions are irrefutable, I want to check out a few last details."

Detective Inspector Rosario Martell bent over my recumbent husband and asked, "Kayne, how was the woman killed? She appears to have collapsed near the doorway. There is no blood or evidence of physical trauma. Massive stroke or heart attack? Not murder. "

"She suffocated, Chief Inspector. The forensic scientists will bear me out."

Kneeling next to the dead woman, Kayne used gloved hands to examine the woman's extremities. He leaned down and smelled her lips, hands, and clothing. My Doctor of Psycho-Criminology gently retracted the victim's eyelids, exposing the orbs' white sclera with great care. He beckoned to the county's medical examiner, Dr. Timothy Leonard, cautioning the young man to be careful where he stepped.

"Here is the evidence that supports asphyxiation as the cause of death."

He pointed and continued. "Please observe -- small red or purple splotches in the eyes and on the face and neck. The autopsy will disclose petechial hemorrhages in the woman's lungs. That is a certainty, Doctor."

I pointed out, "There is also a small degree of foam in the nostrils and the corners of the mouth, Boss."

"Excellent observation, Nick. Our unfortunate victim struggled to breathe in her last moments, and mucus from the lungs created the foam you see as it mixed with the air. It would appear she pulled off her silk scarf and dropped it there as she tried to get air."

The scarf on the lab floor was near the dropped papers, a tablet, and a small broken glass tube. A bagel in plastic wrap and a few other objects that must have spilled off the desk as the unfortunate woman staggered were also scattered near the body.

While down on one knee, Kayne took hold of a metal rectangle from among the ruins and held it in two fingers. He began holding it to the light and sighting down each of its two sides, front and back. A black bang flopped over the left side of his forehead and into his eyes as he looked up, pushed it back, and held up that same free hand as the Police Inspector introduced two individuals who were carefully picking their way into the room.

"Kayne, this is Captain Michael Clarke-Mills, Director of Blackhawk, and Doctor Martina Howard, the Center's Director of Research. Folks -- Dr. Kayne Sorenson and Mr. Nick Sechi, investigative consultants."

"Officer Martell, is local law enforcement incapable of dealing with a simple case of medical complications on its own? The woman collapsed while locked inside her research lab. Heart attack or stroke?"

"Kayne and Nick are friends and colleagues, Captain, and were in the immediate area. No offense to the medical examiner, but the county's resources are sometimes inadequate. Dr. Sorenson greatly appreciates a pristine crime scene, so his prompt arrival at Blackhawk is quite fortunate."

Rosie nodded to the increase in personnel outside the larger laboratory.

Dr. Howard said, "Crime scene?"

Kayne said, "Most assuredly, Doctor. I am holding the murder weapon in my hand."

He turned the mysterious flat metal object, which sparkled in the laboratory's light. I took a picture of it with my phone.

***

The woman still wore the gauzy white hairnet and blue rubber gloves as she slowed down, approaching the exit side of the Center's main checkpoint. Although it was barely dawn, the maintenance worker wore dark glasses. She waved to the guards who were alternating sides of the checkpoint. They sent a flatbed truck piled with machinery under a tightly fastened tarp into the base. As she pulled away, she heard the security's communication system signaling loudly. Speeding up, she saw both gates drop into place in her rear-view, closing the Center to all but essential traffic.

***

After handing me the curious metal object, Kayne reached for the Captain's right hand and gently turned the thumb and first two fingers. He smelled the man's fingers. The officer made a face and attempted to pull away.

"I beg your..."

Ice-blue eyes blazing with a cold fire, Kayne removed his left-hand glove and moistened his index finger. He ran the small amount of saliva over the tips of the Captain's fingers and tasted them. I handed the startled Navy guy my handkerchief while trying to suppress a smile. Two of the guards in the outer room moved toward the door as if to protect their boss.

This is the part about my man that I so fuckin' love — his ballsy and often over-the-top manner of shocking his "victims" into the world of induction science. Things are never what they seem, and the truth is frequently overlooked.

"You are a pack-every-three-days-or-so man, Captain. Filtered and domestic."

He re-tasted his own index finger.

"Marlboro Black Menthols."

Kayne now stepped very close to the tall Navy man and sniffed him, causing Captain Clarke-Mills to move back with a "WTF?" expression on his face.

"You had indulged in your social addiction not fifteen minutes ago. Your aftershave does not completely disguise the odor of a smoker. Besides, your close-clipped mustache is a scent-keeper."

Clarke-Milles looked at Rosie and protested, "What is going on here?"

"Please forgive my dramatics, Captain," Kayne said. "I am merely trying to prove a point. Smokers smell and taste of tobacco, even those who occasionally partake. You have nicotine stains on your fingers. I would say that your habit goes back to your days on the Navy Midshipmen football team, where, in your senior year, you rushed a total of 7,735 yards in your running back career, bringing distinction to the United States Naval Academy."

Now, the dude relaxed a bit but maintained a serious expression. He spoke with the attitude of one who was not happy about law enforcement inviting two rookie consultants onto the military facility.

"But what does all this have to do with Dr. Rockland?"

"She did not smoke."

Perplexed, our audience of four hung on his next words. Kayne took back the "murder weapon." With a slight gesture, he popped it apart.

Rosie remarked, "It's a cigarette case."

"Containing two Sobranie cigarettes. These black-papered beauties are made in Ukraine, although the company is Japanese-owned now. You are looking at Sobranie Black Russians, and there are four more in Dr. Rockland's lab coat pocket."

Dr. Howard observed, "But you said she did not smoke."

"Exactly, and especially not these. The Black Russian variety stains the fingers darkly, the tobacco and the paper dye."

I said, "This case was placed into her pocket."

"Precisely. The case is light, and with the other materials the scientist toted in her coat, Dr. Rockland would not have noticed it."

Rosie Martell asked, "How did a cigarette case kill Gretchen Rockland?"

I interrupted everyone by asking Dr. Howard not to touch the keyboard of the instrumentation computers on the console against the wall.

The Research Director turned from the flashing screen and said one word.

"Quench."

Kayne said, "Yes, the magnet in the NMR quenched."

The young county medical examiner pointed to the deceased woman's body with an inquiring expression.

"Doctor Sorenson?"

"Yes, Doctor Leonard, by all means."

The young medic retrieved and drew a sheet over the dead woman's body.

Kayne next pointed to a double-decker alien spaceship-like instrument station at the far side of the lab. Besides the computers and monitors, it was the only other thing in the lab. The construction consisted of four thick metal legs holding a rounded housing on the first level. The outer casing displayed the logo "Brückner." The undersurface of the beast was a collection of electronic cables that ran into the floor and then into the computers.

On the second story, a round, railed balcony surrounded what appeared to be a waist-high, silver cylinder extending up from the machinery below it and having an array of tubes, dials, and attachments. A small, circular stairway gave an operator access to the instrument's top.

"Doctor Rockland was doing research with Nuclear Magnetic Resonance or NMR spectroscopy. This is an analytical chemistry technique used in quality control research to determine the content, purity, and molecular structure of a sample. For example, NMR can quantitatively analyze mixtures containing known compounds."

"And the rest of her research is classified, gentlemen, which I am afraid creates an impasse."

Martina Howard looked anxious as she said this. She bent and, using a tissue, retrieved the tube containing Dr. Rockland's solid sample. The Research Director also took the scientist's tablet. Rosie Martell took note of this evidence swipe.

From Dr. Howard's behavior, I could tell that we were getting too close to something.

Kayne shrugged and continued. "Our mechanical beast is made entirely of plastic, glass, and non-magnetic metals like…"

I said, "Aluminum."

"Yes. Nothing in this room is or can consist of magnetic metal. It will cause the giant magnet, super-cooled with helium, to malfunction. And then, there's this…"

Kayne held up the silver cigarette case and proceeded to walk us through the last moments of the woman's life.

"Unbeknownst to the unfortunate Dr. Rockland, the metal in her pocket was attracted to the instrument's powerful magnetic field, causing heat in the coil windings. This distorted the magnetic field and forced the device to…

He turned to Dr. Howard, who said, "The term we use is 'quench.' This heat causes a sudden, explosive boil-off of the coolant, liquid helium."

"Thank you. Dr. Rockland's only warning of the impending malfunction or quench was a soft hissing sound caused by a small volume of helium escaping through the boil-off valve. Next, she heard a louder hissing as a larger quantity of gaseous helium was released."

Kayne pointed to a unit on the ceiling and addressed the Director of Research.

"Dr. Howard, this scanner room seems to be designed appropriately. Most of the helium should have escaped through that vent to the outside. Unfortunately, it did not. Once the keyboards have been dusted by the Detective Inspector's team for fingerprints, you will see that the safety vent has been disabled.

"Sadly, the cryogens – sorry, the helium escaped into this scanner room. Dr. Rockland, by now, struggled to free herself from sticking to the machine. She pulled her coattails from the NMR, and the metal cigarette case fell back into her lab coat pocket, spilling most of the Black Russians inside. She dashed down the stairs.

"But it was too late. Through the mist, the victim would have felt the room temperature drop by at least fifteen degrees as she stumbled in the direction of that door."

Perhaps looking to be a part of the analysis, Dr. Leonard took up the narrative. I noticed that his remarks seemed to be directed at the Navy Captain.

"So, gaseous helium is lighter than air and will float to the top of the room. But a lot of helium in an enclosed space like this will completely displace oxygen from the entire room."

"Sir, what happens if she inhales the gas?"

My Boss' newly acquired pupil answered the consulting detective with, "She would lose consciousness in about ten seconds, Dr. Sorenson. She would have experienced asphyxia and death."

"Suffocation."

The Captain was not convinced.

"By my count, Dr. Rockland had thirty seconds to get to the door. Your conclusions are pretty inconclusive if you ask me, Sorenson."

"Ah, but she did make it to the door, Captain, but was unable to open it."

Kayne walked us over to the glass and aluminum opening of the scanner room. He stood on the threshold and turned the inside lock release. Bending, he examined the borders of the door.

The Detective Inspector said, "Then the killer took some kind of outside doorstop away as they ran off."

Kayne said nothing but walked into the outer facility. He opened a chest, tightened his gloves, and reached in. He returned with a pile of smoke in his left hand and an ice pick in the other.

He blew the clouds of carbon dioxide away, revealing half a cube cut on a diagonal.

"The wedge of dry ice in the door," Kayne explained, "A match to this one... it blocked the door and then simply sublimed into the atmosphere."

The Captain looked astonished.

I said, "It disappeared."

Thomas Paul Severino

Chapter Three: Just the Facts

Blackhawk Navy Air Warfare Center, Blackhawk, California

Nick Sechi's Journal

"Thank you for allowing us to use your office, Dr. Howard."

The Director of Research came back with a brusque response bordering on impatience.

"To be honest, and I believe I speak for Captain Clarke-Mills, I am not comfortable with local law enforcement's decision to bring on outside consultants, especially two…"

"Gays?"

"I was going to say 'internet celebrities.' Mr. Sechi."

Rosie held up a hand.

"Careful, Doctor Howard. From what I know of the Captain, the man speaks for himself. I asked for their expert advice, and if you are astute enough to know of their reputation, you also know of their credentials. Their acclaim is international. Nick has been very thorough in publishing their *curriculum vitae* on his blog. Research, Doctor. Give it a try before forming an opinion."

Kayne followed with, "I can understand your frustration, Dr. Howard. It is not every day that a direct report is murdered in the course of doing her job."

"I consider your conclusions premature, Dr. Sorenson, but we will leave that to the medical experts."

The last remark stung, but Kayne flashed me a look that said, "Ignore." We were seated at a conference table in Dr. Howard's office. Rosie's police folk gathered up a few folks of interest, and I could see them waiting in the hallway. Martina Howard insisted on remaining standing.

"How long…?"

She cut Kayne off with more than a bit of impatience in her voice.

"Dr. Rockland had been working here at Blackhawk for three years. She came to us from Case Western Reserve University, where she was the Chair of Physical Sciences. She was an excellent colleague -- never missed a deadline. Her reports met the highest of our work standards, and Dr. Rockland received excellent performance reviews. She followed all facility procedures, all evidence to the contrary notwithstanding."

Me: "The bagel...."

Rosie: "And the apple."

Kayne: "Suffice it to say she was not killed because of her uneaten breakfast."

"Your inferences are obvious, Dr. Sorenson. As I mentioned in the NMR lab, Dr. Rockland's research is classified. No, you cannot have access to her files, and no one here is authorized to discuss her work."

I said, "Non-disclosure agreements."

"Correct."

"If the coroner rules Dr. Rockland's death as murder, her files are evidence."

"Let's discuss that when you come to me with a court order, Inspector."

Through the office's glass walls, I could see law enforcement officers removing a body on a stretcher from the lab in question.

Kayne said, "Doctor Howard, did you have a personal relationship with the deceased?"

That took the wind out of the woman's sails. Howard paused and shot a WTF look. Her large brown eyes slid sideways so that she seemed to be looking at her left ear and away from us. Almost imperceptibly, she swallowed and then said very carefully, "No. I know nothing of her life outside this facility. None of that is any of my concern. I resent your inference."

I couldn't hold back. The tell of a person who is being untruthful was so familiar. Kayne and I had seen this before.

"Seriously?"

Yes, so here's where it pays to have two unofficial individuals involved in the case discussion. Truthfully, I had not much to go on, but the body language. Anyway, I wanted to bust this woman's... Let me say she was a bit too much of a pain in the ass for me. I looked as she resumed her resting bitch face and decided, *so let's rumble, huh?*

I pressed, "Doctor Howard, you are not being truthful. And that means you are hiding something. It is not the research you are protecting, although that is probably valuable stuff. I think Rockland kept a journal or personal notes in addition to her technology. Bet you made her calendar – the outside-of-office stuff, you know? Something went down that you figure needs to be kept hidden, I'm thinking.

"Let's try this again. Perhaps you would care to explain the nature of your personal relationship with the dead woman?"

Martina Howard left the room.

* * *

"Seaman Sanders, please start at the beginning."

Kayne pushed a diagram of the base toward the young Navy man and handed him a stylus.

"And show us on the map, if you will."

The security guard pointed to various places on the diagram as he spoke.

. "Sir, I came in the north gate at 01:30 like I do every day and parked here in the security staff lot. Our office is there. I was making my usual rounds starting at 02:00 outside the buildings. I came into here. That's Research Block D, and I did my usual walkthrough. There is a lot of glass in this building, which allows plenty to be seen, and in some cases, things are not what they seem."

Inspector Martell asked, "What does that mean, Seaman?"

Sanders looked around before answering. "Well, I have only been assigned to security at this building for three days. But it was made clear to me that, up to a point, I was to stay out of the business of the work going on inside. Private stuff goes on in this place, and I needed to avoid interfering with the research and the chemists."

Again, the young guard looked around before continuing.

"The dead woman, Sir. My first day in here, yeah. Two days ago, she had been crying and was wiping away her tears. I started to ask her if there was something I could do, but that Doctor Howard lady, she caught me talking and told me to… ah… well… She wanted me to mind my own business and move on."

Sanders attempted to steer us back to the facts of the discovery. He tapped the building on the map.

"Ma'am, some of the labs have frosted glass as they are used for special projects. All doors to offices, conference rooms, and labs have access panels. I do not have access to high-security rooms, although my boss, Chief Petty Officer Davies, does.

"Well, I came into Chem Lab Four… that's here… the electronic lock had been disabled. I spotted Dr. Rockland on the floor of the little room with the big machine, there. I called the security office and the police. I met Inspector Martell when she arrived at the building."

Kayne said, "When the NMR quenches, the lock is programmed to open."

Rosie asked, "Before you met Officer Martell, did you touch the body, Seaman, or change the site in any way?"

The kid looked worried. He said, "No, Ma'am. I mean, yes, Ma'am, I only took her carotid pulse with these two fingers."

"Lifeguard?"

"Yes, Doctor Sir. Three years during high school, then I joined the Navy."

"How old are you, dude?"

"I am nineteen, Mr. Sechi."

He paused and looked off for a second.

"Anyway. Dr. Rockland was dead," Sanders said solemnly.

Captain Michael Clarke-Mills entered the office, and the Seaman stood and saluted.

"Sir."

"As you were, Sailor."

The Base commander pulled up a chair, and the Seaman sat back down.

"Tell us, Seaman Sanders, who else you saw this morning from the time you began your rounds until you met Detective Inspector Martell."

"Seaman Chambers, Sir. He and I grabbed some coffee when I got here at the office. We shot the shit…"

The kids jumped up and saluted again. In a choking voice, he said, "Begging the Captain's pardon, Sir… Sir, Ma'am… we discussed the Warriors/Lakers game. Then, I started my rounds."

The Captain suppressed a smile and, with one hand, waved the kid back down into his seat.

Kayne asked, "Who did you see in the vicinity of Research Block D, Chem Lab Four?"

" Ah… the usual maintenance crew, Sir. I am not familiar with all of their names, but the roster can be obtained. I just started here at Blackhawk two weeks ago, you see. They clean the buildings at night when most of the folks are gone."

"Anything unusual in or around this lab?"

"No, Sir… wait. There was one cleaner who seemed to be knocking off early. She actually left her mop cart in the back vestibule."

He again indicated where on the chart.

"That's right there. I saw the cleaning woman leaving and figured she may have gotten sick or something."

He stopped and thought a bit.

"She was a nice lady."

"Who?"

"The Doctor. Dr. Rockland, Sir."

***

"I don't have anything to add to the Seaman's account."

"Did you know Dr. Rockland?"

Chief Petty Officer Jacob Davies was one big dude. His body type was similar to a tighthead prop on a rugby team – a strong, impressive upper body. Davies was definitely someone you would want as head of security. Broad of chest and shoulders, he remained at parade rest despite being invited to take a chair.

"How does someone get on Base, Officer Davies?"

The bull answered in a deep voice that indicated some masculinity overload.

"Sir, in your case, authorized personnel have informed the gate that you were to be permitted entrance. You were then given yellow security badges that must be displayed at all times."

Big Man gave me a smoldering look. You know, the one featuring a single arched eyebrow. I stood and took my visitor's badge out of my pocket and clipped it to the neck of my Deadpool t-shirt. I pursed my lips in a cocky "Whateva, Jack" expression. I love bustin' balls, sometimes.

"All other members of the service and civilian staff have badges. White and blue for military, red and white for civilians, worn on a lanyard. Those who work here have barcodes on the driver's side windshield. Visitors get a dashboard card after checking in at the base's gate."

"Building access?"

"The security badges are coded for building and room access. Certain areas require retinal scans to get in, Sir. Arrangement for maintenance in these secured areas is complicated, but we get the job done, Sir."

Rosie said, "Please, Chief Petty Officer, look at the screen. This feed is from the security cameras on the North Gate. Do you recognize this woman?"

After a while, Davies said, "Negative, Ma'am, but her security badge..."

He pointed to the driver's ID, which was generated below the visual feed.

"Carmencita Lopez, Sir. She is assigned to this building. My office is in the process of contacting her as we speak."

Kayne said, "Last question, Officer Davies, did you have a personal relationship with Dr. Gretchen Rockland?"

The man was pissed, and he pretty much dropped the military courtesy. His gaze bore down on Kayne like a predator as he responded.

"Why would you ask me a question like that?"

"I apologize if I am being impolite, Chief. Call it a hunch. Gretchen Rockland was a beautiful woman. The military has a history of improper behavior concerning women."

"The answer is no. I would like to go on record as resenting the accusation."

Captain Clarke-Mills said, "It wasn't an accusation, Chief Davies. It was a question."

***

As we walked down the corridor to exit Block D, Kayne held up a hand to stop us. He began speaking in a low, monotone voice.

" … god-damned fags and dikes. That asshole wanted to know if I fucked her. And the big homo is sitting right there and letting them insult me. Rockland bitch and that fag boyfriend of…

"Jake, take it easy. They can't touch either of us. They don't have anything. We were miles away, as ordered."

Rosie and I followed his gaze through to the outside of the building.

Davies and Howard spotted us. They each tossed a cigarette and walked away.

"Sorry, I lost it. They ended their conversation."

"Holy crap!"

He continued with a smirk, "The bad thing about glass walls is that they are transparent. The good thing about glass walls is that they are transparent.

Rosie said, "Jesus, you were lip-reading."

Chapter Four: Viewshed

Walnut Creek, California

Nick Sechi's Journal

"Yes, Mount Diablo is an appropriate name. On this side, with your back to the western bay, the mountain glows red at sunset."

"Why did she die, Brian? What can you tell us?"

Rosie Martell had chosen the outdoor patio of the Café Bien-Être in Walnut Creek to meet with Gretchen Rockland's partner, Petty Officer 3rd Class Brian D. LaCroix. The young Navy man seemed eager to discuss everything except his recent loss. He ignored the direct question.

"Yeah, so check it out. From here, it looks like a double pyramid with those subsidiary peaks."

He pointed, saying, "That one is North Peak."

Our new acquaintance gazed off to the mountain behind us.

"Not the highest of elevations, but that mountain's viewshed is the largest in the world — or at least in the Western United States. Anywhere you go in the Bay Area, when the air is clear, you can see that badass looming over the Central Valley."

Kayne, Rosie, and I sat in silence. Brian's grief had wrapped around him like an overcoat. His bright, clear, mahogany eyes were glazed over, and he sniffed back tears as he spoke. It would be a long time before this kid smiled again.

Oddly, he pointed gracefully and said, "Certain Native Americans believe the universe was created when the gods came down from heaven on that mountain and the creator beings, Eagle-Man and Creator Coyote, pushed back the waters of chaos. Bingo, all things bright and beautiful sprang into being. It's such a…."

A lost boy, he was now struggling to continue.

"Gretch loved the park… she did… sacred, sacred, she called it… like paradise life, sky, land, and beautiful souls… no death… no death… no…"

His last word hung in the air as if it were a delayed answer to Rosie's question.

As usual, Kayne found a window into the soul of the unfortunate young man.

"How long did you dance, Mr. LaCroix?"

Brian seemed poised to slide back into realness.

"Huh?"

Kayne smiled only slightly. He stared like a mesmerist into the young sailor's eyes.

"Kindly point to the mountain again, Sir."

Rosie and I had no idea – the usual when Kayne was up to his logic demonstrations.

"Stop. And now to the south, please."

He caught the dude's extended hand and demonstrated.

"Every finger and your thumb are visible in the gesture. Please allow me to touch you again, Sir."

Out of the ordinary? Please. This is standard operating procedure for an educator and investigator like my extraordinary husband. Anyway, Kayne took the seated kid's right leg and brought it up to his lap.

I worked hard not to chuckle. Rosie stood to check it all out and did an eye roll. Brian did not know what to do but seemed completely disarmed,

"Please bear with me, Officer."

Kayne took off the man's sandal and pointed to the very attractive man's rather ugly foot. He looked up to give the explanation as Brian said, "Yeah, dancers have gross feet – muscles and bones shaped pretty unnaturally -- a real giveaway."

"You are Nick's age, twenty-six, yet your feet appear much older. Also, one never loses the grace of movement gained through years of disciplined training. Very developed leg muscles, the way you move... I was immediately sure you had been a gymnast until you pointed as you did. Athletes extend the hand so that all fingers are in a single plane with the thumb at a forty-five-degree angle. Dancers do not. It is an artistic display of the human body, a habit difficult to relinquish."

Furthermore, the muscular development of your lower body suggests you are more than gym-toned, Officer. You are a disciplined dancer and have been from a very young age."

Kayne is famous for these Holmesian demonstrations. He often does the "Elementary, my dear whoever" to help someone involved in a case drop their defenses.

"Dr. Sorenson, can I have my leg back?"

"By all means. I apologize for my familiarity."

"Cool. I read about how you can figure things out."

I winked at my beloved and non-fan of my blog, The Kayne Sorenson Mysteries.

Yes! Another point for Nick Boy in the ongoing argument on the value of my writing and our internet fandom.

"Yeah, I met Gretchen at Purgatory."

Rosie said, "So I'm thinking a bar, a restaurant?"

Kayne said, "A dance company. Ballet."

"Jesus, you are on a roll, man. Yep. I'm like that English dancer kid in the movie...."

"Billy Elliot," I said.

"That's it, yeah. I joined the company when I was twelve. My father had a fit. Stayed until I was twenty-three, then caved and joined the Navy. I was quite accomplished and on the verge of becoming a leading dancer in the company. But then I met Gretchen at Dance Purgatorio. She was a member of the company's Board of Directors and a scientific researcher at the Base.

At the mention of his late friend, Brian began to slip a bit.

Kayne said, "I would have thought a family from Martinique would have…"

"Simple, huh? My accented remarks in French to our *maître d'*? Too easy."

"On the contrary, my dear Officer LaCroix. I did not overhear your conversation. You possess a tattoo on the inside of your left bicep of the Nationalist flag of Martinique, the red, green, and black."

"Back to the Caribbean slave trade, yeah. My great-grandfather came to the US, and my dad was a veteran of the Navy. Turns out, I get stationed up in the Old Port Chicago Reach, north of here on Suisun Bay, and Gretchen gets the research job at Blackhawk. We kinda picked up where we left off in San Francisco when I was dancing."

It was Rosie who came back to it.

"Gretchen Rockland was murdered, Brian. Any idea why?"

I was like a bomb went off. The young man was shocked. When Brian was able to regain his composure, he looked around before answering.

"No, ahhh… but… look, so, Gretchen was meticulous in her research, except for the food-in-the-lab thing. Yeah. No rivalries that she ever spoke of."

I went on a hunt here.

"You folks all good in the relationship? Anything going on there? Trouble? Abuse? Family Issues?"

He did a nervous guy, hand-to-the-head hair rustle before answering. His dark eyes flashed at me, borderline pissed or afraid. I could not tell which.

"You asking if we were good together? Yeah, we were. Some ups and downs -- dry spells, like all couples. I don't know anything about the other stuff."

A beat… then he added.

"If there was any of that."

Once upon a time, I was a cop. I was good at direct to the heart of the matter interrogation, and we were definitely into something. I went for the money shot.

"Arguments?"

"I loved her, dude. Back off."

"Gonna get married?"

Brian LaCroix looked at me with eyes that were even more intense.

"We never talked about that."

"Rather unbelievable... a long-term intimate relationship and never any talk of marriage. You must admit it seems rather strange."

No one said anything. Some sweaty hand-wringing was going on.

I could tell Kayne was analyzing this kid big time.

"Hey, am I being accused of anything here?"

Rosie said, "No, Officer, just some routine questions."

"Routine my ass. OK, so I've got stuff to do. We done here?"

It was clear that Brian wanted to get away from us ASAP. He threw us a fish.

"But the cigarette case was not hers. I am sure."

He paused and looked off at the mountain again.

"You know they came looking to take all of her work stuff. There wasn't much she kept at home."

Rosie nodded.

"Yes," she said. "Her work was classified. The Navy has made that very clear."

When next he spoke, his eyes were again glassy in a spooky kind of way. His expression reminded me of a hunted guy avatar in one of those hack-and-slash action video games. Brian's remarks were made in almost a whisper.

"Le char du soleil."[1]

He stood and left.

_____

[1] The chariot of the sun -- French

Chapter Five: The Attack

Summit Trail Trailhead, Mt. Diablo, California

Nick Sechi's Journal

"No, Nick, wait."

The big dude in the backward ball cap clipped Kayne in a flying tackle, and the two of them rolled in the soft meadow grass. The dark blue hat with the gold lettering went flying just as I recognized our would-be assassin.

Kayne and I intended to return to our campsite early in the afternoon. Detective Investigator Rosie Martell thanked us for our involvement and returned to the County Center with some grateful words.

"I apologize again for interfering with your R&R in the mountains, but you were a great help today. I will let you go to get more of that fresh mountain air."

"Please keep us informed," Kayne requested, adding, "Murder is never a simple affair."

I perched on a wooden rail fence and watched the two jocks scrabbling in the summer meadow grass. Grunting and flipping each other like middle school playground rivals. The sun felt good, and I was glad I slathered some goop on to cut back on the rays. Fair-skinned, muscled boys like me who like to show a lot of the old hot torso in public have to be careful.

I yelled, "Don't hurt him too much. I'm going to need him for something later."

It didn't take long to get into our running gear after the meeting with Brian LaCroix at the Café Bien-Être. When we hit the hiking trail at a run, Kayne challenged me to a race to the top. The switchbacks coasted up the foothills and into the steeper range tiers. I teased with a bunch of "old man" name-calling. Although Kayne was six years older than I, at 32, he was in superb condition.

Now, he was just dirty. They both were, but hotter'n hell in the eyes of this overly visual dude. My own private softcore porn – live and in person, I resisted yelling something like, "Yank his shorts off, dude."

OK. OK. Kayne will protest when he reads this anyway. I will behave – not.

"Your blog followers will think we are man-whores, my love."

"Naw, Boss. Just horned-up, red-blooded, American gay boys. 'Sides, sex sells."

"I haven't been a 'boy' in many years, but I will admit to the frisky part."

"Depends on what you include in the term 'boy,' and to that, I can testify that last night…"

"Mr. Sechi, do you see how you are?"

Now, he was cussing in Australian slang. Tossing the bigger man on his "arse" and fly-tackling him to dominate. I did a package adjust and cheered.

As Kayne stood up and off the "bloke," His opponent sat up and grabbed the Aussie Barbarian around the waist and pulled him back down on top of him. He snarled, "Not so fast, Puss Boy. I eat guys like you for lunch." Sweat-soaked and growling, they went in for more muscle-on-muscle action before falling apart, one face up and the other face down.

Kayne scrambled to sit on the guy's back. He reached under the top of the exhausted man's shorts and grabbed the waistband of the dude's jock. He pulled up.

"Fuck! Now you're fighting dirty, bitch."

"I come from a notorious line of Botany Bay convicts. I regret to say I am strong, but not always honorable, ya… oooff… hot bastard."

Kayne looked up at me through a mess of wet, black hair with the expression of an evil imp. He gloated as he twisted the broad elastic band at the small of the agonized man's back.

"Navy sucks, ya bloody brogan."

A cry of pain issued forth from somewhere deep inside the arched-up, prone body of Captain Michael Clarke-Mills, USN.

At that point, I was knocked off the fence on my ass. The ground was convulsing.

Thomas Paul Severino

Chapter Six: The Earth Moved
Devil's Head Ranch, Mt. Diablo, California

Nick Sechi's Journal

"San Andres, men, just a little buckling and sliding. The mountain under our feet is growing and changing shape."

I was jumping up on my feet while Kayne offered a hand to help the Navy dude up from the ground. The sweating jock dropped his shorts and re-adjusted his undergear, which had recently become a bit too snug for what he was packin'.

Ohhh, yeah...

Kayne shot me a wink. He loved messing with big dudes, even if he got a bit inappropriate along the way.

"Quite right, Captain. Considering our bit of gladiatorial contesting, should I refer to you as Antaeus? Your mother seems to be telling me to sod off, mate."

The big guy smiled and broke into a laugh.

"You are as good at wrestling as you are in your research. Such an intellectual in the classic sense. Actually, that was my team nickname in my Academy days, among others. I ate a lot of dirt, you see."

He raised his big arms up.

"Care to try, Herc?"

I piped up, "OK, OK, feeling a bit left out here, boys. You're first, Boss. Go."

"Nick, Antaeus was a giant. What are you, Captain, six-five?"

"And a half."

Kayne continued, "In Greek and Berber mythology, he was the giant son of Poseidon and Gaia, the goddess of the earth. Antaeus was a famous wrestler who could not be defeated as long as he was in contact with his mother, the earth."

The ground shuddered again, and I bounced against our giant. He started with a steadying grab but ended up crouching and lifting me up in a bear hug.

My lifter said, "Oooff. Hercules only defeated him by lifting him up above the ground."

A third shake knocked the two of us to the ground. Again, Kayne assisted with a hand, but I sat, waited a bit, and did a kip-up, pushing up and landing on my feet – meant to impress. Failing to stick the landing without a slight wobble, I grinned sheepishly.

"Fuck, is this volcano about to blow, dude?"

"Mt. Diablo is not a volcano. She was lifted up, beginning about two million years ago, by two tectonic plates moving sideways against each other, one going under the other. They get stuck sometimes and jolt when the energy builds up – like a huge release, Mr. Sechi."

Kayne seemed to be suppressing a smile as he attempted to brush off some mountain dirt and said, "Let's go with Kayne, Nick, and...?"

"Mike is good, Kayne."

Out of uniform, Mike was relaxed and friendly. He easily flashed a killer smile, and I began to think he was very comfortable in the company of men. So, yeah, he was one hell of a studly, rocking the trained body of an athlete and tipping the scales at 225 pounds, I'd say.

I reached out and turned him.

Like Kayne's prowling panther, the Captain had a bright blue tattoo on the back of his left deltoid muscle.

It was a coat of arms with a hand clenching a trident that went straight down and behind a shield. On the armament was an ancient warship, an open book, and a banner with a motto.

Kayne leaned in and read, "*Ex Scientia Tridens.*"

Mike translated, "From Knowledge, Seapower. It is the seal of the Naval Academy, designed by Park Benjamin, Class of 1867."

"I thought there were Navy regulations about career officers and tattoos."

"Another smart guy, eh, Little Jock?"

I crossed my arms in an "explanation, please" pose.

"The policy has changed to reflect reality. The Navy does not want to miss the opportunity to bring in talented men and women who wish to serve their country. In my uniform, you cannot see this."

He gestured to his back.

Kayne said, "Or the other one."

No response.

"Forgive my flight of fantasy, Mike. Go back to when you were, umm, nineteen. Gearing up for the big game against Army. You and your mates on the town in Annapolis, breaking curfew... Many drinks later, we find our hero arse end up in a tattoo parlor, as it was with many mariners back to John Paul Jones."

Mike roared a hearty laugh.

The Navy stud reached out for a headlock, but my man threw a block, stepped back, and pointed to Mike's derriere. The pointing finger made a repeated downward stroke. Down came one side of the Navy Officer's shorts in a somewhat chaste (or was it teasing) lowering. The insignia was small but clear.

A butting Navy ram in a lofting attack jump was at the top of his right gluteal muscle, just below his waist. The mascot was springing off his hind legs, head down, curved horns lowered, and forelegs tucked under. The football mascot was wrapped in a gold and blue blanket with a large capital "N" and two stars.

"Dude, if I had a dollar bill, I'd."

I did the thumb and first two-finger gesture of tipping a male stripper in his thong strap and smiled wickedly.

This time, the big lug connected and wound the two of us around, with me tucked under one of his arms in a hammerlock. He tried not to show the exertion in his voice as he said, "We lost that game, and it was at West Point, not in Maryland."

He twisted and grabbed for my arms, but I likewise broke the hold and stepped back with a cocky stance that said, "That all you got, asshole? Bring it."

Mike Clarke-Mills shook an "I'm-gonna-get-you-sucka" index finger at me and bent to retrieve his ball cap. He said, "Hey, Nick, Kayne. Getting late, men. Let's take a jog unless you are all in from my clobbering you. I wanna show you something."

Big Mike led the way, alternating speed from a jog to a sprint as we took the trail away from the summit, dodging between hikers, dirt bikers, and other runners. We kept up easily. It was an excellent workout.

In about a mile, we took a turn up and around another mountain rise in the park. This stretch was marked "Property of the United States Navy. No Trespassing." We vaulted the fence like three pillaging raiders.

The switchback rose as it wound upcountry. The air was clear and bright, and I felt like I could run all the way back to our campsite. Finally, a cluster of buildings came into view. On a grassy lawn before the compound, a flagpole flew both the American flag and the Navy's Flag.

Mike stopped, and with his hands on his hips, he explained with a touch of pride.

"It was an old tourist destination during the thirties, like a dude ranch, put up by some Hollywood producers. They actually filmed some classic films up here.

"I convinced the Navy to restore it as a retreat center for officers. There are six cabins and the main house. The barn and stables are unused. I'm afraid not many of the officers or enlisted men use it. The creek is pure mountain spring-fed, and the view is even better up there."

As Kayne and I looked around, Mike dashed into the main house and came out with three white towels and three waters.

Tossing these to us, he challenged, "Last one in…"

He sprinted up across a pebbled yard with one lonely black SUV with a Blackhawk security emblem on the lower driver's side window and slipped off into the mountain brush.

Kayne and I took swigs and poured the rest over our respective heads. "Is this gonna be the everybody-gets-naked part, Boss?"

"One can only hope, my love."

We exchanged a goofy look, shrugged, and dashed in pursuit as a voice called from up the chaparral, "C'mon, you babies. Move it."

Thomas Paul Severino

Chapter Seven: The Devil's Basin
Devil's Head Ranch, Mt. Diablo, California

Nick Sechi's Journal

Yeah, this is the naked part, one of them anyway. (Oh gosh, more to come? What will I tell my priest? LOL.)

The viewshed at this summit was spectacular. It seemed we were at a high point in the range, and mile after mile of rock, trees, brush, trails, and roadway fell away and off into the horizon, and then soared up again. It was almost a three-sixty panorama of extraordinarily clear visibility. The range lifted and fell over the darkening mists gathering in the east's Sierra ranges and forests. Opposite, toward the west, we could see the sun beginning its dip into the Pacific. A crop of even higher reaches of mountain rock raised its Jurassic head over this oasis off to the south. It reminded me of a broken tooth, and we had climbed up to a wet, crater-like cavity.

"Starkers," as Kayne would say. The big ram-ass jock sloshed into the water for about 25 yards and then dove under the surface. He looked very much like Poseidon may have been his father, heroic in stature and glistening with cascading water. He made for the "tooth" rock outcropping that stood against one side of the mountain basin.

Mike's powerful arms and shoulders pulled him to the showering rushes of a waterfall that arched over and down into the large pool of crystal water. Just beyond it, he hauled himself up on a rocky shelf at the foot of the cliff and did a hand-over-hand climb up, a conquering warrior, fearless, naked, and shining in the sun.

"Holy shit, Boss."

A smirk and then, "The view? I guess we may say that it meets with your approval, my frisky love."

There was a somewhat raunchy insinuation in his remarks. My husband knows me well.

"Yep. I am liking it a lot. One hell of a lot to say the truth."

I kicked off my running shoes and socks and dropped my shorts and gear. If there's a naked muscle boy party, I'm so there.

"Holy fuck!"

Big Guy laughing...

"It's a mountain spring-fed lake, Nick. You are about to experience shrinkage. I'm afraid."

Kayne came up into the ankle-deep water and slipped his sweaty arms around me. He sucked lovingly at my neck.

"It's only painful at the beginning. Trust me... What'd you say your name was, Boy?"

I pushed his naked arse into the icy waters of the lake and dove away, swimming from retaliation. *Jesus Frog, it was cold! And where did my man junk go?*

I made for the climb-up just as Mike dove through the air and hit the water like an older version of Olympian diver Tom Daley. Well, perhaps not that good, and anyway, Tommy Boy always wears a suit, at least I think so.

(Sometime later...

Kayne: In reviewing this part of the story, Nick, I only want to say, Are you quite sure, my love? Seriously? Your readers will think you have the libido of a fifteen-year-old — all of this drooling over yet another attractive male. You forget our nephew will be scandalized. I only ask that you describe me as a man who has his sexual conduct under close control and always acts with the utmost decorum and appropriate behavior.

Me: Bullshit, Boss. Did you or did you not give that beefcake a wedgie and check out his dreamy, strapped buns? — Talk about middle school hijinks... And as for our son and nephew, Kris is of age, and the longer I am a member of this family, the more I realize very little scandalizes a Sorenson."

So, back to our story...)

I did not go too high up the cliff. I suffer from acrophobia. I was happy to stick to the lower platform diving events in our friendly challenge affair with the top-of-the-world vista.

Kayne called down in mid-climb from an upper outcrop, "Sixes from the judges, Mike. Kinda disappointed, boyo. Too much splash. More practice, mate. Keep watching, and Nick'll show ya how it's done, boyo."

I took a couple of steps and lofted into the air. My diving team skills from high school were largely based on muscle memory, and my body remembered. I piked, twisted, and hit the surface like a hot dagger plunging into ice cream, hands, then torso, and finally, feet.

So, that's how you platform dive, "Bitches."

Bubbles rose as I sliced down into the darker depths of the vast, icy, blue-green pool. A prince in my water kingdom, I saw the bubbling curls of the falling water from underneath. Somersaulting, I tried to see the bottom but figured at least 60 feet down where the tall, freshwater plants waved. Far below me, the currents and waving movements suggested the springs that fed this watery abyss and did their thing. The walls around sloped sharply down from the plateau. It was a sheer bowl of rock filled with Arctic blue water.

Using underwater dolphin kicks, I explored. The crater lake's transparency was pristine and mysterious, with no obstructions, such as fallen trees or forest debris. The light from the surface danced through the dazzling, crystalline kingdom in razor-sharp and glimmering rays. Finally, I arched my body, kicked, and used my arms to change course, starting to rise.

Two white and finless mermen cut into the depths, one on each side of me, and seemed to race to the lower reaches. Kayne and Big Mike cut into the water world like thrown javelins, their naked, muscled bodies training streams of bubbly veils from their noses to their kicking feet. In turn, each did an underwater body arch, reversed their descent, and began to chase me to the surface. We broke through, smiling and laughing.

"High School diving champ. What can I say? I'll take tens all around, boys. Learn from a master. Hardly a splash at entry, right? D'ja see how hot my ass looked?"

"Man. The hell you say, kid. Brag much?"

It was on. I so showed them my butt in a surface dive like Aquaman. I shot through my underwater realm, my two foes in hot pursuit. Almost immediately, my right leg was trapped in a firm grip that even kicking would not release. Like a hero of ancient Atlantis, I turned and faced my nemesis, formidable with wide, cold blue eyes that seemed to convey terror, a mocking grin, and a head surrounded by long, black, waving hair that resembled the serpents of Medusa.

He was strong and fearless, but I prevailed only to face his even more powerfully built hulky buddy. The other evil denizen caught the two of us – the mythic Triton, half man and half fish. He sought to rule, overcome, and punish all rivals. Scrabbling, we rolled over each other as we fell toward the shadowy bottom. Not for long, however. Three pairs of legs kicked to the surface, their owners questing for oxygen.

The game of dive tag lasted a while longer. Mike and Kayne made leaps from higher up, and I followed from the lower perch. Rough and tumble "jump and dunk the guy" interspersed the swan dives, jackknifes, and backflips — fun at middle school summer camp to the max.

As the sun began to set, I got the nerve to get up to the high ledge. I faced the rock wall and balanced on the edge, arms spread. Bringing them down, I turned my head to my aqua-buds.

"Watch this, my sorry-ass bitches."

I had saved the best until now.

Reverse backflip... into a twist (Oh, and your boy did a triple, my fans, hell yeah.) ... into a pike... opening to the layout and down. You know the splash was simply non-existent. My body entered the water like a fuckin' best-kept secret.

They were still cheering when I surfaced.

Nevertheless, I heard clapping from the opposite direction, from the shoreline. A white pickup truck had pulled into the clearing where we first came upon the mountain lake. A familiar figure stood on the shore and yelled, "Spectacular, Nick."

Timothy Leonard, County Medical Examiner.

Chapter Eight: Alpha Scorpii Rising
Devil's Head Ranch, Mt. Diablo, California

Nick Sechi's Journal

"We can get you back to your campsite. You're staying at the Morgan Territory Regional Preserve, right?"

Tim added another log to the big outdoor stone fireplace. Mike was dishing up plates of a quickly prepared dinner. He had loaned us a couple of Navy sweatshirts to ward off the evening chill.

"You are welcome to stay here. The big house has three bedrooms, and the cottages are all unoccupied."

Like most things about this mountain, the view was spectacular from the patio of the main house. The US Navy's retreat compound was on a rise that faced the west. I recognized the double string of pearl lights for each of the Bay Area's two bridges, the closer one, the Oakland Bridge, and the Golden Gate, further away. The hills of the "City by the Bay" were encrusted with buildings that sat like sparkling crown jewels on the slopes and in the valleys. Scattered across the night landscape were the sentinel lights of the city's many signal towers, Telegraph Hill, Twin Peaks, and Alcatraz. We could even see the sentry on Mount Tamalpais north of San Francisco. The stars were clear and bright like a net of pin lights stretched across the dome of the night sky.

The furthest western horizon, beyond the city, was smudged. Where darkness should have intensified as the demarcation between sea and sky was indiscernible, it appeared as if a giant, sprawling beast made of slowly spiraling smoke was hugging the earth and stretching forward to devour the Golden City. Out of the darkness came the fog, which gradually settled over the Bay, coming toward us.

Kayne stepped about and freshened our drinks. He said, "Staying over may allow us to discuss the unfortunate tragedy at Blackhawk this morning, Captain. Any new developments, Doctor?"

Tim Leonard's dark eyes flashed in the firelight. His features hinted at a mixed-racial family line. I suspected an Asian, Native American, and Black lineage. The young County Medical Examiner shared that his heritage went back to a time when Chinese immigrants and formerly enslaved people came to the Golden State. They joined the White Settlers, the Indigenous People, and the Spanish to build the California paradise on the West Coast.

The young man said, "Inspector Martell's office contacted the family, and I understand you met with Petty Officer LaCroix earlier today. Dr. Rockland's body is being shipped home for services and burial in a few days. Please call me Tim, guys. I saw you naked, after all."

"Can't get more casual than that," I remarked.

"Autopsy?"

'Exactly as you said, Kayne. Asphyxiation. No other trauma or marks on the body. The Techies at Blackhawk confirm that the NMR quenched, and I am reporting that the metal cigarette case was the cause of the malfunction."

"Prints?" I asked. I was pretty sure I knew the answer.

"Clean, Nick. Detective Martell let me know and asked me to tell you guys."

Kayne picked up my phone from among our things. He moved his fingers across the screen as he said, "Tell me, Gentlemen. Does this mean anything?"

Using the picture as a guide, he used a stick to trace a soft earth design. The lines resembled a capital M in a script font.

"It appears to be a monogram, Kayne. What does it mean?"

He showed Mike the phone pic.

"This mark was engraved on the murder weapon."

"Could it be the initial of the owner of the cigarette case, Boss?"

"Monograms on cases such as this usually appear in twos or threes. They rarely consist of a single initial, my love."

He adjusted the drawing. The right-hand tip of the letter now bore a point like Satan's barbed tail.

"The poisoned barb – it is the symbol for the eighth astrological sign of the Greek Zodiac, Scorpio."

"Correct, Timothy. I find it a strange set of circumstances that tonight, we are bathed in the light of the constellation associated with this sign. Look there."

Kayne pointed to the southern sky. A cluster of bright stars in a hook formation against the dark background of the night sky was low on the horizon.

"That red star in the middle of the constellation is Antares or Alpha Scorpii. It is actually a binary, and it is rising at this time of the year.

"The Babylonians called it the breast of the Scorpion goddess Ishhara. The Chinese named it the Firey Star because of its color. The Māori people of New Zealand call it Antares Rēhua and regard it as the chief of all the stars. In my country of Australia, the Wotjobaluk Koori people know Antares as Djuit, son of Marpean-kurrk. The stars on each side represented Djuit's wives. The Kulin Kooris called Antares 'Balayang,' the brother of Bunjil, who is our Altair, a star in the constellation Aquila, the Eagle."

Mike settled down with us near the fire and lit a cigarette. He dropped a strong arm around Tim, who moved into the casual embrace in a most relaxed and familiar way. They exchanged a very loving glance.

When I'm right, I'm right.

Mike said, "Coincidence? I mean the murder, the astrological mark, and the stars and all. Omens of evil? Celestial warnings? The cosmic forces of evil?"

"There are no coincidences, my friend. The gods of wickedness and their minions are all around. To quote the Bard, 'The fault, dear Brutus, is not in our stars. But in ourselves.' Julius Caesar."

Tim added, "The Greeks believed that the Scorpion was sent to kill Orion the Hunter because he was overconfident. The beast was defeated, and Zeus put both of them in the sky as constellations and warnings. Divine punishment for hubris."

Kayne stretched back and lay his head in my lap. I caressed his brow and his soft black locks. He was lost in a reverie, gazing at the night sky. After a time, he spoke.

"No. I agree with Shakespeare. Nothing is to blame for all of the world's evil but ourselves. We are the self-made gods of evil."

Chapter Nine: The Night Before the Morning After
Devil's Head Ranch, Mt. Diablo, California

From the Case Files of Kayne J. Sorenson, PhD

"All I ever wanted to be was a Navy man. The usual story -- family members in the arms services. My father and grandfather were in the Navy. When I received my appointment to Annapolis, I thought I had hit the jackpot. Had some gay experiences as a kid, but was pretty sure I could get over it with some discipline."

It was about 2 AM. The night was still clear and crisp. Mike and I were sitting out on the patio after a bit of sleeplessness. Nick and Tim were in that the-guy-always-falls-asleep-after-sex condition. Nick's Big Mike was enjoying a smoke, and I was sipping a whiskey neat.

"Difficult in the Academy, no doubt."

"Cult of the Alpha Male at the Naval Academy. This was 2006. The repeal of the ban on gays in the military would not take place for another five years – the year after I received my commission. So all through school, I was this hypermasculine jock, way too busy for dating women and all that.

"I had this instructor who used the term 'fags' in class, and he even would disclose other people's sexual identity when he felt like it. This was during Don't Ask, Don't Tell. No one made a stink. The idea was he was creating a class climate based on some weird notion of a straight warrior."

"How did you get through it?"

Mike looked at the ground and continued.

"Most of the time, I felt like I was drowning, man. See, in the service, you do not want to stand out at all. Blend in and be the same as everyone -- same as the model Navy man. I was already regarded with suspicion because I was this accomplished football player. If you were different, you got punished and passed over for promotion."

"A culture that promotes uniformity is *de facto,* not a welcoming one."

"Put this on, Boss."

Nick had come out of our cabin with one of the guest robes.

"I thought you were asleep, my love."

He bent and lightly kissed my ear and whispered one word.

"Reloading."

Nick stoked up the fire and then came and sat with us.

"So, I pushed through training and remained an exemplary military man. All kinds of awards – a rapid rise, and my family couldn't have been more proud. Checked all the boxes except having a gal in every port. However, being overseas frequently, I admit that I found ways to get away and have fun.

"I completed Seals training and continued to rise in the ranks. On course to be one of the youngest Admirals in the fleet. Each time I was on a promotion board, I would remember being totally sleepless for days beforehand. Passed over for Admiral last year, although my record was stellar. There were rumors. Came out to a few friends but found out they got religion all of a sudden. Shit canned to Blackhawk -- a small operation where they could hide me."

Nick asked, "What do you think of the trans soldiers' situation, Mike?"

"So unjust is all I can say. The Defense Department lifted that ban in 2016, and transgender troops could serve openly and seek treatment while in uniform. The training of officers was to follow. In a controversial move, Trump announced a reversal of that policy in 2019.

"I served with some of the best, man. No more transgender men and women could come in, but those inside could not be kicked out, and if they had not completed their transition, they had to serve according to their sex at birth. Major fucked up".

I said, "Let's see what the Supreme Court does. Justice Gorsuch wrote in this year's LGBTQ+ employment discrimination case, 'An employer who fires an individual for being homosexual or transgender fires that person for traits or actions it would not have questioned in members of a different sex. Sex plays a necessary and undisguisable role in the decision, exactly what Title VII forbids."

"Repealing the bans did not make it all suddenly comfortable. Lots of fear, I am here to tell you. It is not useful in a loyal and selfless military. So many negative career repercussions from the chain of command – extremely unjust.

"Your physical and personal integrity is all that matters, mate."

The Captain rubbed his palms together and spoke softly.

"Sometimes, it is like trying to maneuver a minefield."

We were quiet for a while.

"So, what's your story, Kayne?"

Nick piped up.

"You would not believe it, Mike. His family is gayer than gay."

"I knew I was gay at thirteen. I only wondered why everyone else was not." I paused, remembering, and added, "You learn to fight."

"Nick?"

"Italian American family – I caused major *agita* at fourteen, caught sexing up my jock crush behind my Catholic high school's field house. My mother was brilliant, facing down those priests. Yeah, you learn to fight, and a family who loves you for who you are are the best allies."

Mike agreed, "Yeah, you learn to fight."

He reached up and took the hand of the boy who had come up behind him. He added, "And to love."

Tim Leonard looked at his Captain with total loving openness and skimmed the man's buzz cut with his free hand. He said just two words as he lifted.

"Come on."

Thomas Paul Severino

Chapter Ten: The Morning After the Night Before
Morgan Territory Regional Preserve, Livermore, California

Nick Sechi's Journal

The woman at our campsite chuckled as we jogged into view.

"Couple of bad boys... your bedrolls have not been slept in. I am, after all, a detective like you. So, tell me, how do you carouse all night at a State Park? You can take the gay boy out of the Castro, but you can't...."

"We live in Pacific Heights, Rosie, a very sedate San Francisco neighborhood. I get it, but the Castro in its heyday is sadly a thing of the past. Totally Disney these days."

"You tell her, Nick. What's up, my friend?"

"I wanted to share the Rockland autopsy with you and to let you know that we are looking for the cleaning woman who was in the research labs on the night of the murder. Carmencita Lopez did not report for work today. She is the assigned maintenance person – a case of food poisoning. The main gate has the tape of the woman who presented proper ID. But that could not have been the assigned woman. Ms. Lopez was at that moment at Contra Costa Regional Medical Center. My guess is the killer had her car, also. I'm swinging over to the Center after I say goodbye."

"Dr. Rockland's research? I am convinced it plays a part in her murder."

"Kayne, the Center's Director of Research, Martina Howard, is not budging on that. Claims it is classified. I will work on it, but it will take some time. I will keep you informed."

Kayne remarked, "The research department of Sorenson and Sechi is headed up by our colleague, Scott Iverson. He is located in Colorado. His investigations into Dr. Rockland's academic publications indicate that the deceased physical scientist was studying rocket propellants for the Defense Department.

"Her doctoral dissertation, "NMR Analysis of the Microstructure and Deformation Mechanisms of Solid Rocket Propellants," caught the attention of DARPA, the Defense Advanced Research Projects Agency, which focuses on high-risk, high-reward research leading to transformational changes in military capabilities and technologies. Soon after she graduated from Case Western Reserve, Dr. Gretchen Rockland was hired by the Navy and assigned to Blackhawk.

"It is therefore reasonable to conclude that the classified research has to do with the microstructure of solid rocket propellants. The top-secret nature of her work is self-evident. In the wrong hands, Dr. Rockland's work could endanger the security of the United States."

"Have you read her dissertation, Kayne?"

"Yes. I found it to be a highly comprehensive study indicative of someone who was at the top of her field. Likewise, her professional associations..."

Before Kayne could finish speaking, a red Mustang convertible pulled up near our rental. Looking dashing in his dress whites, Brian LaCroix jumped out of the car with a manila envelope in his hand. His graceful walk reminded me that the boy possessed the beauty and agility of a trained dancer in addition to his military bearing. We shook hands all around.

"Good morning, Officer. How are you doing?"

"Please let me apologize for my abrupt exit at Café Bien-Être yesterday morning ."

"Quite understandable. Sir."

"I have some time off and am on my way to visit Gretchen's family in Milwaukee. But I wanted to give you this and say that I will do anything I can to help you three find Gretchen's killer. Please let me know."

He pointed to the thin package.

"You know they are prohibited from bringing anything home from Blackhawk, but I found this."

Kayne took the envelope and said, "I suspect there are mysteries upon mysteries here, and therefore, we intend to make ourselves rather an annoyance at Ballet Purgatorio. It would appear that a significant connection to the case lies with the dance company. Brian, please come and visit us in San Francisco. Your connections to the organization may smooth over some rough spots for us.

The officer did not like the sound of that, I could tell.

"I have to get going. I have a plane to catch. Inspector Martel has my contact information."

"How was the hunting?"

"I beg your pardon, Doctor?"

Kayne nodded to the equipment in the back of the Mustang.

"Oh, no. I'm just holding that stuff for a friend. These mountains are all protected anyway."

We shook hands again, and the young man circled to the other side of the car, vaulted in without opening the door, and sped out of the park.

Kayne opened the envelope. One file folder marked 'Private' was empty, except for a single sheet of paper and a business card. The business card belonged to Robert Amenti, Acting Resident Choreographer of Ballet Purgatorio.

The page was blank except for a two-inch circled dot.

Kayne shielded his eyes and looked up at the sky into the bright light.

Thomas Paul Severino

Chapter Eleven: Phaethon
Ballet Purgatorio, San Francisco, California

Nick Sechi's Journal

"I created the piece for him. He has to do it."

The Artistic Director shrugged and raised her hands palms-up on either side of her head.

"He will not dance the lead, Robert. Tyoma is convinced that a younger dancer should be cast in the role. Graciously stepping aside for a new artist, he would consider the secondary role."

Robert Amenti was not convinced of the supposed professional humility of the world-famous dancer Artem Eglievsky. Known to his friends as "Tyoma," the Ukrainian ex-pat's ego was colossal, on and off the stage.

"Bull shit. The starspot is the title role. He is far from gracious. Tyoma is afraid the part is too demanding, given his year-long absence from the stage. The man wants something."

Artistic Director Maria Berman nodded.

"Yes. For starters, Eglievsky wants the second lead, and he wants the part broadened. Helios must be a bigger part. He is asserting his right as the company's Étoile."

The young dancer/choreographer was visibly upset. His master's thesis, "Phaethon," was widely anticipated, and the company's future was riding on its success. With Eglievsky in the title role, the ballet would create financial solvency and pay many bills. There was a lot of arts "buzz" about the work of the wunderkind choreographer and the highly anticipated return of the legendary "bad boy of dance" to the ballet stage.

This was just like that asshole. He just doesn't fuckin' stop. Throughout our time together, he insisted on total control, particularly over my artistic work. Only one of us could shine.

"Nureyev danced the frisky boy in *L'après-midi d'un faune* until he was well into his fifties. Baryshnikov danced roles created for younger men when he was in his late fifties. Tyoma is like all of us in the dance. We possess eternal youth if we do not give in. The Ukrainian star is playing us. He is asserting creative control over my piece. Why are we not surprised?"

"Bobby, be reasonable. There is more of the composer Izabella Hajdú's music that we can use. We cut an entire scene when we tailored the score. She set music to the protests of Helios when the boy begs to drive the chariot. It is the middle part of the second movement."

The speaker was Michael Lee, the company's Musical Director. Amenti rebutted.

"Yes, I know the tone poem, Michael. The ostinato section, where Helios tells the boy about the chariot's passage through the zodiac, is long and monotonous. I am not adding to the cast for this ballet. It is designed to feature the principals, specifically the boy.

"Create a solo for the Sun God -- a *tour de force* for Tyoma. We can do the constellations using technology. An arch of astrological figures moves behind the god, who warns Phaethon and tries to change the boy's mind. Our technical wizzards will create some breathtaking CGI and..."

As the company's Regisseur, Olivia Ortiz-Leon was responsible for coordinating the production's design. Creative insight started and ended with these three artists, but Amenti was not to be deterred.

I will not have a glorified stage manager interfering with my masterpiece. Tyoma has been lobbying for changes behind my back.

"Please try to remember we are not creating a video game, Olivia. This is dance – flesh and blood in motion."

The young artist slapped the table and said, "It will require a reworking of the entire ballet. This is the story of the boy who literally set the world on fire. Phaethon is the focus of the entire piece, with his feelings and passions at its center. His search for authenticity. Nothing will stop him from becoming who he is, despite his ineptitude. Phaethon was born to this."

Ashraf Sah, Chair of the Board of Directors, quoted from Ovid's Metamorphosis, Book II, "Here Phaethon lies who in the sun god's chariot fared. And though greatly, he failed, more greatly, he dared."

"Exactly. The plot is profoundly existential. That is why Hadjú set it to stark, minimalistic music. The zodiac section has some problems, Michael. You said so yourself. Eglievski's demands will throw the work out of balance."

He continued raging.

"You are ruining my masterpiece!"

Robert angrily paced the office. Through the floor-to-ceiling windows, he saw across the plaza to the rehearsal studios in the Marsden Building, a gift of John Shepherd Marsden. The technology billionaire named the complex for his wife, the late Elena de Céspedes Marsden, the Cuban-born *prima ballerina assoluta*.

In selecting an architect for the center, Marsden insisted that artists be seen in all their artistic phases. In addition to luxury condos, which overlooked the arts district and San Francisco's City Hall, the tower featured offices, studios, and performance spaces behind an undulating glass façade. Ballet Purgatorio was chosen as the resident company, and every stage of its productions was opened to the world.

Watching the young dancers, Amenti said, "This work is a fable, a parable for every kid who somehow felt he was different and was taunted because of their uniqueness. Mocked with illegitimacy, Phaethon is a tortured soul. The demi-god begs his father, Helios, who swore to give the boy whatever he wanted, the chance to prove his paternity. The boy asks to drive the chariot of the sun through the heavens for a single day."

Now, the passionate artist and choreographer turned to the production team.

"One day to shine to prove he is who he is – special, unique, and authentic. It is not about the Sun God and his place in the hierarchy of the cosmos. It is about the boy. When we previewed it at the arts festival in Spoleto last year, the critics gave us raves."

An unexpected voice, thick with a Slavic accent, came from near the doorway.

"You danced the role in Italy to critical acclaim. And so, you will triumph as Phaethon here in San Francisco, my Robert. I will see to it."

Chapter Twelve: *Iaijutisu*
221 Baker Street, San Francisco, California

Notes to the File by Andi S. Rodrigues, Administrative Assistant

"More coffee, Miss?"

"Yes, thanks, Andi. Please tell Mrs. Trasker the eggs were perfect. Any stirrings from upstairs? What the hell are those guys doing? That clanging noise is making me crazy. May I see that bracelet, Darling? It is so faboo. Damn, what a beautiful day, warm and sunny. Hope it stays that way. Can you sit and dish? I need to get caught up on my boys. Hello, you guys. Loving an ear scratching? Alice, go tell your daddies to stop that racket and come entertain their guest. Sorry, Chouko, Darling, my Japanese is very rusty. Nope... got nothing... OK *Sayonara*. How's that? Go with Alice. Good boy."

I just gotta get Trasker to really do the decaf thing.

It's easy to see why this woman was Dr. Kayne's bestie. After three cups of the "high octane," her brain was flying at 100 miles per hour and going in an easy dozen directions at once, just like my boss' ADHD. I extended my wrist and turned my jewelry for inspection while pouring a refill.

"No. All's quiet on the second floor. That guy is Jiro Ishida, a friend of Kris'. He is teaching some martial arts stuff to Doctor Sorenson and Mr. Sechi. He goes by 'Jack.' Nice guy."

I added, "My boyfriend. It's from Guatemala -- Bracelets for Change. Funds go to help rural kids and families. Trasker insists on no bling in her kitchen, but I really love the piece."

I attempted to respond to her other items in the breakfast conversation. As the dogs raced off in the direction of the lords of the manor, a yawning barefoot man in boxer shorts strode across the flagstone patio, scratching his butt. He bent and kissed his woman, snagged a gulp of her coffee, checked out the mock fighting, and said, "Morning, Beautiful... Oh shit, that looks like fun. Andi, can I get a..."

He dashed in the direction of the Parkour course and the other jocks. I must have looked perplexed.

"He wants juice. I'll get him some of Kris' green goop. You know it's some kind of secret spornosexual fraternity, don't you? All males and so obsessed with fitness and the best grooming, showing off their fit, toned, and virile bodies — a cult of male beauty. They dress the same, exercise in unison, even eat and drink the same shit."

She stood to retrieve an ashwagandha shake from the kitchen. However, she was intercepted by Mrs. Trasker, who handed her a plastic sports bottle filled with the concoction in question. I stood up and began to pick up a few breakfast dishes.

"Thank you, Trasker."

The chief cook and housekeeper almost smiled as our guest added, "Athletes. You can't cook 'em. You can't eat 'em."

"You sound convinced, Miss."

Yeah, definitely a bit of sarcasm in that remark. The old bird has a twinkle in her eye. She knows more than her rosary, that one. I tried to look busy with the breakfast sideboard and the patio table.

"Andi, please remember the Doctor's 9 AM."

"Thank you, Mrs. Trasker. My laptop is right here. I will remind him. Any word from his Highness?"

"Mr. Krisof Sorenson is not down yet."

Trasker went back into the house. The clanging stopped.

"Rebecca, my lovely. Did you sleep well?"

"Kayne Darling, you are ignoring two alluring women to fight with broomsticks?"

"These are real, not wooden katanas, my lotus. Nick and I have graduated under the tutelage of young Sensei Ishida."

"Thanks, Girl, is that for me?

Rebecca Quinto lifted the tumbler of supplement slop up and away from the hands of Mr. Sechi. My bosses held Japanese wooden swords and were sweating like gay circuit party boys going to confession.

"No, Darling, after last night, Mr. Gadarn needs some intense revitalization, if you know what I mean."

Rebecca pulled back her long mane of mahogany hair and winked lasciviously. I poured them both tumblers of water and handed them a couple of gym towels.

Referring to the sports shake, Nick said, "You had better take it to him, Miss Thang, because that young Sensei is about to destroy his spectacular reporter's ass. Thinks he is such a hotshot with all that..."

Nick gestured to the course where Jack was taking Mark to the grass with some lightning-fast moves and loud shouts in Japanese. The younger man extended a hand and brought Mark back to his feet. Jack coached a few blocking maneuvers with the handsome journalist.

"I swear if I have to pull one more male off my man on this trip..."

As she moved away, I was caught by how lovely she was, graceful and sensual in a chic Camilla swim ensemble, the pink and gold silk coat catching the breeze and trailing out as she walked.

Rebecca slipped one shoulder bare. Placing a hand on her hip and holding the drink aloft like it was an offering for a sultan, she sallied forth to meet the warriors. Rebecca knew how to get even the most preoccupied man's attention.

Nick carefully placed the sheathed swords on one of the chaises. Kayne leaned over my shoulder until I handed him my tablet. He gnawed on a dragonfruit and continued to review the case notes.

"Need anything from the office, Boss? I'll just hit the kitchen. We have just enough time to do a grub grab before..."

In an instant, Trasker was there with a big tray. I helped her unload their breakfast victuals and more green shit. Nick held up the coffee pot.

"Dr. Sorenson, I am lodging a formal protest concerning the appalling lack of clothing here at 221 Baker." As she spoke, she handed Kayne his Versace robe. With a guilty look, Nick grabbed an oversized t-shirt with some superhero logo I had never heard of and pulled it over his upper body.

"When I came to this job ..."

Trasker would always frame her complaints by saying how surprised she was and that she did not expect such-and-such when she accepted the job. As if she had been misled and compromised...

"... I did not expect so much nudity and... well... to be frank... the free love that seems to..."

She was helping Kayne into his cover-up as she spoke. Dr. Kayne lifted an arm, then another, and stood for the belt tie-off. He never stopped working, scrolling through the documents on the tablet. He had been down this road before.

As always, Kayne was half-listening. He resumed his seat and held up one index finger while reading as if to pause the conversation. A point about the murder investigation or concerning the improprieties surrounding the Sorenson-Sechi business and personnel, I do not know, assumed importance.

Nick took his tablet and began to power it up before sitting down to his egg white omelet and juice. Trasker would not be hushed up.

"Sir, I am only thinking of the boy and how his Catholic upbringing is slipping and..."

Nick did a very comic spit-take.

"T, gimme that again. No offense, but did you ever think that the Catholic thing and the sex are..."

Kayne placed a restraining hand on his husband and addressed Mrs. Trasker in an earnest voice.

"I understand completely and will bring up the issue with my family. I apologize if you have been made to feel uncomfortable. We will make adjustments where necessary. Thank you, Mrs. Trasker."

Nick looked at his Smart Watch and added, "Speaking of the phony-baloney prince..."

He raised his eyebrows in a questioning expression.

Mrs. Trasker looked up at the windows of Kris' room, looked back, and shook her head. She went back into the kitchen, wondering if the situation would go from bad to worse. Most likely, it would.

Kayne slid the tablet back toward me. He tapped the screen.

"Andi, this section on Ballet Purgatorio, see what you can get on the members of the Board. Reach out to Scott at the Aerie. He can get the secret files on just about anyone. They are quite a fascinating group."

Nick said, "Yeah, and that dancer dude, um..."

I said, "Eglievsky. He was there last night, Mr. S. I will lay you eight to five, those are from him. They came just before breakfast."

I pointed to the nine giant, yellow, black, and green sunflowers in the ceramic pitcher at the end of the long patio table. They reminded me of a Van Gogh or that scene in Dr. Zhivago – you know, where the petals on the sunflowers slowly dry and fall to the sound of the balalaika's sensuous playing of "Lara's Theme."

Before Nick could snag the card, a beautifully manicured set of fingers picked up the note and read, "The Honorable Kristof Saxe-Coburg Gotha-Koháry Sorenson."

She lowered it with a somewhat exasperated movement.

"Darlings, nobody has that many names."

Kayne and Nick exchanged a rather dramatic look as Rebecca dropped into a seat next to her bestie and rested her chin on his shoulder.

"So, when I marry your gorgeous nephew, can I get a royal title? Lord knows I will never get Mr. Gadarn to make me an honest woman or the countess I have always been destined to be."

Oh brother.

"I can just keep him on the side. And then what will I be to you, Kayne Darling?"

"Quite dead, my dear, or incarcerated. Do not molest my child."

She made a face that ran the gamut from a pout to a smile, and then to a friendly kiss as she read over his shoulder.

Nick said, "Just so you know, Miss R, we seem to be coming down on the side of homosexuality these days if my tally of his loves and sexual conquests is accurate. Hey guys, breakfast is waiting for ya."

Right on cue, Jack and Mark entered the patio and made for the breakfast bar. They loaded up plates while talking.

Sidebar: Rebecca stuck her tongue out at Nick.

"No, Mark, *laijutsu* is not an aggressive attack art. It is more counterattack. It is classic *bujutsu* swordsmanship, not for the battlefield but for training the body and the mind.

"You saw what I had Dr. Sorenson and Mr. Sechi doing. The challenge is to strike that metal pole with their swords at least one thousand times a day. If the technique is perfect each time in the standing *tachi-ai* position, your body and mind enter a state of warrior strength and awareness that is embedded in your unconscious."

"Cool. I learned some of this with a guy when we were in Egypt and Greece last year. Show me the *lai-goshi* again."

Mark called, "Hey. Beautiful, watch this."

Jack set down his breakfast things and swung his body out and into a low crouching posture. He shouted in Japanese. Dropping to his left knee, he placed his left hand on his waist, turned his torso to face forward into the plane of his legs, and raised his bent right arm, holding a butter knife above his head.

Mark did the same, but he held up a spatula.

"Your chest should be turned more in the plane of the kneeling thigh. That's it, Sir."

"Darling, is Little Mark trying to say 'good morning?' Oh, my stars."

"Oh, shit."

The hunky guy stood up and used his hands to cover the opening in his boxer shorts. Nick was howling, Kayne was deadpanning, and I was tapping keys and slyly smiling.

Probably realizing that most had seen cute Little Mark, Big Mark said.

"Sorry, Andi."

I said, "Not a problem, guy."

I pointed to a pile of towels and terry robes on the wicker bench. The warriors covered up and sat down to eat-- Little Mark tucked modestly back under his covers.

Thomas Paul Severino

Chapter Thirteen: A Phone Call from Purgatory

221 Baker Street, San Francisco, California

Nick Sechi's Journal

"No, I'm awake. Slept too late. Partied too much after the performance last night. Damn, what time is it?"

"Almost nine. Did you get the flowers, my boy?"

"I haven't been downstairs yet. Our housekeeper most likely put them in water. I'll get back to you. Oh yeah, hey, thanks, though."

"The sunflower is the national flower of my country. As they grow, they turn toward the direction of the sun from its rising to its setting."

"Nice."

"Perhaps they are symbolic, my young friend. I enjoyed the performance. It is one of my favorites. I saw a revival in the West End last year, but your company was much superior."

"Were you able to see both parts? 'Angels in America' is an epic, I will say."

"No, I have been in rehearsal this week. Last night was the first opportunity."

"My character is interesting. The dude is a fuckin' mess. I like playing broken people rather than heroes."

"Your listing in the program indicated you have experience in musical theater. I would like to hear you sing sometime."

"My uncles say I am a very accomplished showoff. I do a lot of sports also, if you really want to know the rest of my story."

"Your dedication to body training is most evident in the nude scene. I am aware that you play football at your University. Good for grace, coordination, and muscle development. I, too, must train for long hours for my art. Interestingly enough, I will be almost naked in this piece. As I age, I am concerned about roles such as this.

"When I danced Martha Graham's exotic 'Lucifer' in Kyiv at age eighteen, my costume was shockingly brief. The impresario was afraid the government would shut us down. Happily, they did not interfere. However, the present part also calls for this body to be on display. Alas, the critics will make the comparison."

"Oh, hey, you said you are opening soon."

"We are delaying the opening. I am dissatisfied with the work, to speak frankly. I insisted that the choreographer rewrite it and change the staging. Also, the title role is being danced by a young man… ahhh, well… he is one whom I have agreed to… ahhh, … coach, coach, I believe you say. Yes, I have trained young Robert over the years."

"Cool. So yeah, so, I'm standing at the window and watching my family gather outside, and I should get down there before Cook closes the kitchen so…"

"A prince of the stage such as yourself should have others do your bidding with no restrictions. You will soon have a fine personal staff if you stay with this vocation, which seems to suit you well. It is your destiny, Kristof."

"Got a long way to go, I am thinking."

"I will let you attend to your family. You must have dinner with me, my young friend, when the theater is dark, and I am not in a grueling rehearsal."

"All good. Text me when you want to set it up."

Chapter Fourteen: A Death in Fremont

221 Baker Street, San Francisco, California

Nick Sechi's Journal

"The whole thing went out of balance, and the load came crashing down. It makes no sense. None of the on-site operators would have left that thing hanging in the sky like that."

"An accident, Rosie. More coffee?"

"Yes, thank you, Nick. No. I am doing a Kayne Sorenson here. 'It was murder most foul.' Not to inject levity into the situation, but I am becoming more convinced this was also no accident— first the murdered scientist and now this. Something's odd about all of this. Murders disguised as accidents?"

"Yes." Rebecca said, "But, where is the connection?"

Kayne said nothing. He was in his meditative pose -- fingertips steepled and staring off into the distance.

Rosie continued, "The victim, Wade Bronson, was a tech engineer in the aerospace industry, one of those private design and manufacturing firms. He was headquartered outside of Fremont in the South Bay area. Only he was killed."

"Crushed?"

"Flat as a pancake. The coroner had a hard time getting the body out of his mangled car. Bronson was a bit obsessive-compulsive. Predictable. Always did the same things at the same time. He was leaving the gym when three-quarters of a ton of construction material dropped from the sky while he was in his car."

"Damn, and say again, what makes you suspect murder, Officer?"

"No one parks under something like that, Mr. Gadarn. That crane was brought into place after the guy went inside Fremont CrossFit. There is a construction site next door. The load was high up, so I suspect he either did not see it as he exited or thought he could get out from under it safely."

Kayne, still staring, said, "Please describe in detail the condition of the cables."

Detective Inspector Rosie Martell took three photos from her folder and handed them to Kayne.

"Those babies are wire rope, strand cables made from carbon steel."

Kayne mumbled, "A metal alloy of carbon and iron with traces of manganese, silicon, and copper – very high tensile strength."

"Darling, how do you know this shit?"

"Common knowledge, my girl." Kayne pointed to the picture. "Nick?"

"Melted, Boss. No doubt about it."

"Right. One of the women exiting the fitness place thought she saw a spark and heard a pop just as the load fell. "

Andi pulled up a figure on her tablet.

"Olvid 537, miniature explosive. Remotely operated. That's one powerful bitch, folks."

Mark said, "They used those in Syria and in Yemen when I was there. Andi is right -- capable of lifting a tank four feet in the air if played right. Cell phone detonated."

"OK, so why not just attach it under the car? Seems a lot of trouble."

"Quite right, my love. Why indeed."

Jack came back from playing "run and catch" with the dogs. He did a nod to a wobbling figure striding out onto the patio. The newcomer got halfway to the table and was accosted from behind by Trasker.

She came quickly out of the kitchen with a large, blue and white, Polynesian-patterned cotton wrap.

"Ba, ba, ba, bap. Hold on Master Sorenson."

Jessie Trasker caught the brash jock in his red Andrew Christian thong and wrapped one of the sarongs we brought from Hawai'i around the boy exhibitionist's hips.

"Oughta be ashamed, Master Kris."

"Hey, Mrs. T., getting a bit too familiar over here. Hey, that tickles." He pulled away, butt covered.

"There is no hope for the likes of you. Your Gran would…"

Trasker did not finish. She shook her head and went back inside.

"Morning, all." He raised his arms in a triumphant pose.

Rebecca did golf claps.

"Darling, you were exceptional last night, as I am sure you well know."

Kris did a bow complete with hand flourishes right out of the court of Elizabeth I.

I said, "Careful, shy boy, you lose that, and Trasker will chase you with the wooden spoon."

"Ahhh, my public, all you wonderful little people."

Andi said, "Oh, brother."

Jack brought him a plate, and Kris kissed his bud. He leaned over the table to inspect the floral arrangement. I placed a tea towel over his rump as a security upgrade. Kayne did an eye roll. The toast of the San Francisco theater scene (in his own mind, that is) picked up the card and viewed its contents.

As he read the note, he said, "Such a very nice man."

I introduced him to Rosie Martell.

"Nice to meet you, Kris. 'The Chronicle' said 'Angels in America' was excellent. I think they named your performance in the role of Joe as outstanding."

"No kidding? Well, isn't that nice? I mean, all of this is just kinda a sideline while I am in school. But the compliments… so very kind."

Oh, brother.

Kayne did an eye roll. Rebecca moved in and dropped her arms around the boy Barrymore. She was goofing around with Kris in an exaggerated manner.

"I have decided you must marry me, my beauty. This one is not interested in all this voluptuousness or walking down the aisle. Carry me off, Darling." She indicated Mark, who was scrolling and examining the pictures of the case.

She added, "I can keep him as a trophy lover. Quite trendy these days, it seems."

Kris laughed, "Who is this diva? Have another mimosa, Aunt Rebecca."

Never looking up, Mark kept his eyes on his tablet but lifted his right arm to flex a bicep. Rebecca squealed and slid out of the arms of Star Boy and into the lap of the famous and quite hunky brown-haired journalist.

"You're so easy, woman."

Mark looked around her to concentrate on his screen. He growled and ensnared a free hand in her luxurious hair – heterosexual hijinks.

Pretending to struggle, she continued to make conversation.

"How's your dad, Darling?"

"Hoping to hear pretty soon, thanks." Kris looked at Kayne and me, and I nodded. Rebecca got it – subject change.

Jack said, "Kris, can I see you inside for just a moment?"

"Wow, sounds serious. Sure."

He picked up his plate and drink and followed Jack into the sunroom.

Kayne looked over Mark's shoulder and asked, "There on the crane, Rosie. Is that a graffito? Looks like something-H E-M-I, and the next letter is also too stylized to make out."

The Inspector took back the photo and shook her head.

"I am not sure, Kayne." She handed it to me, but I was at a loss as well.

"Doing a search on Wade Bronson, Doctor Kayne. I should have it for you shortly."

"Thank you, Andi."

"Rosie, I do not want to hold you up, so I will ask if we can review this file a bit more and have Andi get it back to you. There are connections here to the Blackhawk murder. I am sure of that."

He added almost gravely.

"I feel the stars are out of alignment. Most peculiar…"

Thomas Paul Severino

Chapter Fifteen: Living with a Star

The Morrison Planetarium, Golden Gate Park, San Francisco. California

Nich Sechi's Journal

"Holy crap!"

The sky above exploded with an intense, fiery yellow, orange, brown, and white mosaic. The surface of a massive star erupted in a shower of burning plasma and flaming gases that blurred the edges of the sphere and blasted out into space.

"Respect the fear, young Sechi. You are looking at the fate of the Earth and, in fact, the entire solar system. This star will expand to engulf both Mercury and Venus' orbits and make this, our planet, uninhabitable. But you have some time."

Kayne said, "About five billion years or so?"

"Correct, Doctor Sorenson. You are looking into the heart of a giant nuclear reactor. The Sun fuses 600 million tons of hydrogen into helium every second, converting 4 million tons of matter into energy instantly. However, given its mass, 330,000 times that of Earth, it will take a long time to flame out."

Priyanka I. Ngwogu, Ph.D., was a distinguished astrophysicist born in the Yoruba community of Ibadan, Nigeria. She was a recent recipient of the Dannie Heineman Prize for Astrophysics for her work on stellar atmospheres and stars' composition. The Professor was on the faculty at the University of California, Berkeley, and a regular lecturer at the Morrison Planetarium.

The distinguished academic pressed buttons on her handset, and the 75-foot dome's NanoSeam projection screen disappeared, producing a true-to-life recreation of luminous, faraway space and black skies.

Kayne said, "Priya, again, thank you for agreeing to this private lecture. We find ourselves on the edge of what could be a critical case, and I know very little about your field, I confess."

"Oh, Kayne, it is lovely to see you again, and you are just a most delightful young man, Nick. It's easy to see why the two of you are a couple.

"But I have a question, Nick. How do I explain all of your, shall I say, salacious adventures to my Kayne? She is thirteen and follows the exploits of her namesake with a passion. All I hear is 'Nick and Kayne, Nick and Kayne.' A proper Nigerian-American girl does not understand the specific dimensions of your exploits, perhaps."

I did not even blush. Nick Boy makes no apologies for who we are.

"She is thirteen, you say?"

"Almost fourteen, actually."

"I think perhaps the way kids are so precocious these days, she will explain it to you and not the other way around."

The professor laughed, smiled, and said, "You are most likely correct."

Kayne and Dr. Ngwogu were friends at Notre Dame in their graduate school days. I cannot reveal the details, but I can say that he saved her family's reputation in a scandal that involved government secrets. In those days, Kayne was a rookie detective and was fast becoming one of the foremost psycho-criminologists on the planet.

"My dear friend here was most extraordinary in matters of the heart ever since I have known him."

She patted Kayne's cheek and continued with cosmological theories.

"So, why do we study the Sun and, in particular, the solar wind?

"The Sun is the only star we can study up close. By studying this star we live with, we learn more about stars throughout the universe. Its effect on the Earth is vast. The Sun is a source of light and heat for life on Earth. The more we know about it, the more we can understand how life on Earth developed.

Now, the observatory ceiling seemed to grow closer as the floor actually rose up into the dome. *Very cool.* Dr. Ngwogu typed, and the images changed to show colorful streams flowing off our blazing star toward the Earth. Lines of energy met and poured around emanations surrounding our home planet, missing a cosmic bombardment as if the Earth were wearing protective armor.

"The Sun creates a vast and powerful solar wind, which affects Earth in less familiar ways. Here, you see the flow of ionized gases from the Sun that streams past Earth at speeds exceeding a million miles per hour. Disturbances in the solar wind shake Earth's magnetic field and pump energy into the radiation belts. These changing conditions in near-Earth space are known as space weather."

Now blue planet was surrounded by flashing, orbiting dots dancing within the green magnetic field lines.

"Space weather can change the orbits of satellites, shorten their lifetimes, or interfere with onboard electronics."

To illustrate, Dr. Ngwogu made the Sun pulse brighter, and the golden fires streaming from its surface flared up and showered the protective field like a bonfire. A few of the satellites winked out.

"The more we learn about what causes space weather and how to predict it, the more we can protect the satellites we depend on for communication and intelligence on many subjects.

The animation changed again and seemed to pull back for a longer view of our neighboring planets and space phenomena.

The astrophysicist continued. "The solar wind also fills up much of the solar system, dominating the space environment far past Earth. As we send spacecrafts and astronauts further and further from home, we must understand this space environment just as early seafarers needed to understand the ocean."

Now, we saw shadowy overlay images of 15th-century exploration vessels sailing through space, combined with modern-age spacecraft. The mythic adventures into outer space unfolded before our eyes.

"Understanding and being able to predict space weather during this time of global warming is critical to solving the challenges posed by climate change. As the Earth's protection against solar radiation is compromised by the greenhouse gas effect, the damaging effects on life on this planet are increased. Joint international cooperation in researching and understanding space weather is essential to our survival."

The floor returned to its previous level, and the display presented a series of sun-shiny days, dawns, and twilights. The lights in the observatory came up.

"And now, my young friends, what questions do you have for me?"

"An observation, perhaps. Research on solar weather and astrophysics is essential for the new privatization of space exploration. Is that a correct assumption?"

"Correct, Kayne. The space industries are competing for the finest scientific minds on Earth to develop solutions to costly space travel and green solutions for a dying planet. SpaceX comes to mind, but many other start-up companies are willing to pay top dollar for important research."

Kayne mused, "Yes. Or perhaps some companies are willing to do whatever it takes to obtain technologies that will advance their enterprises."

Chapter Sixteen: Mr. T and Company

Golden Gate Park, San Francisco, California

Nick Sechi's Journal

"I've got your location. We will meet you there. Not too long. We're kicking it."

I showed Kayne Mark's text and remounted.

"Wait, Boss. C'mere. Turn around."

I adjusted his backpack straps and gave him a "good to go" shoulder cuff. We had come over from our house in Pacific Heights to the Morrison Planetarium in Golden Gate Park on our mountain bikes.

"How's mine?"

He made a similar adjustment.

"We cannot show up with our rucksacks hanging off into the street, my love. Too tight?"

"Perfect. Let's work up an appetite, Big Guy."

We headed out of the lot at Burger Boys on Balboa and back into the park. Our rendezvous with Rebecca and Mark was at the San Francisco Model Yacht Boat House on Spreckles Lake. They were coming from a meeting at the de Young Museum and on the park's north side.

"There they are, Boss."

Our friends were pulling up to the Boat House's green doors just as we came over the northern border on Spreckles Lake Drive and continued along the west side on 36th Avenue. The cottage headquarters of the SFMYC Boathouse was tucked up a short lane just steps away from the southwest corner of the lake and the takeoff landing for the model yachts. About a half dozen clubbers were coming out carrying their boats and launching rods for a sunny afternoon of boating. Morning model yacht people were returning their crafts to the clubhouse.

Mark greeted us with, "So cool, guys. This place is a combination meeting hall, storage facility, workshop, and library. And folks, do I have to use the Men's!"

He dashed.

Kayne asked, "Your meeting at the art museum?"

"They're in. Now comes the hard part. Putting together a pre-Columbian art exhibit at the Fritcher that will be cutting edge," Rebecca said.

"Our plan focuses on the ancient Maya city-states of Guatemala and Mexico. Mark and I meet with the folks at the Museo de Totonicapán in Guatemala City in four days. They have one of the largest collections of Maya art in the world."

"I know it," Kayne said. "I visited the campus of El Universidad San Pedro in Guatemala City. I was part of a symposium there. The Museum is run by the University and is known for its extensive collection of pre-Columbian and colonial art of the Maya culture."

I asked, "What did you present, Kayne?"

His blue eyes seemed to flash.

"As I recall, it was a cultural psychopathology framing of human sacrifice in Pre-Columbian America."

I snickered, "Wow. Blood, gore, and religion – all that good stuff."

"Hey folks, let's get into some of that grub. What do you say?"

Mark was back and remounted his rental.

I pointed to our friends' colorful bike pants and shirts. "You two look like you are ready for the Tour de France. How did you pass scrutiny at the de Young?"

"Mark was rocking 'jock chic' with a pair of workout pants and a polo, now stashed. I have a skirt and blouse in my knapsack, and these little darlings are ultra transitional -- sport or fashion."

The Evil League

Seated on her bike, the CEO of the Fritcher Museum of Fine Arts of Ft. Lauderdale lifted one leg up and posed one of a pair of pearl and rhinestone bedazzled sneakers.

"They're Steve Maddens, Darling. It is essential to look the part."

"You are a fashionista on two wheels, my girl. Where to, Nick?"

I pointed and said, "There, near the Bison Paddock. I thought I saw an empty table."

We rolled on over and staked a claim.

I brought out a tablecloth from my kit. Simultaneously, the gorgeous bovine beauties placidly ignored us, either grazing or resting and chewing their cud. I looked into our knapsacks and groaned, "Uttt, Ohhh."

Kayne said, "Nick, the food!"

Mark was miffed.

"Hold it, hold it. You mean you set up this picnic and forgot the food? Seriously, dude? This boy is hungry enough to eat an entire..."

Rebecca put an index finger on her man's lips.

"Don't say it, Mark. You may start a stampede, and then where would we be?"

She nodded to three bison who decided not to fake their usual shyness and see what we were up to. They watched us intensely through the fence.

"Sechi?"

"Me, girl."

The young woman in livery from Chauffeuse placed the red and puffy, temperature-controlled package on the table. She pulled out the burgers, salads, and sides, all of which were wrapped in recyclable materials and contained in planet-friendly containers. The burgers were still warm.

"Got yer card on file, Sir."

I nodded and handed her a tip. She thanked us and dashed down to her Rav4 on the swale below our spot.

"Enjoy, folks."

Mark grinned, "Saved by delivery. Ya had me going, I will admit."

"Drinks, Darling."

"No cups -- gotta pass the bottle, kids." Mark withdrew and opened two insulated bottles of lemonade. "Cold and refreshing and alcohol-free. You fellas and gals are driving, remember."

Kayne just took it all in, but I could tell he was doing a "present-in-the-moment-but-really-not" thing. His mind was running at least two channels at once.

Rebecca helped set out the eats. She asked, "Was the lecture in astrophysics at the Morrison rewarding, my Darlings?"

"Definitely. I learned a lot. It is incredibly difficult to comprehend the vastness of the universe and all that comprises it. Humans suffer from such ignorant pride and hubris when it comes to living things and our place in the cosmos."

Apparently, one of the bison agreed with my assessment of humanity -- the demons that caused his kind's ecological extinction. The big guy snorted and mooed as if on cue.

Mark said, "You tell 'em, Mr. Tatanka."

He looked at a smiling Rebecca.

"The Lakota word for 'bison.' Common knowledge, Beautiful."

He snuck a French fry.

I waved my half-eaten burger at the bull behind the fenced enclosure. "Hey, studly, this is not one of your ancestors or any member of your evolutionary line. I bought us all Impossible Burgers. We're chomping down veggies just like you guys."

Kayne pulled me down next to him.

"You are an amazing boyo, my love."

He resumed that peculiar look as he traced his thoughts back to the investigations.

Rebecca said, "You have something you are not saying, Kayne. Out with it, Darling."

"The clues are in the stars, the cosmos. I am sure of it – the energy, the physics, all of it."

He looked at three somewhat startled faces.

"This case of ours. The two murders so far are related -- scientists working on top-secret astrological projects. While you were in Burger Boy, I got a text from Rosie down in Fremont. They cannot find Dr. Bronson's computer files. It seems his office was broken into."

I said, "Amazing, Dr. Rockland's files are also unavailable, although the Research Director will not say directly. That specific project is MIA, you can be sure."

"I agree with you. The common thread – missing research… that and the signatures."

Rebecca asked, "Are the victims being staged?"

"No, my dear. Signed. The murderer is signing the murder weapons. The 'monogram' on the cigarette case…"

Kayne moved a fry through a catsup smear on a burger wrapper in a familiar pattern.

"Scorpio."

Mark asked, "And Bronson?"

"The graffiti on the crane's cab – Nick?"

I showed him my phone. "This is an encryption program. I set it to letter combinations – find the two missing letters to the 'blank-h-e-m-i-blank' word. I have fifteen possible."

Kayne scrolled, "There." He pointed, and I took back my mobile. I made a scrunched-up face as I read, "Themis?"

"She is the ancient Greek Titaness, the goddess who built the oracle at Delphi. Themis is the personification of divine order, fairness, law, natural law, and custom."

Mark showed his iPhone.

"Statue of Themis outside the law courts in Brisbane."

The mighty and divine one held a sword in her right hand and raised the Scales of Justice in her left. The two pans were slightly out of balance.

Rebecca said one word as if it were a state secret.

"Libra"

Chapter Seventeen: Just One of Those Things

The Bison Paddock, Golden Gate Park, San Francisco, California

Nick Sechi's Journal

"Senator Diane Feinstein."

I raised my head from Kayne's lap and asked, "What? Did you invite her, Boss? VIP guests and the food's all gone. Damn."

He tousled my short hair and clarified, "No, my love."

He pointed to the bison who were imitating our post-meal reverie by kneeling in the meadow doing an asynchronous cud-chewing. One little guy was having a meal from his mom's underside.

"The story goes that when she was mayor of San Francisco, following the assassination of George Moscone and Harvey Milk, her husband, Richard Blum, gave her a gift of two bison. Over the years, the Blums have added to the herd, but they believe the bloodlines go back to the original two."

Mark did a Sir Walter Raleigh and spread the tablecloth near us for his love. Rebecca moved over and joined us on the grass. He rested his head on her lap as she said, "So gallant, Darling."

Mark entwined one of her hands in his and directed his attention to us.

"So, the Prince Boy is in rough shape, Uncles. Given his star entrance and all that glitterati crap he was pulling at breakfast, the kid is pretty heartbroken. We had a brief man-to-man conversation after you guys left for the Academy. Rebecca was in our room, getting some work done."

"Jack?"

"Well, Nick, I would say 'no' to that. Kris is smart enough to know the difference between playing and true romance. Jack, too, I would say. It seems the Sensei told Kris he was heading back up to Mendocino County. Apparently, there was no offer to continue their affair. Affair? Is that what his tribes are calling more than a hookup and less than romance these days? Generation Z or whatever – I cannot keep 'em straight. What is the saying in the world of the late teens and early twenties?"

"Liaison, Darling."

"Naw, too literary, Beautiful."

Mark continued, "So he tells me, 'All good, Uncle Mark. I have no time for relationships. I suck at them anyway.' Bitterness out the ass there, but he is trying hard to find courage."

"Matt."

"Right, Kayne. So, I talked to him about his aspirations for a happily ever after. He told me that they were taking a break, and it was Matt who made the suggestion in the middle of the Jack 'liaison,' – naw, really sounds all Molière and shit, Rebecca. In the middle of the Jack Ishida sex-up – there we go. We journalists are plain-speaking. Kris is now two for two, and he is having problems with that."

Rebecca commented, "He is so young and seems to be dancing on air. Exceptionally good-looking, an accomplished student-athlete…"

"Excuse me, but his grades could be better. The lad knows of our expectations in that regard, my friends. And as for his athletics, I believe Coach McDaniel is having a hard time keeping the lad disciplined and focused on collaboration with his teammates."

"I hear you, Kayne, but in the process, the boy is learning about what it means to be a loving man – an authentic man."

"I have thought for a long time that the kiddo has let his sex drive get pretty much out of control," I said. "He's getting into some of the clubs in the City with a fake ID. I know that for a fact, and now the theater thing. His Grandma Sechi would throw a shoe at him if she found out."

I looked off at a gathering of Canadian geese who had dropped over from Spreckles Lake to see what the lawn around our picnic table held to appease their appetite.

Thinking for a moment, I finally added, "I will talk to him again. Soccer practice starts next week for the fall season. As the play's run ends, Kris needs to make sure his priorities are in order. Perhaps it is for the best that Jack is out of the picture, and Matt is on hold or whatever."

Mark came back with, "You will find him, as I said, pretty embittered about the chances of finding a truly caring guy to share his life with."

"His ego... and I have said this before -- star quality, alpha boy, jock phenom, male beauty, whatever you want to call it. I think he believes his own fandom raves, and that drives guys off. The kid escaped from kidnappers when he was seventeen by kicking the asses of the Big Bads, for fuck sake."

Mark said softly, "Nick, it's simple. He wants to be a studly player, that is for sure, but he does not want to be left behind. And into all of this is one more important element."

"Eric."

"Yes, Kayne," Rebecca said. "What's the latest?"

"Young Kristof wants desperately to go to Europe and visit his father at the sanitarium. His doctors agree that this is not the right time. Eric is in a very volatile state at this time, and his caretakers have some essential security concerns for both the boy and his father. The spy-verse is electric with wonderings about his disappearance. So far, his location has not been compromised."

Rebecca said, "Anyone looking to settle scores with the Super Spy needs only to track the comings and goings of his son."

I added, "Correct. Kris needs to keep a low profile. Kayne and I have been talking about a bodyguard for a while."

"May I say that I am at a loss when it comes to parenting our nephew? I am following Nick's lead, as he is much more understanding, insightful, and compassionate regarding young Kristoff. It is with some regret that I admit that I am my father's son."

"Don't sell yourself short, Boss. The boy idolized you."

Kayne looked off over the grassy meadow.

He said, "One thing we have resolved regarding our case involvement is we are going to make sure that one of us, at least, is never too far from home. Australia is not a good choice. Ace and Darana have a child on the way."

I added, "And Kris would never agree. No offense, Boss, but it would be like banishment."

"Colorado?"

"We did talk about an arrangement with my brothers for an extended vacation, but Nick and I want to keep our 'son' here -- with us. A commitment among the three of us would necessitate that."

Rebecca had the same concealing expression that she had earlier accused Kayne of. I went for it.

"Now you have a secret, girlfriend. Come on, give."

"Nicky, you are spending too much time with your husband. You sound just like him."

"You have a tell, Rebecca. I am an expert at body language, given my Italian heritage."

Mark sat up and turned to look at her.

Kayne mused, "You looked guilty as can be, and you examined the back of your hands. How many times do you need confirmation that your manicurist got it right?"

"You know, he's right, Beautiful. You are doing it now."

Kayne smiled. "Very good, Mark. Tell us what you are concealing, my girl."

"I peeked."

"What?"

The flowers, Kayne. After Kris read the note, I swiped it, and I peeked."

"And?"

She finished, "It said, 'To a rising _Étoil_ – burn brightly. Yours fondly, Tyoma.' Somewhat dramatic, and I will venture to add, Darlings, subtly passionate."

Mark said, "Jack's body isn't even cold. That boy is a man magnet."

"Excuse me, did you say Tacoma?"

She shook her head and said, "Tyoma, Nick. It is the diminutive used by the ballet legend Artem Eglievsky."

Thomas Paul Severino

Chapter Eighteen: Firelight

221 Baker Street, San Francisco, California

Nick Sechi's Journal

"You guys are up late. What's up? Casework got you edgy?"

I stirred on the couch, and Kayne reached for his nightcap after placing another log in the library fire. Kris unzipped his light jacket and walked over to each of us, delivering a kiss.

"Getting chilly out there. Fall is on us, and with it, soccer weather, men. Bet! At fuckin' last."

"When?"

"Practice starts the day after tomorrow."

He looked at Kayne and added, "And your favorite, Uncle Kayne— classes start next week."

"Good, Lad. Very good."

"How about a beer, Shakespeare?" I checked Kayne's expression as I asked. "All good?"

"Would love one if that's OK... my last days of being a party boy, at least for a while."

He helped himself from the sideboard, cracked a Mick Light, and settled on the floor between the two of us on the carpet.

"How was Part One tonight?"

"Yeah, we got it together so fine tonight. You know when the angel comes through the ceiling... now I am not on stage, you see, but even watching from the wings, I get goosebumps."

Kayne reflected, "Kushner is a genius -- one of the outstanding playwrights of the age. 'Angels in America' is the definitive epic theater piece of our time."

"Yeah, definitely GOAT. I've been reading a lot about AIDS as I prepared for the part. The play is so packed with things that make you think."

I stared into the fire and said, "We lost so many to that plague. So many beautiful people, every one of them. We live within an absence of souls. A divine abandonment… "

"Reagan said nothing while thousands died," Kayne said. "And Americans hold him up as a great president. I am astounded and filled with despair at the thought."

Kayne took another swig of his Hibiki. For a while, the only sound in the library was the crackle of the fire and the settling of the logs.

"OK, so, what'd I do?"

Kayne and I looked at the boy.

"OK, boomers. Yeah, don't give me those eyes, you guys. I know something's up. Uncle Kayne is five paragraphs away from slipping into his Australian slang, which he does when he's been drinking and thinking, and Uncle Nick is grinding his teeth. He only does that when he's extra fidgety. What stress, guys? What?"

I started to say something when a soft, zapping sound was heard. I looked for the extra-terrestrial life forms with the ray guns when Kris said, "Oh, shit. Sorry. Mind if I take this?"

Without waiting for an answer, he hopped up and crossed the room to the terrace.

"Hi. No, yeah, it's cool. I'm still up. Oh, it went fine…" Kris stepped out on the terrace and closed the door.

"iPhone popular at 12:55 AM? We have our work cut out for us, Boss."

"At least he's home, my love."

Kayne stood up, poured another three fingers over new ice, and pointed to my beer.

"Naw, I'm good. Thanks."

As he came back, he reached over and touched my face. "You *do* grind, my love. Did you not know?"

"Yeah, bed partners mentioned it in my former lives. Usually, just before we went into breakup mode."

"Now, you have me shakin' in my knickers, boyo."

I kissed the back of his hand.

"Stuck with me, Bossman. Not going anywhere."

"On another note, my love, I find it interesting that our nephew is perplexed by my quaint Australian phrases. He has become the master of Gen Z speak. What, in all that is reasonable, is the meaning of GOAT? A reference to a farm animal?"

I laughed as I explained.

"GOAT – Greatest Of All Time. Couple of language barriers in this family, mate."

The terrace door opened, and Kris ended the call.

"… you too, sleep well."

He tossed the phone on the divan and sat back down.

"Sorry. A new fan..."

He looked us over and said, "Mark and Rebecca – a good day with them?"

"Yep, biking around town. The hills of this Golden City kicked their straight asses, and..."

I checked my tracker.

"… they hit the shucks about three hours ago."

"Cool."

Kayne said, "Mark told us that Jack left, Lad."

Kris took a swig.

"Yeah, he had to get back to farm living, I guess. City life makes him tense. He has too many negative associations with his ex. Said to tell you thanks and all that. Also said to train tough."

I waited a moment and then said, "You good?"

He shrugged as he looked into the fire and said, "Oh, yeah. We're just friends. It was never gonna get serious. As I said, he's still hurting from his break-up. The dude was cheating on him. Loyalty... monogamy... that shit fucks you up. Sorry"

The firelight, the only illumination in the room, played over him like a caressing lover. He was indeed a handsome young man. The part of Joe Pitt, the young Mormon lawyer in "Angels in America," called for a mid-1980s conservative hairstyle and a few more blond highlights. He had a deeper version of the Sorenson blue eyes, complete with the long lashes. The planes of his face tended to be a bit more dramatic than the Aussies. Cliff-like cheekbones descended to a strong jaw. Off-stage, his voice had a bit of an English accent — a remnant of his young days at the Bulgarian court and the boarding school.

He stretched his athletic frame on the rug between Kayne and me and said, "My Unks are worried tonight. This has gotta be good... so, tell me."

I reached out and touched his jaw. It was a question. He rubbed the light blue bruise, but sort of chuckled.

"Spouse abuse... the woman playing Harper, my wife, is supposed to pull the shot. She has been having trouble with it, and it looks phony. I told her to just do it. So, ouch."

Kayne said, "Young Matthew... how's he doing?"

"Yeahhh... so, Matt. Matt. Matt. Matt..." Kris pulled up into a seated position and hugged his knees to his chest. He heaved a sigh.

"Fucked if I know, Uncle Kayne. Ghosted me big time. Moved on from the best of the best – his loss is all I gotta say. Working a lot at the Medical Center, I guess. Can we just, not... like... just leave that?"

He was drawing with his finger on the oriental. Grabbed his phone. Checked the screen and smirked. Kayne touched his shoulder.

"No."

Kris looked up.

"Huh?"

Kayne leaned forward into the boy's field of vision.

"No. There is nothing off-limits between us, Kristof. We love each other in this family. We discuss even the most problematic issues. We communicate. There are no secrets, and there is nothing... nothing any of us could do that would end the love we have for each other. It is unconditional, Son."

Kris looked up as if he were looking into the face of an angel. I was totally overwhelmed and raised a hand to my mouth to stifle getting a little *verklempt*. The firelight made the visuals almost cinematic.

Kris could not sustain the intensity and looked away, saying, "I don't know, Uncle Kayne... bedroom bull shit. Matt and I agreed to be open. Like with Jack, you know. But I felt like I was being pulled... confined – him getting all possessive and stuff. Yeah, we kept running like that, and I guess he couldn't handle it."

He got a bit angry as he said, "Finally, I was like, 'No. You say playing around is OK, and then you say it's not, and you want more. More what, dude? Make up your fuckin' mind.' There is a saying in Bulgaria, '*I dvata nachina ne sa nachini*.' Means 'Both ways is no ways.' That's my playbook."

He shrugged.

"So, he walked. Fuckin' split. Full stop."

Now, he was pacing and well into his beer.

"So fine. Whatever. *Dovizhdane*. Don't let the door hit you in the..."

He paused.

"We had words. Jack walked in on it. He knew he was caught in the middle. I think Jack decided to split soon after. Major shit storm, and Jack is all about getting along and shit."

He took a deep breath like he was pulling it all back in and down where he had imprisoned those feelings.

Kris stared at the fire for a moment. Then he said more softly, "Fucker hasn't even come to the play, man. Whateva."

We did not say anything for a bit.

"Like I give a shit…"

"Kris, is there anything either of us can do or say? It will heal, kiddo. Give it time."

"Yeah, Nick, you told me all of that last time, and all that stuff about, suddenly you'll know and shit. Well, I am done."

I stood up and faced him.

"C'mon, quit the acting, Kris. This 'I'll never love again' scene is right out of some sixties musical theater piece. Show some realness, man. Stop feeling sorry for yourself. You're nineteen and just getting started. But hear me out, kiddo. At some point, you gotta begin… begin, I am saying, to decide if you want to be a player or real, that's all."

Kayne said, "If it is love you want, Kristof, please try to understand it is a process of learning that often involves setbacks, but only in being true to yourself can you fully become an authentic man for others."

Kris shook his head.

"I'm a man, Uncle Kayne. A man. I am a man. I am over this crap, big time. People getting all clingy and jealous. It's sex, bro, and sometimes, that's all it is, but that can be good. It can be what I want, and right now…"

"Make up your mind. You done, or you ready to go deeper?"

"Seriously, Nick? With all of this? I'm through. A mindless trip to Hustlerville is looking pretty good right now – boy toy for hire. Getting what I want and no strings… auditioning for a daddy… bring it, fellas, this Studly does not disappoint."

"Stop."

"No, really. My Dad – no one ever tied *him* down. He takes what he wants. And even you guys… fighting and sexing like champions. Right now, I'm gonna enjoy myself, and the hell with it all."

"Kris, you go down that road, and I will… "

I stopped. My hands at my sides were clenching into fists. The expression on Kris' face was, "You will what?" We were nearing a dangerous spot here. So. I sat back down.

Silence. He finished his beer.

What he said next came out like a lost memory.

"My Dad?"

Kayne said. "No change. We have to give it time."

He stared stone-faced as if asking the question for the hundredth time. "Can I see him?"

"Not a good idea. Those who have sworn revenge are watching, Kristof. Despite our best efforts, you will lead them right to him."

"So, he and I are never to be together? Is that what you are telling me?"

"Lad, I am not saying that. We just have to work this out. Call in a few favors and move everyone into a more secure position. You will need to trust us."

"Deal. I have something I need you to promise."

"OK"

Using his fingers, he counted off, saying, "No bodyguards, no guard dogs, no boarding schools, no guns, no Nonna Sechi babysitting, no Australia. I am capable of going to school, playing soccer, living my life, and taking care of myself."

"Kris."

"I know you have a few new cases, and you may not be home, but I will be fine."

"Your Uncle and I need to think about this, Kristof. We are your guardians."

"Right. Not my guards."

He tapped a side table and continued to make his point. His blue eyes flashed in the firelight as he spoke.

"Uncle Kayne, it comes down to this. You ship me off to Inala, and I will bolt. You will never see me again."

Our nephew was making himself very clear. He softened a bit as he said, "Look, I love you both, but I will not be anyone's burden, and I will not be caged up. That goes for here and anywhere else, Aspen, Sofia, or anywhere. I am no one's victim, including my own. Let 'em bring it. I'm not afraid."

He took a deep breath and continued. "I will live up to my word at the University, but if I need to move out and live somewhere else, I will. You and Uncle Nick face danger a shit-load of times. I can do that too, man."

Kayne stood up.

"Kristof."

The boy left the room.

Chapter Nineteen: Lamplight

221 Baker Street, San Francisco, California

Nick Sechi's Journal

"Total fuck up."

"Why?"

"He's hurting, and he refuses to listen to reason."

We had adjourned to our bedroom.

"Who's reasoning, Nick? His or ours? Refusing to obey us? Not true. He is an earnest student and a dedicated athlete. Remember, he is emotionally a teenager and, in his mind, an abandoned boyo. It is a scene that seems to play itself time and time again.

"He overcompensates physically. Finds gratification and star-quality affirmation where he can get it – sports, theater, sex. But he will not be confined. Thus, he plays the field as it were..."

"A lot, Kayne. A lot. Kris beds a lot of people and doesn't seem to understand the effect he has on those who get more into him, more emotionally involved than he expects."

"... and they leave. Kristof gets hurt or is puzzled by it. That would be a better explanation. It does not fit into the boy's understanding of how relationships work, including their intricacies and responsibilities. In the world of our young prince, love and sex must be totally apart and without the restraints of commitment – what does his Generation Z crowd say? – NSA, no strings attached."

"Which is a nice way to say he is totally controlled by his sexual passions, and they are record-breaking. Hmmm, where have we seen that before? Oh, yeah, your brother. Right."

Kayne said softly, "Take that off."

He was seated in an armchair, with his stocking feet up on the ottoman, hands behind his head. His Oxford shirt's cuffs were rolled up, a casual style he preferred when we were kicking back in the Pacific Heights house for an evening at home.

He pointed to my Suicide Squad t-shirt. Without thinking, I pulled it off over my head as I paced the room. As I passed him, I was hardly aware that he took it.

"There is going to come a point in that kid's life when the hero worship he has for Eric will crash and burn, and we have to be there to pick up the pieces. I love your brother, but I have this sinking feeling he's doomed, Kayne."

"We will be there for him in that and everything."

The atmosphere in the room seemed to change, tilt a bit, and grow somewhat feral.

I asked, "Are you going to take a shower?"

He took my T-shirt away from his face and spoke softly, "Not right now."

I stepped over a sleeping Chuoko and Alice and cracked the window. I held onto the casement and grabbed at my socks, one at a time, tossing them toward the hamper.

I heard Kayne say, "Kristof deeply resents what he sees as abandonment by his father."

"What I don't get is how much he underestimates the shit that is hanging over his father's head."

My thinking was a bit messy as I continued, "Overprotective, my ass, Kayne. You and I both know and have seen firsthand what the Big Bads can do. He thinks that because he is so good-looking and fit, he can take on the fuckin world and…"

I turned away from the night lights and sounds of the City to face him. Kayne seemed lost in his thoughts as if exhausted by the case, our struggles with the boy, and the whole Sorenson worldview. His stare was somewhat deep, dark, and wicked in the velvet glow of the bedroom lamps.

"I saw it, Boss. I'm a cop's boy and a former... I know what they can do. I was there when my father got it on the 72nd Street platform of the Number Two Uptown Train. Kris has no fuckin' idea."

"And he is so much like you in that he will not be compromised by fear, by love, by physical challenges or restraints."

He gazed at me with an intense expression as he said, "Please put the dogs in the hallway, Nick."

His tone was measured and mysterious.

"Alice, get up, girl, good girl. Come on."

The Australian border collie followed my directions to the bedroom door. Alice's buddy cocked one open eye in our direction. I knew my Akita was thinking, "Are we going to get a treat now?"

Chouko, Kurisu o mamotte hoshī. Arisu to issho ni ikou. Īkoda.[2]

Our Akita raised up and followed his lady love out the door. They took up sleeping side by side on the landing outside Kris' door.

I closed the door, saying, "Whether he likes it or not, I think extra security around here for a while..."

I was heading for the bathroom, doffing my jeans, intending to have a wash-up.

"No."

"You gotta be kidding, Kayne. He's already going out a lot with his friends down to the bars in the Folsom. Life can be pretty dicey on the streets of this town."

"That is not what I mean. No shower. Come over here."

It wasn't until I was three feet from his reclining form that I realized what was going on.

"Stop. Stand right there."

---

[2] Chouko, Kris needs you to guard him. Go with Alice. Good Boy.

He made a one-handed motion that indicated I was to drop my briefs.

"Really, Kayne? We are having a serious discussion on how the two of us…"

"Do as you are told and stop speaking."

He put his hand out, and I placed my underwear in it. He gestured that I should widen my stance. His stare was dark blue in the lamplight, and his breathing came faster. He slowly brought my gear up to his nose and mouth as my body responded appropriately to his descent into the realms of kinkdom.

Kayne made a turn-around hand signal, and I did. I lowered my head as called for by the role. He leaned forward and said, "Hands at the small of your back, boy."

He took the restraints from the bedside drawer, stood, and fastened them on my wrists.

Outside, the night sounds blew in through the open window – strong wind gusts, hot, wet Bay sounds, and the erratic shush of night traffic as two glistening hard bodies battled for total submission in the lamplight.

Flaming desire, burning passion, and exquisite ecstasy…

Chapter Twenty: The Entire Cast and Crew
221 Baker Street, San Francisco, California

Nick Sechi's Journal

"Sorry, I wasn't paying attention. You were saying?"

Kayne smiled slyly. He knew the signs. What's it called, "morning after syndrome?" I was feeling amazing. Our shenanigans lasted almost to dawn, and he was a titan, never letting the dominating character slip until well after we had both been satisfied a few times.

("Just do as you're bloody well told, boy."}

We said and did things that would frighten most, but we seemed to be inches from mental and physical oblivion each time the endings came. The tension and frustration of the late-night convo seemed to fuel our intensity. It was a night for the record books – no brag, just fact.

Under two hours, boys and girls... I had no idea how to make up for the lost sleep. This was going to be a jungle of a day, but I did not care right now.

Andi tapped the keyboard and remarked, "I'm bringing Scott online for our scheduled Zoom meeting. They are an hour ahead, as you know, in Colorado, so they have been up a while."

A familiar gruff baritone who a few hours ago had been growling the foulest commands said very sweetly, "More coffee, my love? Andi?"

He refilled and called out, "Get up, Mugo. The game is on."

One of two members of the Sorenson and Sechi Research Department, Scott Iverson at the Aerie, came on-screen. He tapped some keys and reached for his mug of tea. My brothers-in-law's ranch and resort were a major tourist attraction and equine industry in the Aspen area, and Scott was the Aerie's resident techno-geek. His work station was the Kitchen island in the main house.

"Hey, folks. Sending you the latest."

He tapped. Andi adjusted the media on the big office screen. I scrolled my tablet after a caffeine jolt, and Kayne leaned back in his chair, steepling his fingers. The team was set to go.

"Hoy there, you hippies. All good out there in 415?"[3]

"Never better, mate. And it's 'oy.' Are you and Gints keeping my brothers on the straight and narrow?"

"Not a term we use much here, Doctor S. -- straight-bad, gay-good. Mr. Kick bought a new mare when he was in Calgary, a Cheval Canadien. A one in a million beauty — literally. She is scheduled to arrive this morning. He is doing backflips; he is so excited. Gints is out doing a security upgrade to the lodge, and Doctor Mitch is in bed with a cold. I just brought him his breakfast."

"And the wrong kind of juice. Bollocks this. You know I hate grapefruit."

Off-camera, Mitch was heard rummaging in the refrigerator.

"Bloody hell, no orange?"

On-camera, Scott did an eye roll and slipped off his stool.

Kayne called out, "Stop whining, ya, big baby. He always was a poor thing when he got sick as a lad. Pitiful, just pitiful. Studly Aussie, my lavender balls."

We heard a croupy snarl, "Could, still break your arse, Mug, then and now."

"Here is your orange juice, Sir. Please, I have a meeting. Go back to bed now. That's a good Sir."

Mitch's head came on camera. He looked "like who done left it and ran." Golden brown bed hair and three-day scruff. Bloodshot eyes and red, runny nose... He was in his Captain America "jam jams," Kick's last Christmas present. Still hunky in a mussed-up and cuddly way.

He waved

"Hello, everybody. I'm sick."

---

[3] A nickname for the City by the Bay -- 415 is the Area Code of San Francisco

In unison, the three of us crooned an almost sincere "Awww."

He flipped us the middle finger and went away.

Mitch's voice gradually faded as he said, "Scott, if my husband comes back, please, tell him I'm in the office... fucking spending every cent we have on more bloody horses..."

I called out, "Catching a cold in Colorado, humm. Bustin' too many nudies with your main squeeze in the hot tub, Stud Man? Keep your long johns on."

Andi tried to reel us in for business.

"So what do we have here, Scott? Highlights?"

"I see you got my file on Doctor Rockland's research. So, using AI, I was able to pull together murder cases that tie to Rockland and Bronson. For lack of a better file name, this time we're talking about 'Dead Crime Bosses and Other Disreputables.' I'll start with the most unusual murders.

"Kalisto Serian: Head of one of the largest international drug cartels operating out of Quito, Ecuador, and Barranquilla, Colombia. Serian inherited the organization, Volcanic Dawn, from the father, Hector Serian-Ochoya, when the Don was assassinated four years ago. Serian, the junior, was non-binary. Ze was found hanging in a warehouse in Rio alongside..."

Tap, tap, tap.

The monitor image changed to display a bearded Asian man in a fur hat and deep blue silk shirt cinched by a broad leather belt. He looked big, bad, and dog-ugly.

"... Gantulga Nergūl, aka the 'Great Khan.' His organization, the White Road, is a massive conglomerate of Asian illegal drugs distributed over three continents. As the head capo of the White Road tong, he is wanted by the Chinese, the Koreans (North and South), and the Japanese, to name the top four. The pair was in Brazil for a meeting of drug lords. Somehow, the hangman or woman shut down both sets of security guarding these individuals. They were abducted and hung out to dry, literally."

A media photo showed the two dangling bodies, their heads and necks at a deadly angle.

Mark came into the conference room and asked, "Hey, can I jump in? I could get a story out of this. Hey, Scott."

"Mr. Gardan, good to see you, Sir."

The next up was an elderly Afghan in Taliban gear, a Kalashnikov slung over one shoulder. Not a beauty contest winner, either.

"Since 1998, Esmail Faiz Haqqani has been the leader of Alkhinjar al'Ahmar, aka, the Red Dagger, the underworld militia forces supplying armaments to at least four armed insurgencies in the Middle East, Syria, Yemen, Pakistan, and Afghanistan. He was in retirement until his son disappeared two years ago. At that time, Haqqani came out of retirement."

I asked, "How did he get it?"

"Poisoned at a wedding. A traditional dish called *Saji Kabab* was laced with radioactive polonium-210, a Russian favorite – the poison, not the entree."

Andi asked, "Scott, any suspects in these three murders?"

"Not for these. The authorities are coming up with bupkis. But the last one is slightly different."

A very attractive brunette with violet eyes came up.

"Diana Calvert-Sans. She was the girlfriend and business partner of Carlo D'luca, Corsican head of a human trafficking group that supplies underage sex workers, boys, and girls to a very high-end clientele. You may remember. D'luca was killed last year while awaiting extradition to France to stand trial. Throat cut by a fellow inmate. Ms. Calvert-Sans was recently stabbed to death by a fourteen-year-old girl who has been captured by the authorities. The girl is presently in custody in Vallejo, East Bay."

Kayne asked, "And all of these murders took place over the last three weeks?"

"Yes, Dr. Sorenson."

Scott went on, saying, "There are some other commonalities we have found. The resulting disruption to the criminal organizations due to the murders of these bosses has shut down operations almost totally. There are signs that they are regrouping, however. The most striking commonality for Sorenson and Sechi is that each of these organizations is a part of the bounty vendetta of one they believe committed these atrocities. Yeah, an ordered revenge op for the live capture and handover of this man."

A blurred and very unidentifiable picture of a dark-haired man came on the display. We waited for the other shoe to drop. Scott is supposed to tell us who the dude is, but he paused considerably.

"Doctor Sorenson…"

"Yes, I know, Lad. It is my brother."

***

"Pictures of my brother, Eric, after he was fifteen and my father sent him to boarding school in Switzerland do not exist. These and other crime organizations marked him for assassination because Eric's career in espionage caused his shadow to fall over some of the most Dangerous gangs and criminal organizations in the world. Please allow me to explain."

"The criminal operations under consideration are noted for their global reach, extreme violence, and powerful influence. Consider, if you will, the 'Ndrangheta, originating in Calabria, Italy. It is a mafia-type entity network that is extremely powerful and pervasive. It has expanded its reach to over 40 countries.

"Together with the other sects of the Italian Mafia, the Cosa Nostra, Camorra, and Sacra Corona Unita, the 'Ndrangheta is involved in drug trafficking, murder, bombings, counterfeiting, illegal gambling, fraud, theft, labor racketeering, loan sharking, and illegal immigration. They are believed to control a significant portion of the cocaine trade flowing through Europe."

"So, Eric is their poster boy for a targeted killing."

"Yes. From 2004 until approximately 2020, Eric was a special agent for an international militia cartel that worked to unravel these webs of transnational organized crime through carrying out assassinations, destroying infrastructure, foiling their attempts to blackmail and kidnap heads of government, and thwarting hostage scenarios. To be able to get in and out of North Korea's Tongchang-ri's armament facility for aircraft and missile deployment at the ripe old age of 22 and leave the place in ashes was part of what promoted him to the top of these rogue organizations' most wanted lists.

"The Yakuza of Japan, with a long history dating back centuries, is another prominent criminal entity. They have offered a bounty of 500 million USD. Other significant groups with a vendetta include various Mexican cartels, the Triads of China, and the Russian mafia, all known for their extensive criminal networks and activities."

He pointed to the image on the screen.

"Through a source which I cannot reveal, I know who is responsible for killing Hector 'The Beast' Serian-Ochoa and the kidnapping and handing over of the son of the arms dealer el Haqqani. This series of violent incidents tore through the White Road's organizational headquarters in Dushanbe in the Republic of Tajikistan, as well as in the militia alliance, the Red Dagger, out of Jarablus, Syria."

Kayne spoke softly, reminding us of the highly sensitive nature of any information about his brother. Rebecca had joined the meeting after Scott had signed off. Kayne stood and walked to the conference room window. Our offices were on the second floor of the carriage house at our home at 221 Baker Street.

He watched the strollers and the traffic along Vallejo near the Baker Street Stairs as he said, "Additionally, Eric Sorenson was single-handedly responsible for the arrest of Carlo D'luca, the child slaver. He paid the billionaire a visit at his villa near Monte Carlo. In the morning, D'luca turned himself over to the authorities with a complete set of documents detailing his crimes. Law enforcement was completely baffled as to why the man turned himself in, and the thug would not say.

"Realizing her complicity had been made public, the publishing heiress and socialite Diana Calvert-Sans went into hiding near Tripoli, Libya. She continued to supply children for sex to other organizations."

"Darling, you are saying that Eric was involved in the lead-up to the death of these four. The double hangings, the poisoning, and the stabbing in Scott's report cannot be by his design. Someone else is the cleanup batter.

"Your brother does not have allies, Kayne. We all have worked with him, and he runs most of his operations solo. If Eric was receiving treatment at the time of these other killings, who did them? The coincidence is much too strong. Another group is carrying out the assassination game."

"You know that I have always denied coincidence. It simply means we do not have all the facts. Eric is indeed at the center of this enigma. Each of these groups wanted his head on a spike. The question is, who or what has renewed the call for his capture and extermination? That, in fact, is the motive for the murder of these four—to draw him out."

He asked his dear friend, "Rebecca, have you ever had *Saji*?"

"Darling, no, but 'Boots-on-the-Ground' here has, I am sure."

"Quite right. Mark?"

"Yes. I had it a few times in Kabul and once in Kandahar. It is very spicy, especially when prepared correctly -- lamb, chicken, but the most authentic version features goat as the main ingredient. Yeah, and goat is really not that bad. Scott is correct about the wedding. *Saji* is a special occasion dish."

"Nick, is there anything that strikes you in the photo of the two hanging crime bosses?"

"Ahhh… wait a minute, they are in identical… ahhh… what are they wearing? It looks like they are wearing identical tracksuits. Unusual. "

Andi had it.

She said, "The child murderer of Calvert-Sans… the girl was protecting her innocence."

Our Professional Assistant looked at Kayne like she had just hit the lottery.

"Capricorn, Gemini, and … and… *Virgo*."

Andi, Rebecca, Mark, and I said the last word simultaneously.

Thomas Paul Severino

Chapter Twenty-One: The Prize
221 Baker Street, San Francisco, California

Nick Sechi's Journal

"What's all the excitement, fellas and gals? And more importantly, Uncle Nick, I'm gonna need to reschedule our training. Gotta get over to USF for a pre-season meeting. Yeah, and so can't tonight…"

Kris eyed the champagne bucket on the patio table as he made his entrance. After a long night of theater and conversation, he had slept until 2 PM. Our workout routine was a regular part of our lives when we were home together, especially during the start of soccer season. Once the season started, we would take our workouts on the fly.

Kayne was ending a call.

"Capital, Darius. I appreciate your kindness as always, my friend. We will be there at eight-thirty. *Antio.*" He clicked off and made a silent, hands-up gesture, indicating an easy-peasy success.

Rebecca approached with Mark's phone. She showed him the announcement. Kris read aloud.

"The Pulitzer Prize Board is privileged to announce the winner in the category of International Reporting: Mark Ceffyl Gadarn, CBN Incorporated, for a set of enthralling stories, reported at the author's significant risk, exposing the atrocities of the war in Yemen, entitled, "Yemen: Nation of Carnage, Nation of Hope.""

Mark was beaming. Kris handed back the phone.

"Ceffyl? Your middle name is 'Ceffyl?' What the hell kind of name is 'Ceffyl?' You musta had a bull's eye on your back in middle school, dude."

We all did a lurching double-take.

Mark said, "It's Welsh for 'horse,' Bud."

Rebecca was a tic away from slutty when she whispered, "Stallion."

125

Kris could not contain his joking and rushed Mark with a hug and a cheek kiss.

"This is fantastic, Uncle Mark. Congratulations. What an honor."

Kayne said, "We are going out to celebrate. You are welcome to join us."

"Oh, crap. I made plans with some friends tonight. Damn.'

I said, "Hey, kiddo, how about rescheduling and coming out with us? It's the fuckin' Pulitzer Prize."

Kris hesitated, and Mark broke in.

"When we come back from Central America, we'll do it. Kris can pick the place. This way, I get two celebrations."

Rebecca moved in for a semi-hug. She tousled Kris' hair and said, "We are leaving in the morning, Darling, so we have to say, 'Thank you and goodbye for a while.' I hope the run of 'Angels' is off the charts, and the start of the soccer season is also a smash."

Mark added, "When you talk to your Father, please give him our love."

Kayne's silence was thunderous.

Andi came into the conference room.

"Which of you has been bad? What a question, I know, right? Look who I am talking to. Anyway, the police just pulled in and are on their way up."

I said, "Someone's been killed."

Chapter Twenty-Two: The Celestial Hunter
An Unspecified Location

Nick Sechi's Journal

"In the matter of 'Operation Night Jaguar,' four assassinations in the underworld have been completed to close out the first phase. We know the bounty on Orion the Hunter was the main objective of the international organizations that have oversight of the operations run by the four criminals we have eliminated, namely, Volcanic Dawn, The White Road, Alkhinjar al'Ahmar, and the child sex operations of late Carlo D'luca.

"The Confederation struck at the heart of the crime web and made it look like Orion is again active. The assassinations have thrown those criminal organizations into chaos. Consequently, the revenge threats to the Hunter have become a top priority among criminal enterprises, gangs, mafias, and syndicates. And this is international, dear colleagues, tongs and outlaw motorcycle gangs, as well as terrorist, militant, and paramilitary groups – all want him liquidated."

A media screen scrolled the faces of the four dead mob leaders for the group. The final visual added the physical scientist and the aerospace engineer.

"Two additional contracts have been executed, for want of a better word. The body of scientific work of the deceased has come into our possession and is critical to sustaining the financial position of this body."

The light in the conference room flickered. Another member addressed the gathering in a heavily accented voice.

"I will state my objection to the choice of your strategy one more time. How do we know Orion won't be put down by the crime families? They are quite powerful entities?"

"Orion will escape their clutches as he has always done in the past. And he will come to us. Once we have him, there are endless possibilities for strengthing this Confederation."

"Orion the Hunter will never kneel before us. What force do you propose?"

"Coercion, I believe, is a much better word. We will force him out of hiding."

The screen changed.

"This is the man who will lead him here. Orion's brother — what better Judas? However, we must not underestimate him."

The leader continued with much conviction.

"This group will apply relentless pressure where it is needed. The Hunter will have no other choice, I assure you. We need his power, his bravery, and his intellect. It is quite matchless, I assure you. He is also a master of secrets. And secrets are the lifeblood and muscle of the League."

The speaker let his point sink in before continuing. He expected no further objections.

"Enough. We will hear the updates on the next group of contracts. I understand we have two contracts near completion."

"Once more, Master, if I may? Our master spy and expert militia operative will know he is walking into a trap. Why would he acquiesce to our demands?"

"Simple. To save him."

The last image was of a nineteen-year-old blond soccer player.

The group continued their work in the semi-darkness that filled the secret space. There was no more discussion.

Chapter Twenty-Three: Revisions
Ballet Purgatorio, San Francisco, California

"Is this right?"

"No, I want to see more of your ass, Raymond."

The choreographer turned to the costume designer and added, "He looks too much like one of those horses in a damn road company of 'Equus.' You have to do better. These horses are immortal. Their bodies are perfection."

The young dance master had hit his limit. Revisions of the choreography had the potential to sever the unity of the original vision for the piece. The Purgatorio's executive team had to be kept focused on the creative vision of the ballet.

"Ass, Justin, ass. Raymond has a terrific one, and so do the other three. The audience should see the hindquarters of a horse, sinew, and muscle. I want the old queens in the front row to gasp when these beauties come on stage. Carousel mounts are not divine. And naked... nude... figure out how to drop the tail so that ... and color the fabric over their genitals must match the skin color, even the black horses should appear to be naked. A horse, get it? Big, powerful, and bestial."

"But Mr. Amenti..."

"That reminds me... someone... I want to see the changes to the design of the Chariot of the Sun. Mr. Sherwood promised that his redesign would be award-winning, total Noguchi, and I haven't seen it yet. Please call Jason and see if he is available to talk. And that thing better sky-fall like a mother... sorry, what?"

The costume designer, Justin Graham, lowered his voice and said, "These four dancers... well, they have incredible bodies and..."

Ballet Purgatorio's Regisseur, Olivia Ortiz-Leon, came into the studio and handed the two dancers coffees. She took a seat at the computer console. She remained silent but tracked the progress of the creative process.

Robert Amenti continued, "Right, Justin, that is why they were cast in the roles of the divine steeds of the sun god, Abraxas, Bronte, Pyrois, and Steropethops."

He turned to the warming-up Artem Eglievsky.

Amenti said, "Tyoma, we need to rehearse the *Pas de Cinq* with the horses before we go over the other additions you requested for Helios."

The choreographer ran a hand through his hair and added, "Wait, Justin. I apologize. You were telling me about the bodies of…"

"Well, Sir. Um… so, they are very healthy men, and… ahhh."

"OK, yes. I get it. Listen to me. Your costumes cannot geld the equines – not that shit we put on them during the European run. Covered, yes, but not confined in a cup. Think about a loose pouch colored to match their flesh makeup. Use their physical gifts to best express their character. Be bold and daring, but above all, be classy erotic -- like a work of art out of the Greek Golden Age."

The costume designer smirked, "Got it, Sir. You're gonna thank me for this when it's over, Robert. The gays and straight women will kill to get tickets to this."

"Yes, but my dances will be the reason history will preserve this work. But it must work together: movement, music, costumes, sets, and lighting. We are presenting religious fervor. Myths that unite the human and the divine…"

He waved the two of them away, pulled off his sweatshirt and warm-ups, and joined Tyoma before the mirrored wall. The older dancer was covered with sweat from his warm-up. He smiled as Amenti joined him, remembering how well they fit together.

"Are you selling sex, my Bobby?"

"Beauty, Tyoma. Hold my arm. Beauty of form and movement. Head up and right leg on point. And lift."

Leaning on his colleague, Robert reached for his right leg and pulled it up so that it now pointed flat-footed to the ceiling. Slowly lowering it, he made the same stretching move with his left, adding more muscle-lengthening movements. Now, they both transitioned into a dynamic mobility warm-up routine, moving their bodies in multiple directions. Joint-specific training then followed. Ankles, knees, hips, spine, shoulders, elbows, and wrists moved with and against each other for balance and strength performance.

Tyoma said gently, "Try this. Come around to the back and turn. Excellent, my beautiful one."

Amenti stretched a bit more and called out to the accompanist, "It's the *pas de deux*, and then we'll go into Helios' Olympus solo. Someone alert the horses to be ready."

The dance artist then said, "Olivia, please be sure you make the revisions to the Benesh as we revise." The choreographer reviewed the dance notation system on the woman's monitor. He pointed to the notations for the movements of the ballet.

"We are here. And this is all new. I have put in a solo for Helios. If it changes as we practice, encode the final movement sequence."

He returned to the *Étoile*.

"This is the initial confrontation, right? You expected a worshipper, and Phaethon is a cocky bastard with a chip on his shoulder for Daddy. So the final arabesque – this."

He demonstrated.

"Becomes this."

"The boy has Daddy issues, Bobby. He is a spurned lover. Try more leg extension here. Yes. Good. Try to color it all with incestuous lust.

The young choreographer ignored the remark.

Spurned lover, my ass. This shit's hitting too close to home, and I know it.

"No! When I lift you and lower you in this series, it is better if I keep you close to my body. Try it again."

They finished the movement, a bravura piece of male intimacy.

"So I sit down on stage left, and you have this extended solo. Helios is divine; he is the epitome of beauty, the source of all life, and he fuckin' knows it. Let's take this in tandem. Please follow my movements. Remember, please be more modern and less classical."

Eglievsky commented, "Less Fokine and more Martha Graham."

"Or Twyla – whatever. Amenti. Do Amenti."

Together, they built the solo piece for the god. The younger man instructed the more experienced dancer, who made Tyoma repeat and add more flair as the expression warranted. The accompanist and the regisseur kept up.

"Lift your head as you move into the bend, hand flat and pointed… now, behind your back. Look at your other hand… right, and follow it… follow… yes… straight up. You are the god of heaven. Nothing surpasses you. They need to see that and understand it up in the highest balcony."

He followed the moving dancer across the stage. "*Revoltade…* *sissonne…* lay out more Tyoma... and the *gran*. Yes. Yes. Very fine. Remember, we are shattering the classical forms to echo the passion of the story. "

"Like the pending wreckage of the Chariot of the Sun, my Bobby?"

"Yes, exactly. Wrecked lives and disastrous consequences."

On the periphery of the rehearsal room, Dancers stood or sat and watched.

"Now, do it again from the beginning."

Amenti stepped back to give the star room. The dancer was incredible. No one was more graceful. No one leaped higher. Eglievsky, in the late prime of his career, would yield the crown to no other dancer. He was beauty and grace personified, a being of light and movement. Robert Amenti and the others in the rehearsal room were transfixed.

Robert was a bit breathless as he said, "Melanie, please give us the end of Phaethon's meeting with Helios. I believe it is 153. Yes, right where the Sun God crosses stage right. Yes, there. Tyoma, remember it's a *fouetté*, but rougher — break it and leap. Yes? Ready?"

Eglievsky launched into space as if he had descended from a great height. He executed seven *grands jetés* in which the working leg brushed into the air, appearing to have been thrown. These were interspersed with leg-fluttering *cabriole* to the side, the head thrown back, and the arms up in perfect form. The *Étoile* flew across the rehearsal room.

Amenti could hear the critics now. "Immortal... a divinity in every aspect. Eglievsky is ageless and dazzling... as fresh as the day he leaped onto the dance stage from ballet's heavenly realms."

As Helios, Tyoma now transitioned to an array of set pieces. After a few minutes, he halted.

"Stop. This part... right here... this combination... is not possible."

Covered with sweat, the superstar stood with hands on hips and protested. The choreographer looked at the dancer with a questioning expression.

"Not only is it too difficult, but there is also no meaning in what the hero is doing. Bobby, you want the story to move forward, but you are taking liberties with the storyline. The work stalls."

"What? You are the star of this piece, so this is what it looks like. I agree it is pure padding for your fans. We revised the edited music sections. Helios performs a series of bravura pieces, followed by the second *pas de deux* with his son. It is a showcase for your excellence."

He wanted to say, *'You told me to rewrite the ballet to glorify you, not the title character.' Make up your fuckin' mind.*

He did not.

"It is crap, Robert, come here. This is shit and quite unworthy of you. It is filled with your anger and hostility. Helios would be strong and somewhat indulgent at the same time. That is the source of his relenting on the bargain. Only he can control the Chariot of the Sun, and yet he loves his rebellious son. This portion makes the god look like a marauder, a cheap showoff."

The watching dancers shifted uncomfortably.

Eglievsky rounded on the young man, saying, "Tell me, what is the inner conflict of this young choreographer that you need to get out? What are you keeping bottled up? Your dance creation should release that."

"Please stick to talking about the ballet."

Amenti was trying to read his star and reason with him. They needed to reconnect with the dance between Helios and Phaethon. He turned to the accompanist.

"No music here, please. Just follow my count."

"You show me, young teacher. Show this antique of a dancer. Yes?"

Robert stepped into place and bent into a one-legged crouch, one arm tucked.

The incomparable Artem said, "No, Bobby. Right there on the rise. Put your arms out. Now, do the steps, and now it is better to triple back on the turn... no, after the push-off... the turn there, lay-out, lay-out. No, a higher extension. Stop. That should be a *battement frappé*. Faster and more forceful. Do it again. Yes, and again. Now, with me... no pre-empt my step, and... Wait. Do not upstage me, boy."

The ballet legend went into the lift. Amenti was not in place. Tyoma tossed the young dancer to the floor. The kid spun on his butt.

"God damn!"

"Blast! These are your steps; do them properly!"

Bobby Amenti got up and turned into his partner. "Slip back in. Point your hand behind my neck and take me with you as you turn. Let's go back to the counter-balance... and take my weight... no, no, straighten the back leg when you twist.... Fuck!"

They both tumbled to the floor this time.

"This is impossible. I insist you put in something I can do."

"Fuck you! Are you the star or the choreographer?"

They exchanged a glare.

"Obviously, you have chosen to be both."

The accompanist stopped and folded her hands on her lap. Olivia Ortiz-Leon left the studio, shaking her head and muttering something about the fast-arriving premier. She shooed the other dancers out of the room.

"Out!"

Robert lowered his aim on the legendary dancer.

"The emotions that your character is living with are minor to the rejection felt by the boy. You are shallow and arrogant and will do anything to get your way."

He stood up and walked towards the older man.

"You are the one…" He stopped, took a breath, and restarted.

"Helios is the one… who played around… fucked anyone and everyone to create a posse of sycophants, demigods, and minor goddesses…"

"Radiant! My character is radiant. A force of light! Give him the choreography that he deserves, Mr. Amenti."

The anger was returning as Robert lost the direction of his argument.

"And you… Your character, that is, has this incredible existential power without which countless numbers will perish. Helios embraces his celebrity. He exists to shine and is a complete fuck wad with no empathy… none. His destiny is to be a star."

Now, the young artist stood inches from his former lover. "You are right. These additions make no sense. Rather than reinforcing your ego by exerting power over… Listen to me, Tyoma. This work is about the abandoned one. We are now glorifying a cult of personality. You."

He stopped and tried to control himself. At some time, the accompanist left the studio. Amenti could not remember when. He stumbled to finish with, "Your character, that is."

Artem flipped the door lock and strolled to the boy. He pushed down the yoke of the lad's cut-off t-shirt and kissed Robert's wet right shoulder. Amenti felt the shudder like a minor earthquake.

Robert asked in a low whisper, "Was I… that bad?"

The dancer cocked a hand-on-hip pose. He exclaimed, "Whoo-hoo, you were a complete fuck. We parted, and now we both are much better."

Robert Amenti blinked, digesting the honest answer. The florid-faced boy grabbed Artem by the sides of his head, tangling his hands in the curls of the man's hair. Amenti executed a hate kiss and pushed the man's head back and away from him.

The angry boy glowered and said one word.

"Rot."

***

The device chirped, and Artem hit the iPhone's side button that sent the call to voicemail. He waited for the rumble to see the ID and then turned back and buried his face in the boy's neck.

"I regret that I must ask you to leave. I have an appointment for this evening that cannot be changed. My agent and some musical theater producers from the West End."

Robert Artem rolled into the one last pillow on the big bed. He pressed his face into it. When they were together... yes. Tyoma... this is his fragrance – like a singular, rare spice generated by his body, skin, sweat, rare whiskey flavors, smoke, and salt. Wafting over and through him when they danced earlier... when they kissed in the studio ... when they made rough love here. Tyoma... the savor of his scent and flavors.

The dance legend never used cologne or aftershave. It was like the scent of sanctity, but more like a rich and powerful aroma of passionate sin. He remembered when they shared outfits, how he would dress in Tyoma's clothes. Even freshly laundered, the air of the man's magnificent body lingered and reminded the boy. He took the molecules of his lover's body inside him, inhaling deeply.

He huffed one last time and stood up to find his clothes.

"I can always tell when you are lying. It's a slight change in the sound of your voice."

"My Robert, I..."

Briefs, torn jeans ... hoodie... looking for tennis shoes. Got them.

"I do not care who you fuck. I stopped caring more than a year ago. Just dance, Eglevski. It is what the company is paying you to do – a total visual orgasm for anyone who buys a ticket."

He pointed to the bed. "You are exceptionally good at that. You always were...

"... a manifestation of your fire... and I will always hate you for it."

He left the apartment.

Thomas Paul Severino

Chapter Twenty-Four: The Good Herb
San Mateo, California

Nick Sechi's Journal

"She was strangled. The body was found in the brush at about 6 AM in a ditch off the North Trailhead of the Sawyer Camp Trail, the part that goes along the San Andreas Lake. She was jogging, it appeared."

"Sexual assault?"

"No evidence. Mr. Sechi."

Jasmine Elizabeth Stokes, Ph.D., age 39, lay on the stainless steel table at the Northern San Mateo County Morgue.

Kayne was doing a forensic examination of the body, turning the head, pronating large and small musculoskeletal groups. Eyes, ears, mouth, fingernails, and soles of the feet underwent close inspection.

"Nick, please tilt the head back and distend the mandible. Thank you."

He used a tongue depressor and a scope to get down into the back of the throat.

On the outside, Kayne moved his fingers over the woman's neck muscles and trachea. He paid close attention to the ligature marks and asked for a pair of tweezers while popping in his jeweler's loop. Kayne brought extracted fibers from the battered neck to the microscope and peered closely.

"Let's turn her, gentlemen, please."

At the back of the neck, the flesh and muscles had been bruised and torn in a pattern identical to the one on the front of the neck. Kayne pressed softly on the cervical spine.

"C4 has been obliterated, and C5 compromised. The carotid arteries have received lateral shearing, and there has been significant blood loss as well as the loss of oxygen to the brain."

He unbagged the woman's clothes and tennis shoes and scrutinized them under the intense light. Picking at fibers and surfaces, he stopped to feel, smell, and taste particular spots. The yoke of the running shirt was torn and bloodied.

Kayne pointed to the Medical Examiner's computer screen.

"I am confused, to be quite candid. Have my husband and I been called in to verify the work of the county medical examiner? He got it right. Time of death, et cetera..

"One thing. The killer took her from the front and not behind. Considering the intense force and torque that was applied laterally to the cervical spine, the pattern of destruction to the neck, including the windpipe, bears that out, along with the direction of the ripping of the cord as she strangled. She first tried to fight off the murderer and then clawed at the rope, cutting into her neck and taking her life. The killer was right-handed and male. He wore gloves."

He stopped and picked up the photos of the deceased as she was found. He asked again, "So, why were we brought here?"

The Medical Examiner said, "Dr. Sorenson, I am Ruben Martell. Detective Rosario Martell is my sister."

Still looking at one of the pictures, Kayne reacted as if he had been punched. Without acknowledging the officer, he moved quickly to the dead woman's feet and removed the sheet. He said, "No one jogs with their running shoes untied. Observe this photo, if you please."

Turning to the body, Kayne moved the digits on each to expose the toe web space.

"These marks have been made with a permanent marker. Please observe these small case letters of the Greek alphabet.

"Delta, epsilon, sigma, nu, and beta."

***

"She was not killed here. She was, in fact, jogging elsewhere when she was attacked. None of the particulate matter on the shoes or the socks contains the material that makes up this trail. Her running togs smell and taste of *Mentha spicata,* also known as 'Yerba Buena.' There is no spearmint to be found anywhere around here."

Kayne had asked to examine the site where the body was found. Officer Ruben Martel arranged for us to be driven to the lakefront recreation areal. The police cruiser was parked near a picnic area and the jogging trail. Police officers were carefully combing the area for clues.

"This way, Doctor."

Kayne wasn't following.

"Excuse me, please, would you move that police car? Please do it carefully. Thank you."

Kayne inspected the parking space closest to the spot where the body was found. With a neoprene-gloved hand, he picked up some debris on the asphalt and placed it in a plastic envelope.

He next turned his attention to the jogging trail. After a close examination, Kayne looked up at me as he picked at the surface.

"It's a rubberized track, Boss. Made from rubber particles bound with latex or polyurethane. This surface offers excellent shock absorption and cushioning. It is durable, weather-resistant, and low-maintenance."

I sounded like a sports equipment salesperson.

"Thank you, my love."

He turned and carefully stepped down.

Facing the Pacific, the park ran along the jogging trail on the east side, while the shallow ditch marked the western edge, providing a transition between walkers, joggers, bikers, and bathers. Numbered yellow cones outlined the place where the dead woman was found.

Kayne squatted to extract some material from the ditch and bring it up for a closer inspection. He bagged the sample.

Looking up, he said, "There is a municipal pier near here, am I correct, Officer Martell? A beach, boats, fishing, and the like? The closest one, please."

Martell responded, "Pacifica Pier at Sharp Park Beach, about half a mile north of here."

"Before we leave, please take a picture of that footprint, the whitish one near the yellow space marker. Careful! Yes, that's the one. Thank you."

***

During the ride, Kayne was silent. He pointed to the end of the Sharp Park Beach parking lot near the boat rentals and parasail, and sail surfing docks. Stepping out of the Examiner's SUV, he examined the surface of the lot.

He hurried off.

Animal trails through the shrubbery led down to the beach. A long, stone and wooden pier extended out to the Pacific. The deep blue ocean was relatively calm, seeming to wait for the bright afternoon sun to slide down into its twilight embrace.

Kayne turned south, away from the pier and closer to the sports equipment renters. He examined various stretches of the ground, sometimes flattening against the earth.

"The parking lot here at the beach is surfaced with crushed seashells and limestone. It gets stuck in the large tires of High Mobility Multipurpose Wheeled Vehicles. What most call ahhh…"

"Humvees, Boss."

"Thank you, my love."

He held out his hand, which cupped a small amount of material.

"Please observe. The white crumbles are oyster shells. Off-white and yellow-white are clam shells. The brown is scallops. Back at the asphalt lot adjacent to where the body was found, there are pieces of the materials I have just mentioned, and even some in the treads of the police vehicle's wheels that intruded.

"The sun whitens this material, and you can see that the whitening rate is the same in both samples. They are identical. The murderer's transport was here."

He stopped and looked at his posse.

"When you want to dump a body in a ditch in the early morning hours, you park close by. We have nature's fingerprint dust if you will. Please consider the limestone and crushed shells, a distinct white powder that invades the treads of work boots and leaves tire prints similar to those on the asphalt of the previous lot, as well as in the sand and rock of the depression where the body was found."

Pointing down, he added, "The murderer walked from his Humvee across the synthetic surface of the jogging trail, leaving even more white dust and off in that direction.'

He pointed to a patch of packed sandy earth surrounded by greenery.

"Dr. Stokes was killed here.

"Please note two directions of footprints. One is deeper coming back this way. He was carrying the body away, which had been assaulted there."

He pointed to a tangle of trampled, grown cover.

I squatted and picked up a soft branch.

"Mint"

Kayne continued, "… with that."

I picked at where he was pointing with a stick. It was a bright yellow nylon cord, similar to the rigging on a sports watercraft. It was almost totally below sight level in the thick greenery. Lifting it with my probe, we could see it was knotted and taped at both ends and covered with a coating of fine dirt that had adhered to the blood.

Thomas Paul Severino

Chapter Twenty-Five: Harmony and Understanding

Millbrae Station to The Civic Center to Pacific Heights, San Francisco, California

Nick Sechi's Journal

"This has got to be an all-time record case, Boss. Sorenson Sechi, Star Detectives. The count is seven corpses and six astrological signs. Those fuckin, Big Bads, Man -- killers on the loose."

We had decided to forgo the police escort and take the BART back into the City from the Millbrae station. Our destination was the Civic Center, Seventh and Market. We would walk the three miles home from there. Dinner was not until 9 PM.

We managed to find a corner of a pretty empty train car. Rush hour had begun, but trains coming south had more occupants. No one was eavesdropping, as far as I could tell. Kayne did a run-down.

"The psychopathology of the murderer tends to suggest similar themes found in the signatures -- a serial killer who stages his victims with insignia or references to the signs of the zodiac. Six signs – Gemini, Serian/Nergūl, being a double.

"Research statistics show that a serial killer chooses victims with a similar background — the same race and/or ethnicity. However, we are seeing Blacks, Whites, Asians, and Latinx – a diverse community of the dead."

"How about the professions of the diseased, Boss? Rockland, Bronson, and Stokes were researchers for the aerospace industry. The other four were connected to high-end crime.

"Stokes? You Googled her."

"While we were waiting for the train."

I flipped through my tablet.

"Stanford. Her doctoral studies encompass investigations of astrophysical plasmas, including stellar atmospheres, atomic structure, and data analysis. Bla, bla, bla… She received her degree from KTH, the Royal Institute of Technology."

"Stockholm."

"Yes."

"If you could, pull up her publications. Please send them to Andi for the files. Request that she send me the abstracts for each."

"Yep. Boss, is this one case or several?"

"Good question, Nick. We need to apply more inductive reasoning to the case in order to answer the question."

He was silent as the train unloaded and loaded passengers at the next station. As the car started up again, Kayne stood and swiped my laptop to a shot of the first corpse.

"Rockland – the asphyxiating sting of the Scorpion. Behold the Gemini (the hanging drug Lords). The calamitous fall of Libra (Bronson's assassination). The answers are right before our eyes."

I pulled him back next to me as passengers were watching with some curiosity. He continued.

"While each of the murders carries a reference to astrological signs, many problems arise as we attempt to go deeper to find motive. For example, are we in the realm of astrology, and therefore, should we look at the astrological profiles of the victims?"

"You mean like, 'beware of Thursday. Not a good day for you. You could get strangled.' Horoscopes?"

"Something like that, yes. I would venture that this is not the case."

"Birth signs?"

"Again, no. The birthdates of the diseased do not line up with the five signs that marked the seven victims. Doctor Gretchen Rockland, Ph.D., was born on June 23rd under the water sign of Cancer. This incongruity is also evident in the other victims. Bronson was a Sagittarian and not a Libra baby."

Kayne steepled his fingers and tried again.

"So, that puts us in the realm of the science of the heavens. Astronomy. Astrology is its very mystical sister and is heavily based on mythology.

"The clues are in the stars themselves. Each sign of the zodiac is connected to a constellation. Witness the constellation Scorpio and our nights on Mt. Diablo. Do the dates of the murders align with the Sun's appearance in certain constellations?"

"No, Kayne. This is out of sync, also. Bronson was killed last week, and Libra is not visible in the Earth's northern hemisphere until November. The sun is not in Libra until the fall equinox. Therefore, the dates of the assassinations show no direct connection to the time of the appearance of their signature stars, Gemini, Capricorn, and Virgo."

"My love, let's go in another direction. Please consider another factor in the case. Suffocated, crushed, hung, poisoned, eviscerated, and, if the Stokes case fits, strangled. Consider: a serial killer usually has little variation in how he dispatches his victims. He kills in the same way.

"So, how do we conclude? Several *modi operandi* and only one sure link – the stars."

Again, we rode in silence for a while. I flipped through my tablet, frustrated with little or no internet, mostly when the BART went underground. Sixteenth and Mission – Civic Center/UN Plaza was next.

"Bingo, Big Bossman. Check it out. I showed my screen to Kayne. He announced before looking, "Of course, the location of the Stokes murder itself – water sign. Could this be the link we seek? Air, earth, fire, and water…"

He looked at me with a concentrated stare.

I said, "Nope, way off. But Stokes *is* definitely in the zodiac mix. The marks between her toes: Delta, Epsilon, Sigma, Nu, and Beta. Kayne. These are the names of five meteor showers associated with the constellation Aries."

"Our seventh victim has been marked with a zodiac sign."

***

"So, a beer and a bit of a nosh to tide… to tide us over until… dinner?"

My husband's ADHD was raging. Kayne was super distracted and just about yanked me into Zia Zia Carol, a trendy bar, on our walk home. The address was Fillmore and Clay. Something big was up and about to go down. I could sense the vibe.

The crowd was diverse and substantial. Kayne snagged a server and a high-top table towards the back. He scoped out the crowd as unobtrusively as he could.

"What's up, Boss? I know when you have something going on. What's cooking?"

"Three tables over, my love."

He nodded to a trio of guys just behind us.

Brian LaCroix was out of uniform and talking to two gentlemen in a back corner of the establishment. He saw us and came over as our drinks arrived. One gent disappeared before I could make him.

"Officer LaCroix, I did not realize you were in the City. It is good to see you again."

Out on the town so soon after the tragedy. Interesting.

"Um… had to come into San Francisco to do some personal business."

The man was not comfortable, like a priest at a drag show. While not a gay bar, Zia Zia Carole had a clientele that was referred to as "gay-friendly," which meant the party boys took over at about 10 PM when everyone else went home to watch "Mash."

"This is Ashraf Sah. Dr. Kayne Sorenson and his um… associate, Nick Sechi. They are consulting detectives."

"I am familiar with the ballet company for whom you serve as Board Chair, Mr. Sah – an extraordinary group of artists. You most likely do not remember, but my husband and I met you at Ballet Purgatorio's gala last year, soon after we were married."

Kayne loves to set the record straight (husband, not associate). Ah, make that exact (not straight).

"Yes, I do remember. Thank you both for becoming two of our top supporters, the Dress Circle. I hope you plan to attend this year's offerings. You will be able to see our donor wall in the foyer of the... well, right now, we are calling it the Marsden Center for the Performing Arts."

Kayne gave the man one of our cards, saying, "Yes, Nick and I are interested in naming opportunities in connection with your company's new complex. Please get in touch with our office for an appointment at your convenience."

"Thank you, gentlemen. This seems to be a good evening for Ballet Purgatorio. The chance to increase your support, perhaps, and an additional opportunity to add a new member of the Board."

He looked at Brian.

"Yes, I have been asked to join and serve out Gretchen's term."

"So very sad. Brian tells me that you are working to find Dr. Rockland's killer."

"Yes. Local law enforcement asked for our firm's assistance."

"Brian, here, is an alumnus. Joined the junior company at twelve. I think. Right? A promising student. He even danced with Artem Eglievsky before leaving us and signing up for the Navy."

Outstanding body language, especially the sailor... napkin twisting at the mention of the dance troupe. So many secrets... for example, who meets a prospective board member at a bar? The dude should have at least offered lunch, no?

The young Navy guy said, "Yeah, we'll see how this goes. I'm not sure how much I can do, having been out of dancing for so long."

"Dr. Rockland said you still kept up with your training. We should feature an alum program sometime. Get you back in your tights."

"Um... I like to stay fit. Dance is good cardio. I combine it with free weights and diet to keep my weight under control."

Sah looked at his watch. He called the server over and ordered the three of us another round, flipping some bills on the kid's tray.

"I am afraid I must be going, my friends. I have a dinner engagement. Brian, I will be talking to you soon. Dr. Sorenson, Mr. Sechi, a real pleasure."

He dashed.

Brian made a move to stand, saying, "Yes. Sorry, I have…"

Kayne put his hand on the man's arm. Brian LaCroix was startled and looked at the mildly restraining hand and then at Kayne. This dude was making me nervous.

"You do not have another appointment, Officer LaCroix. You simply do not desire to speak with us."

Brian shook off Kayne's touch.

"Hey, what is this?"

"Secrets can injure you and those you care about, Brian. Especially if those secrets give others power over you."

"You are out of your fuckin' mind. I don't know what you are talking about, and I'm leaving. I've had enough of this place and your…"

Kayne touched him again, and the young man reacted as if he had been tased. He actually drew up his balled-up fists. I didn't respond except to hit my brain's first level of alert. *Warning! Warning, Will Robinson!*

Kayne said, "Listen to me. It may save your life."

He continued in an even more serious tone.

"You are not a child nor an adolescent, Sir. Remember who you are and be truthful about it. Live with authenticity, starting right now. No one can take that away from you or hurt you if that is so."

The man pulled away, looked around, and jostled people as he headed for the exit of Zia Zia Carole.

Chapter Twenty-Six: Coming Home and Going Out
221 Baker Street, San Francisco, California

Nick Sechi's Journal

"I saw them when we were crossing the street, my love. Brian is rather hard to miss, even at twilight."

We crossed the Alta Plaza Park diagonally from Clay to Jackson, heading further into Pacific Heights. The park has fantastic city views. As we watched the lights come on in North Beach and over in the Financial District, we deconstructed our meeting at the bar.

"Huge closet case."

"Sah or our LaCroix?"

"Sailor Boy. He was having a shit fit with all the gays around at the Bar. And not everyone was our tribe."

"Our server seemed particularly attracted to the handsome Officer, but I digress."

I dove in with, "He is in a particularly precarious place, professionally, to be blackmailed, Boss. That is what you were going for, there at the end, right? And who was the third dude – the guy who made tracks just as we spotted Bri Boy and Sah?"

"Exactly, Nick. There is more to this than it appears. But I will bet that the anxiety we witnessed is grounded in the Navyman's struggle with his sexual identity and the loss of his beard..."

Took me a moment.

"Gretchen Rockland?"

"Yes, and her secret Navy files. Young LaCroix is a vulnerable man and could be in real trouble. He wants out of the spider's web of blackmail, murder, and sexual indiscretion, my love. Remember, he gave us the envelope with the only clue. He wants us to solve the case before it destroys him. But young Brian wrestles with bigger devils. "

We reached Vallejo and were nearing Baker.

"Finally, as a minor, the boy, Brian LaCroix, was sexually molested by a man. He cannot stand when a man, and I say this in all humility, especially one he finds attractive, touches him."

***

"No, no, no. Wait right there. Go back, go back."

Rebecca made the waving hand gesture one does to ducks in the barnyard.

"Girl, you shooing us?"

"Better do what she says, men," Mark said. "Rebecca is in a 'making-a-fierce-impression-on-the-town' sort of mood. Take it from me. This is a fashion-forward force that cannot be stopped."

The four of us had champagne as an accompaniment to our dressing for dinner.

Rebecca was stepping out in a drop-dead black and teal, sequined dress that showed a lot of bosom and was slit to the thigh. Impossibly high open-toed shoes shimmered with the same sparkles and gave her that runway walk. A grey shawl in a sheer jacquard print crossed from shoulder to opposite hip, enhancing her cleavage. Her mahogany-colored hair was coiffed with style and taste, setting off her diamond bling, ear dangles, and necklace. A vintage black velvet purse with a long silver chain hung from her shoulder.

Mark wore a tight-cut dinner jacket and a tux shirt, black skinny jeans, and ebony, silver-toed cowboy boots. She tucked a silver scarf in his breast pocket. It matched her accessories and drooped down in a very jazzy way.

"What did you do to his hair? Those golden-brown curls..."

"Highlights, Nicky. It washes out. And the sexy wire-frame glasses are just so Matt Bomer. Now you two..."

I said, "He looks hotter than hell. I think I may have to take him right here, right now, on the oriental."

Mark and Kayne howled. The former raised the back of one hand to his forehead in a damsel-in-distress gesture.

Rebecca said, "Keep your hands off of my Pulitzer Boy. Now, strip. Everything to the socks, and I hate those shoes, Nick."

She went to our bathroom and came back with a tube of moisturizer.

"Please hold this." She went into our walk-in closet and pawed through the racks. Three shirts were held up against Kayne's chest. For each, she stepped back, pursed her lips, and tilted her head in an appraising posture.

"Stand still, darling."

"Rebecca, Nick, and I are capable of dressing ourselves. What was wrong with what we…"

"Umm, humm, right. You are talking to a head museum curator. This woman makes things visually stunning. And Kayne Darling, there are times when I feel a need to revoke your gay card. *Capisce*?"

She lowered the third sample, a pale blue with a soft, white, misting design. She nodded to herself, took it off the hanger, and handed it to him. Turning, she added his formal leather pants and pointed to a pair of velvet rhinestone loafers on the top shelf.

"Breaking News, boys: Ms. Rebecca Quinto did not spend the last of her clothing budget to go out with a pair of Mormon Missionary Elders. And in San Francisco? Hello?"

The Diva Rebecca spun and drew me up in her sites.

"Nick, are those Amiri's I saw on your side of the closet, the slashed skinny jeans? On you, they will be pure sex, Darling. Put them on, please. P.S., you're going commando, Darling. Ripped jeans were not designed to show tighty whities."

I'm not shy. I did as I was told.

"The blue shirt. Oh, hell yes, Kayne. Matches your eyes. Wait, don't button it yet."

She reached for the skincare.

"Kiehl's. Impressive. You girls know how to stay wet."

Mark laughed again. "Beautiful, you are too much. Leave the menfolk alone. You will *make* them gay."

Kayne and I chuckled and said in unison, "Opps. Too late."

She stepped to Mark, unbuttoned his jacket, and opened his shirt to the first set of his abs. Rebecca smeared him with goop, teasing his scruffy chest hair. She touched his very flat belly and stepped aside so Kayne could see the demarcation spot.

"Don't button the jacket or shirt higher than here. This quartet ain't going to church tonight, babies. Nip slip – very hot. "

Kayne, in just his briefs, said with exasperation, "Crikey, woman, are you pimping us or what?"

"Thinking about it, Darling. I can use the cash. But Boyfriend, we would have to do something about those laugh lines..."

"I know. I know. Ya, brogan Sheila.' Nothin's that funny.' Crikey."

She pointed and winked her assent. As Kayne got both legs into the Rebecca-selected slacks, the fashionista turned him by one shoulder and smeared him.

"Devastating. Keep this hunk close, Nicky. He slays."

Mark laughed as he slumped ino one of our club chairs. Rebecca reached and pulled a Superman curl onto his forehead. She spun.

"You, my ginger darling. I will get top dollar for you. No shirt, thank you."

Wiping her hands, our own Anna Wintour Adjacent stepped back to the closet. Rebecca came out with one of my black jackets, the one with the jade green, gold, red, and black dragon in rough textile threading on the back. Kayne got a black suede sports coat with a light dusting of deep blue glittery stuff. We were total glam-glam for a night of sensuality.

She tossed me a pair of my seldom-worn meteorite-blue patina high sneakers. Kris gave them to me last Christmas and wore them twice before buying a pair for himself.

"Those, Nicky. Air hose."

I checked my phone.

"Limo's here."

"Right. We are leaving, Beautiful."

"Wait. I haven't done hair or makeup."

Kayne, Mark, and I upended our flutes and made for the bedroom door like three convicts running from the screw.

"All good. I can finish on the ride over, Darlings."

Thomas Paul Severino

Chapter Twenty-Seven: Estiatório Darius Sastre

North Beach, San Francisco

From the Case Files of Kayne J. Sorenson, Ph.D.

"Good evening, Dr. Sorenson. Your table is almost ready, but Mr. Sastre has asked you to join him in the lounge for a drink before dinner. If you and your guests will follow me..."

"Thank you, Spiros. Is the food tonight as delicious as you are?"

The handsome maître d' flashed bedroom eyes and whispered as he said, "Do not embarrass me, please, Doctor S. I am in enough trouble with the Boss. But thank you for the compliment."

The young man smiled and indicated the way to the bar area.

Estiatório Darius Sastre is located in a remodeled, small Byzantine Church where North Beach meets Fisherman's Wharf. A construction firm was hired to strengthen the earthquake-weakened structure. The international design firm, Dalloyau Clementi, preserved the structure's classic elements – the Greek-cross plan with a domed polygonal crossing and four arms of equal length. Many of the mosaics in various stages of decrepitude had been likewise saved.

The bar was designed in shades and patterns of blue and gold. The decor featured a stylized, floor-to-ceiling brass gate with pieces shaped into six figures resembling Orthodox saints and other heavenly beings. It was a stunning frieze of golden cut-outs, a great jigsaw puzzle, blending classic forms and modern expression.

Above us, a cream-colored dome raised circles of images connected to the creation and fall of humankind. The mosaics were spectacularly smoky illustrations of the invasion of sin into paradise, complete with the fabled serpent tempting the naked Adam and Eve, whose descendants, dining below, came close to foretold damnation while surrounded by decadent luxury.

An elderly gentleman, who had been speaking to the bartender, came away from the bar and crossed the space as we entered the lounge. He stopped, smiled, and spread his arms wide.

"Doctor Sorenson, how lovely to see you again. And this must be your extraordinary husband. I am delighted to meet you."

The very ebullient restaurateur and I exchanged the European triple-cheek kiss. My beautiful husband was turning the heads of the patrons — a real glitterati crowd. Nick is an extraordinary beauty in his own right, but Rebecca's stylings brought his masculine beauty to an even more heartstopping level.

I introduced Nick, Rebecca, and Mark to our host.

"This is Darius Sastri, an old friend and a direct descendant of Constantine XI Palaiologos, the last Byzantine Emperor."

In a dark suit complete with a wine and grey tie, the very gracious gentleman did a small head bow. He took Rebecca's hand for a very conventional continental kiss.

"You grace my home, Ms. Quinto. I am acquainted with your exploits in the world of fine arts, and I must say, you have made an important impression on the international art world."

Rebecca smiled.

It promised to be a night of superlatives.

"And it is indeed an honor to meet you, Mr. Gadarn. Many congratulations on your journalistic accomplishments. You also do our establishment a great honor."

The elderly prince extended more compliments to Nick. As he showed us to the owner's table in the elegant lounge, Darius said to my dazzler, "I am not sure who I am more in love with, you or your extraordinary husband. I have read your writings, Mr. Sechi, with avid interest and..."

He paused to speak to a server.

"No, Margot, my dear. You know what I want for my guests. Yes, from the crypt. Here is the key."

She disappeared, taking a tray of four wine glasses and a bottle with her.

Darius continued, "I was saying that I am in great admiration of your crime-fighting abilities, Mr. Sechi. You and the doctor here are true heroes."

"Thank you, Sir. I am never quite sure how my books and blogs will be received. We usually stir up quite a bit of trouble, I will say."

"And those lusty encounters... it is so reassuring that someone out there is having an enjoyable time."

I could see Nick blush at that one, deep red, and I could not withhold a chuckle.

"Darius Darling, your restaurant is breathtaking. I am reminded of nights and days in the Peloponnese – sacred and opulent. The preserved artwork and modern flourishes are so tasteful and glorious. A lost age of beauty and mystery here in North Beach..."

Darius gave Rebecca's hand another kiss.

"My Estiatório was formerly San Francisco's Church of Theotokos Panagiotissa. This is a neighborhood where there were once many families of Greek fishermen."

He continued, "The Theotokos, the Bearer of God. You will see her in the dining room, by the way. We attempted to pair the old elements with the new. This is a revered space, after all."

Rebecca said, "Tell us about the gate."

"The designers had it made near Ravenna. I wanted something in the building to represent the iconostasis – the wall of icons in all Orthodox churches. I was very pleased with the modern abstract feel of the piece."

He gestured to the ceiling.

"We also worked to preserve the mosaics. It was done by local Greek artisans who came here before the Great Earthquake. The art is not as old as that in my home country, but it is nonetheless quite beautiful. Where they were damaged, we stopped the decay but did not completely restore the images for the sake of authenticity."

Darius waved a hand to take in the church turned restaurant.

"The gold you see, above and around, is quite historic. It dates back to the California Gold Rush of 1849."

"Simply divine, Darling."

Darius signaled to the returning server.

"Yes. Thank you, Margo. Please ask Giánnis to send over the slices and a sharp knife, my dear. I am making 'The Empress Theodora' for our guests."

He poured the green-gold wine/liquor into five cut glasses, then added ice while scoring and garnishing the edges with orange slices.

"This is my family's reserve of Lillet. You will not find it anywhere except in the wine cellars here. It is the best of the best aperitif wines. It opens the stomach and stimulates the appetite."

Our host turned to Mark and, proposing a toast, said, "*Eíthe na échete kalí týchi kai na agapáte pánta.* May you always have good fortune and love. Opa!"

"The Empress Theodora" was a tasty quaff, I will say. Margo returned with hummus, stuffed grape leaves, and small plates of spanakopita. Mark and Rebecca were delighted with the evening so far – the ambiance, our friend Darius, and the warmth of being together.

"If you will excuse me, I will see to your order."

Nick looked slightly puzzled.

"Oh, no, Nick, if I may call you 'Nick,' a fine Greek name. No menus tonight. You are guests in my home. I am cooking for you tonight. You will find no better food in the entire universe tonight. You will be served at your dining table by my most excellent staff for an unforgettable evening."

Darius rushed off after speaking to the bartender.

I lifted my glass.

"Quite a guy, Darius is – old world elegance. His brother John's firm, Dalloyau Clementi, did all of the restoration. They are quite close."

"How did you guys meet, Kayne?" Asked Mark.

I pointed to the maitre d', who had come into the lounge to speak to waiting patrons.

"Actually, it was through Spiros. Giánnis..." He pointed to the bartender. "... and Spiros are step-brothers, and Darius had been their ahhh... benefactor for several years. This is, in fact, their home. The priest's convent adjacent to this building has been remodeled as the owner's residence. The church's bell tower... well, let's just say it now affords quite interesting meeting spaces for some unholy activities.

"Kayne Jason Sorenson! Do not tell me you have blasphemed this once-holy edifice."

"Please, my girl, you of all people... Remember, I knew you before this amazing Welsh-American beauty did."

She love-swatted him.

"As I was saying, the eminent Mr. Sastre had a bit of a family problem. Missing documents connected to the sexy and somewhat reckless Giánnis over there. Pictures, to be exact. Like all of us, the boy has a past. With luck and some mental insight, I was able to locate the damning photos and convince the blackmailers to play elsewhere."

"Excuse me, I wanted to say hello."

I stood, kissed up the intruder, and introduced our table to Giánnis. Handsome and fit, but a bit blurred around the edges. One could see that the boy had a difficult life, marked by some challenging years.

A set of five different glasses and a bottle of crystal clear liquor appeared.

"My Darius loves the piss-elegance of his custom-made cocktails. This is for manly men and their beautiful women."

He raised up to toast Mark.

"Ouzo in honor of the beautiful man.

"Εβίβα!"[4]

---

[4] Cheers!

One got the feeling the three of us were *non-sequiturs* at this point. Rebecca, I could tell, did not appreciate the proprietary remark about belonging to a man or the gregarious boy's over-attentiveness to Mark. She just let it happen and sucked down her aperitif.

"Opa!"

We slammed down the shot glasses.

I asked, "Life is good, my friend?"

"Oh, yes, *Γιατρός*[5] business is very good. The *Αφεντικό*[6] has been very happy, even with Spiros and me. Both of us are doing classes at the community college when we are not working at the Estiatório."

He poured another round.

"But you, you bring us a star. This man. I will read your book, Mr. Mark. It will be outstanding, I know. I will tell all my friends, also."

"It is a documentary, Darling. And yes, my man is quite exceptional in very many ways."

She was sweet and gracious.

"Doctor Sorenson, your table is ready."

---

[5] Doctor
[6] Boss

Chapter Twenty-Eight: Starlight

Estiatório Darius Sastre, North Beach, San Francisco

Nick Sechi's Journal

The domed nave of the church/restaurant was the main seating room for Estiatório Darius Sastre. Two large mosaics presided over the voluptuaries' epicurean activities of taste, smell, and exotic presentation. Above us, Mary, the Mother of the All-Holy, stretched her arms to reveal a miniature Jesus who extended a blessing over all. In another icon, the Savior's older self, *Christus Pantocrator,* presided over the universe's creation in a swarm of exotic, broken, and mysterious art above our heads.

Gold tables and crescent-shaped banquettes lined the walls. Round tables and their chairs filled the center. The entire area was filled with tiny lights suspended on invisible wires of various lengths from just above our heads and up to the ceiling's mosaics. The effect was a heavenly galaxy under the firmament of heaven.

The meal was incredible, with course after course of Eastern Mediterranean food paired with delicious wine. Our conversation covered family, our adventures, Rebecca's and Mark's respective projects, and random happenings of mutual interest.

We centered on the theme of the evening, celebrating the journalist Mark Gadarn. He was a hero in every sense. A dedicated journalist, he went behind the lines to get the story while embedded in peacekeeping troops. Our dashing reporter had performed acts of bravery and rescue in Syria, Afghanistan, and Yemen.

I was in the middle of saying, "So, tell us again why the Taliban leader thought you were just an American reporter. He could…" When the applause began.

Two couples entered the large dining room, and several of the restaurant's patrons stood to send an ovation their way. The alluring quartet was enveloped by a tasteful wave of praise. One of the four, a man who moved with the grace gained by years of strict training and physical discipline, stepped away from his friends and did a stage bow. Bending from the waist, hands clasped in front of him. He did the requisite palm tap to the heart and smiled.

Rebecca said, "Sunflowers. Well, for shit's sake."

Artem Eglievsky stepped back to his young date and their two women companions. His female friends were also dead giveaways for ballerinas — thin and with legs that seemed to stretch from here to there and back again. With a regal posture and goddess-like beauty, their movements exuded a graceful elegance. They scanned the room and shared whispered *entre nous* behind opera-length gloves. Their facial expressions had two iterations: from extremely bored to a dazzling fake smile.

The ballet legend's date was a dead ringer for a familiar jock boy, and I do mean boy. I was slack-jawed. Kayne was unreadable and composed. Mark was fascinated, and Rebecca was ready for trouble as only she could dish.

"Now, my Darlings, that is how a muscled-up young male shows what he built and makes no apologies. A chiseled physique clad in a satin and leather vest and nothing else... look at that magnificent upper body. Painted on metallic pants. And the rest ain't too shabby either, the hair, the *maquillage*.[7] Your Bulgarian prince uses more mascara than I do. Ahhh, the notorious – they can get away with the most provocative couture."

Tyoma made a gesture to his friends that, from what I could see, read as, "My dears, what can I say? Fame is such a task." He threw an arm around Kris and tousled the boy's hair.

Darius buttoned his jacket and moved from the kitchen entrance to greet his celebrity guests. He escorted them to a table against the opposite wall.

Mark said, "The dark-haired woman is Antonia Ivanova. I saw her dance with her husband at some gala in Rabat three years ago. Her Dying Swan, I think it was – really super."

The woman of interest was also very much of interest to her fawning female companion.

---

[7] makeup

Kayne said, "Ballet Purgatorio's newest Juliet for the coming season, Dominica Guillem... she is destined to be the next Pavlova.

Mark suggested, "Now if I were someone with a prurient mind, I would say that..."

Rebecca said, "Sex and relationships are so fluid these days, Mark. Spouses and lovers, everyone is leaving room for an assortment of others. Triples, multiples... Treat each other kindly is all I have to say."

I had made my personal distinction concerning matters of the heart and the libido many times in my writing. I saw no purpose in chiming in. However, where my self-righteousness did kick in was about the age difference of the man who boy-napped our nephew. I was pissed.

Before I could say anything, Kayne stood up, excused himself, and walked across the room.

I threw back the rest of somebody's wine -- mine, I hoped.

"OK, so here's where Kayne comes walking back, pulling that boy by one of his ears. If my mother were here, she would have gone into the kitchen for a wooden spoon."

"This is getting good. More, please, Mark." He filled Rebecca's glass and leaned into me.

"Whatever the nature of this... this... whatever this is...." He nodded to the errant boy's table. "And it could be many things... do not... wait, look at me now, Nick. Do not get all loud and ass-kicking on Kris. He will resent it, and it may even drive him into the arms of the aforementioned Dancer Daddy."

"How do you know so much about kid-raising?"

"I *was* a kid once."

Rebecca advised, "Nick. Kris knows when he is being taken advantage of. Just look at him -- a bit starstruck tonight. He is an intelligent young man. Chill, Sweetie."

I growled, "Yeah, the perpetual bad boy who thinks with his..."

Kayne returned.

"Well?"

"I ordered them a bottle of Armand de Brignac[8] to celebrate Eglievsky's return to San Francisco." He settled back into his chair. "You know, I once saw him dance '*Le Spectre de la Rose*' in Melbourne ages ago. It was breathtaking. In the days of his youth, Tyoma took the ballet world by storm. Truly a marvel."

I harrumphed, "How did *your* nephew react?"

"Oh, he's *my* nephew, is it? When he's bad, he's Bad Sorenson. When he's amazing, he's Good Sechi. I get it now, ya mug."

I said nothing and just cocked an eyebrow.

"He was pretty much deadpan, polite. He introduced me. It was all very cordial. One can easily conclude from their body language that they are intimates. So, apparently, there only seems to be one person in the immediate vicinity who is appalled by Kris' ventures into the world of older and wealthy gentlemen."

I retorted, "Twenty-one years older, Kayne. Can you say 'daddy's boy?' Seriously?"

"How can anyone say otherwise, my love?"

Mark poured and said, "You're acting so much like an overprotective parent, Nick. Let Kris make his own choices, man. We have all had experiences with older men and women."

He patted Rebecca's hand with a sly smile.

Rebecca snapped, "Two years, Boyfriend. It's not like I used to babysit for you." She picked up Mark's hand and continued, "Besides, it's all the rage, Darling. So very sophisticated..."

"I seem to remember the first entry into your teen boy diary, Master Nicola. The high school pole vaulter who helped shape you into the man you are today. He was much older, as I understand. A freshman in American schools is what? Fourteen? Your jock studly was four years your senior."

---

[8] Armand De Brignac Ace of Spades Blanc de Blancs Champagne

"Three – we're rounding down. Minor differences. But back to the issue at hand. Just look at the way Kris is dressed. He looks like a hustler. Rocking those naked arms -- pretty rude in a place like this."

"Nicky, there are plenty of women in this place with bare arms."

"But, Rebecca, he is a man."

"Correct, Grandpa. He is a *man*. Let him be one... the one who sometimes chooses unwisely and one who makes mistakes. But the one who knows how to rock it. Go gently, Bud."

Mark stood up.

Kayne said, "Viola, Mark is right."

"What? Kayne, I am not acting like my mother, you Australian bush baby."

Holy shit, I had resorted to name-calling. Well, Kayne started it.

Mark continued, taking Rebecca's hand.

"Come on, Beautiful. We are going to say hello and goodbye. We have an early plane in the morning -- your chance to meet a real dance sensation."

"Darling, I thought I was out with one."

"She smooched him."

I glared at my husband.

"Nick, my love, young Master Sorenson, has never been all that successful in his love choices, save one, and I think that this..."

He gestured to the table across the room.

"...is far from love. I agree with Rebecca, my love. Kristof knows that. This is his rent-boy persona, born of anger, frustration, and fascination with the limelight. "

We were both a bit twisted and so not sober enough to have a serious conversation. Nevertheless, Nick from the Bronx persisted.

Before I could continue, Kayne glanced off to Eglievsky's table and said, "When the dance rockstar is done with him, Kris will curl up in a fetal position in our bed, yet again, and ask the answers to those existential questions that come with being a discarded boy toy and a fellow seeker of true love. You and I remember those dark nights of the soul well enough, do we not? I most certainly do. We can only hope it is part of the growing process."

"Kayne, he is too young for this. It is one thing to play around a bit, but he may be venturing onto the cliff ledge of a very high-powered and phony world. The celebrity, power maneuvers, the way people climb over each other, and God knows what all. Kris is barely two years out of high school, Boss."

He poured another shot of the Ouzo for both of us.

I pointed to my husband and added, "Your that-which-does-not-kill-us-only-makes-us-stronger attitude in my thinking, Kayne, is bullshit. He has been pampered his entire life, and given his situation with his Father, I think this is a step in the wrong direction. I'm willing to draw the line if you're not."

Kayne took my hand and said, "How, Nick? How? Our house, our rules? 'As long as you are living under our roof…' That lad will be right out the door."

He sighed and said, "Kris is nineteen, my love. Ultimately, we need to trust his judgment and allow him to make his own decisions. If he should fail, we can show him a supportive love that will help him rebuild himself. We can only hope that Tyoma will be kind. Come what may, we will both be there for Kris."

"I think I need to speak to Mr. Dancing Star. The is no fuckin way that…"

"Nick, are you hearing any of this? I appreciate your concern; however, please let this affair run its course. Kristoff will be all the better for it. Remember what Big Nick would say. 'Non stuzzicare il can che dorme.' Don't poke the sleeping dog. He and your mother raised six daughters and a son. As wise as the day is long."

(Images of my Father wagging the index finger of parental advice.)

Balls! Sometimes, I hate it when Kayne is right.

I pouted.

He made leaving movements, checked his watch, and smiled.

"Come, my love. Tonight is about Mark. Flex should be in high gear right about now. The head of security is a former close mate. We will skip the line like rock stars. Shall we bust our dear Rebecca's chops, as you say, and dangle her hunky boyfriend in front of an assortment of energetic gay men at San Francisco's newest dance club?"

I took a deep breath. This was not over by any means.

"Why the fuck not?"

Thomas Paul Severino

Chapter Twenty-Nine: The Map

221 Baker Street, San Francisco, California

Nick Sechi's Journal

"Any last words?"

"Yes, aside from a throw-away about you drinking too much, Rebecca and Mark thanked us again for last night and for their stay with us. They invited us back East. Thanks for driving them to the airport, my love."

I poured myself a cup of coffee and plopped down in a seat at the patio table next to him. Some dog love was called for, it seemed. Chuoko and Alice did a bit of a snuggle and dance, putting dog noses in some very private places.

"Rebecca drove, actually. I was her co-pilot. That girl loves a Mustang convertible. She only ran one red light – amazing."

I leaned over and gave my husband his good morning smooch, and asked, "Did you wake up with a nickel on your nose this morning, Bud? No?"

He smirked, "Yes, yes, I know, then you owe me five cents. You need new jokes, Sechi."

"I'll tell you what I need, Bossman, my big hero Bossman."

I could tell my eyes were twinkling.

He folded his arms and said, "Well, now I wonder what that would be."

"A kick-arse fight, Big Man... on the Parkour course before we load up with breakfast. We can try some of those Iaijutsu moves Jack taught us."

"Sounds capital. I should go into punishment mode after the way you behaved at Flex Club. May I remind you that you are a married man, Mr. Sorenson-Sechi, and make the observation that the purple mark on your neck is not of my creation -- and after all that sanctimonious talk at dinner. Nichola Michael, for shame!"

"Hey, Boss, it wasn't my best gal pal that was pimping me, and you too, for that matter."

I turned his wrist and said, "Gosh, not my phone number on your forearm. Hmmm ... now, where did that come from? Some muscled monkey needs to learn the cell phone capture if he really wants to be a trick at the gay disco."

Kayne chucked and said, "I don't think tall, dark, and muscled-up owns a mobile – a bit of a Neanderthal, that one."

I looked in the direction of the kitchen.

Kayne said, "Not home."

"I am *so* surprised. Did he text you, at least?"

"Yes."

***

Andi handed me a cold compress and placed a bottle of ibuprofen in front of Kayne. I put the ice on my neck, and Kayne took two gel caps.

"Did you see any of it? The katana fight, I mean, not the ahhh..." I motioned to my passion bruise.

"Yes, Mr. Sechi. I saw you and Darth Vader here, squaring off. I missed the 'Luke, I am your Father" part. Lemme see that. Damn, you look like a leper. And you need to go easier as the head of the company. It looks like you were trying to devour his neck here. I thought our company was founded on logic and not passion."

Knowing the truth of the purple mark of lust, I felt the heat of a full-on blush and waved her back as Kayne began.

"Andi, we need to do some follow-up, Blackhawk, Fremont, and San Marino. Personal relationships... research topics... details of the murders. We may have overlooked some critical details."

Andi had used one conference room wall to do a detectives' briefing room collage. Portrait shots of the seven deceased and photos of the six murder sites, including pictures of the corpses, were grouped across the wall. Beneath each, Andi had added their professional or criminal affiliations and major research topics in the case of the scientists. A horizontal line above the victims had each of the zodiac symbols associated with the killing.

- Gretchen Rockland, Ph.D. -- Scorpio

- Jasmine Elizabeth Stokes, Ph.D. -- Ares

- Wade Bronson, Ph.D. -- Libra

- Esmail Faiz Haqqani -- Capricorn

- Diana Culvert Sans -- Virgo

- Kalisto Serian -- Gemini

- Gantulga Nergūl -- Gemini

A left-side vertical axis listed the names of persons of interest, from Brian LaCroix to Ruben Martell. A red string connected each of these folks to the individual who had died. Our administrative assistant moved our map of the Bay Area to the adjacent wall. A pin indicated where each of the bodies was found. Clues – images of the etched cigarette case, the text of "Themis," etc., were attached to each crime scene around the outer rim of the display.

"Damn, Girl. You have worked hard on this. I feel like I'm on Hawaii Five O. Super cool..."

"I know you both are hyper-visual, and given the complexities, I thought I would turn the case into a crime storyboard."

Kayne steepled his fingers and crossed his long legs, heels on the conference table. He examined the wall plot.

"Groupings... La Croix and Rockland... Ballet Purgatorio... Ashraf Sah and their Board... add them, please, and also the staff. Robert Amenti, the new choreographer. What's his story?

"Also, the maintenance woman who did not show up for work the day Gretchen Rockland was killed, Carmencita Lopez. I believe Blackhawk's Chief Security Officer, Jake Davies, ID-ed her."

He pointed at the picture of the security goon.

"Boss, something was going on with Rockland, LaCroix, Davies, and Howard? We have some nasty games going on there. Which one of them is gonna crack on this?"

"LaCroix is two tweaks away from going psychotic, I would estimate. I say we go after Davies. He is just macho and hot-headed enough to spill the muck up, as we say. Let's put the pressure on him a bit, my love. Your special assignment."

"Andi, can we find where the gay military dudes hang out in the areas over in the East Bay? Pleasanton, Concord, Berkeley, please? And can I get a photo of Davies, preferably not in uniform?"

"I have a friend who networks with many East Bay clubs. He is a distributor for OUTGay News Magazine on that side of the Bay. Even knows some of the gay bars in Sacramento. He is buds with all of the bouncers. I'm on it, Mr. Nick."

I looked at Kayne.

"Let's roll, Dano."

He had no idea.

Chapter Thirty: Pony
North Richmond, California

Nick Sechi's Journal

"See, the thing about being in a gay bar when you are on the down low is that anyone who is going to blow your cover is usually hiding something himself. It's a wash. So, sup, Ginger Boy, your Daddy not satisfying your itches? Don't tell me he's not man enough. You power bottoms sure are a lot of work."

Jacob Davies was in a complete cruise bar kit -- boots, jeans, athletic T. A weekend scruff on his strong jawline, coal-black eyes, and that fit-as-fuck body made some of the cruising patrons of Pony Bar turn and take notice. He was a gay boy magnet with his military tattoos and aggressive style. He was hunting up sex tonight and wore his preferences like a Grindr profile -- red hanky left.

He pulled in next to me at the bar about a quarter to midnight.

Pony was pretty crowded this Friday night. Andi's contact had zeroed in on a bouncer who recognized the Chief Petty Officer and nailed the location. Earlier, I had shown up at Pony Bar outside of North Richmond to confirm the chances that Davies would be there tonight.

"You a cop?" The bouncer, Raymonda, a do-not-fuck-with-me female at the door, punctuated her question by spitting off to the left.

"Naw, just want to hook back up with my man here, is all. Sorta lost him, ya know?"

She looked at my cell phone a second time.

"Good luck, Sweet Cheeks. Ole Jake here usually walks outta this place at last call with one or two playmates. He used to come in with this one boy hottie, but word is they split up. The kid must dislike crowds if you know what I mean. He'll be here. Buy him a drink and wiggle your ass. May get lucky. Again."

Pony was near the oil refineries on a back road. Service buildings and warehouses seemed to fill the immediate landscape, alternating with tractor-trailers and fuel oil delivery trucks. I convinced Kayne to let me go alone. Flying solo fit my hook-up story, considering Davies may be spooked if we both corralled him.

It doesn't take much for me to rock out shirtless in a down-at-the-heels place like Pony. So there I was, sucking down the Mick Lights and leaning against the bar like I was definitely out to steal someone's man tonight. Or so I wanted the fans to believe.

Oops, is the top button of my jeans really undone? My, my, my... Oh, well.

"He's out of town."

It was Davies' basso growl.

"And you're strayin' and playin'."

"Not that it's any of your fuckin' business, Shithead, but we're open."

A leer crossed his rugged face. He leaned in and grabbed his beer with two hands. Davies smelled of whiskey, sweat, and smoke.

"Who isn't, Boy? Know anyone who isn't cheating? It's called a relationship enhancement – adds to the excitement. But, I'll tell you one thing, Trouble. I ever catch one of my boys stepping out on the Stud, and I'll fix it so he'll never wake up. "

He shifted and placed a hand on the back of my neck. The Bull started to grip as he said, "And show some respect, son. I got two inches and prolly ten, fifteen pounds of muscle on you. Could be a problem if you don't play nice with Jake."

Now, the drunken lecher tightened his hold, and he spit-snarled his next line in my ear.

"Am I clear, Boy?"

OK, I could have so taken this asshat. Guaranteed. But, you see, I had gone undercover, as it were. I had ratcheted my ballsy swag down to a muscled-up sub boy with a big mouth. I faked submission and answered in the argot of dominance play and the posture of not meeting his eyes.

"Sir, crystal, Sir."

Now, his hand moved off my neck and went on an exploratory mission down my back.

"Nice, kid. You pump those muscles hard for your man or the other men he lets use you? Damn solid, boy."

I did not say anything but shifted under the touch of his calloused hand, arching my back. He signaled for two more beers.

"So what I want to know is why you told Big Ray, the bouncer, that I was your studly? We never got together, as far as I recall. I would have definitely remembered this."

Now, here is where it starts to get really shabby. "This" referred to my ass, and the placement of Jake's hand, the waistband of my jeans notwithstanding, now made it clear that he was claiming it for himself. 'S all I'm sayin'.

He tasted the muscles of my neck, pulling me into his arms for an assault kiss. Jake was swaying and struggling for control of his drunken state.

What the hell information... mmm ... ohhh shit.... was I supposed... ahhh... to be getting... from this guy? Oh, yeah, oh, yeah – I began to think with my big head again.

"Hey, can I get a Coors?"

The man who squeezed next to us announced, "Still waiting for that call, Mister Davies. I saw the posting, and it was smoking hot. The choke fuck in the second round should get you a shitload of new subscribers."

Jake came off me a little to have a look. Coors Guy made like I was not there.

"You gotta admit... much better than your regular butt boys, Sir. I'm wilder and do more things than he does. You know I can increase your cash flow. I am still waiting for another collab, Stud. Let's make some more porn, Sir.

"And so, who the fuck is this?"

Jake freed a hand, grabbed the kid by the back of his head, and pulled him close to us. He rough kissed the man and pushed him away. Still holding on to me, he pointed across the bar.

"I don't even remember your name, bitch. Now you get the fuck over there by the pool table and wait until I'm done here. You go over there and pray like the whore you are that I even consider smashing you again."

The pornographer went back to making out with me. The other man backed away. Eventually, I came up for air.

I said, "So, yeah, so, the bouncer woman also said you have a special regular. Second time I heard it tonight. Who is he? And how come he's not here?"

Davies put an index finger in my mouth to stop me from talking.

"You fucking know who he is, Sechi. I can't figure out if you are hungry for that Petty Officer boy – a little night of group play? Huh? Huh? Or are you just nosey? Out to get something on ole Jake, huh?"

He grabbed my head again and continued to explore my mouth, going deeper with a sense of ownership. I backed up, trying not to gag.

Jake turned me loose and leaned with both forearms on the bar. He shifted his powerful body and said, "Baby Brian can't seem to make up his mind despite my many attempts to bring him to face the facts of his life or whatever. Baby Boy was born to serve a man like me. He's good at it when he follows orders.

"Trouble is, he kept going back to that woman. Then he found her videos. She was a wild one. Even with the face swap, he knew it was Princess Pretty Ass. So, Baby Boy is even more messed up by it all. Brian is one fucking shitstorm, and a fuckin' lot of work. But he'll be back. Can't stay away from this."

Jake eyed me in the mirror, turned, and pushed my hand down to his very substantial groin. He swigged his beer and looked at me with intent. He pulled off his tank top and yanked me back into a clinch. He was seriously out to make a conquest and did not care where.

"You wanna know if I killed her or had something to do with it. Right? I'm making out on you like a bandit, muscle boy, and you got crime shit on your mind."

He popped a bicep and pushed my face into his muscles. Lack of enthusiasm can be a dead giveaway. I was pretty cold in my response, considering what he had to say.

He stepped back a bit. Jake stared at me and scratched his head.

"Jesus, man. You really are playing me. This I can't figure out. Anyway, I got this place not too far from here, back near the town. We can get something searing hot going, boy. I'm thinking we start with some bondage and go from there. Way hotter and wilder than anything you'll ever get from the professor. When we are done, and I'm satisfied, we'll give him a call to come and clean you off and take you home. Then, you can show him the video to turn him on."

This guy is a total pig. That's for sure.

No, he didn't kill Gretchen Rockland or have her killed. Unless he is way more complicated than he appears. Jake the Snake was pretty frank about sexing up each of them. That being said, I was becoming convinced that he had no interest in clearing the field so he could have Boy Brian all to himself. I think he was clearly making some serious cash with each of them.

He looked into the corner of the bar for the Coors Guy. The appeal on the part of the pornstar wanna-be seemed to have faded. The kid was hitting on two other guys.

Yeah, Jake Davies was a total libertine with no moral principles or a sense of responsibility in sexual matters. Total user... and that made him quite savage.

My reasoning was disappearing, but so was the attraction. Meanwhile, Jake was working me into some pretty heavy action. His sexual energy was almost overpowering.

"Need to get you in some crisp white Navy rig, Sechi. Tight in the ass and crotch. Make us some film – all about a sailor bad boy on shore leave whose teasing goes wrong, way wrong. Throw that Brian bitch in as a guest slut."

He raised his big arms up like Rocky on the steps of the Philadelphia Museum of Art.

"Produced by, directed, and starring Iron Drake Crusher. Hell Yes!"

Davies took a wide stance so that he could get me in a hold that pressed our bodies together. His taste was somewhat intoxicating.

His powerful fingers and hands moved up. I felt pressure on my neck muscles as he ate more of my mouth and lips, sloppy and slick. The Crazy Ass was insistent.

"You know what the ultimate thrill is, boy? Snuff films. Ever want to kill just for the rush? The total control? The rage inside, boy. It needs to come out and slaughter."

Shit! Even in the dim lights of the bar — crazy fuckin' eyes. Drunk or insane? Yeah, gonna say both. Still, I was convinced he did not kill Dr. Rockland. If he had, the gig would have been more stagey and more pornographic.

About this time, I began to figure out my defense and escape moves as he eased off.

Did I get what I came for?

Jake Davies upended his beer and ran a paw over my chest and shoulders.

"And they pay, Boy. They all pay Jake. Secrets, secrets, secrets."

I dropped my hands over and around his hips.

The big creep swayed as he said, "Let's go. All you have to do for the rest of the night until I let you go is do whatever I tell you. That's all it's gonna take to please me."

It was an easy move, really. Simple. I took Jake's right hand in both of mine. I pressed down on the back of it with my thumbs to apply continued pressure, slamming the palm down into the inside of his upper arm. The pain was meant to be excruciating.

He knelt.

He howled.

He collapsed.

I let go.

"I'm gonna take a hard pass on the audition, Big Guy. Thanks for the beers. Looking forward to checking out your vids. Not!"

He was using the bar to get back on his feet. I took his truck keys.

"On the way out, get 'em from Big Ray, Bozo."

As I turned to go, I said, "Oh, and just so you know, Kayne sexes up like he invented it. Compared to him, you are an amateur. Yeahhh, count on it, Asswipe."

Thomas Paul Severino

Chapter Thirty-One: The Third Watch of the Night
221 Baker Street, San Francisco, California

Nick Sechi's Journal

"What are you doing up here?"

"Couldn't sleep, my love."

I plopped down on the brown Chesterfield sofa in the conference room. It was well after 2 AM. I had checked the rest of the house and saw the light on the second floor of the carriage house that served as our offices.

Kayne was in his robe, barefoot, legs up and crossed at the ankles. He was staring at Andi's case map. A glass of something golden sat on the side table to his left. Outside, the night was chilly and soundless, creeping in through a partially opened window.

"You ever think of taking up a pipe, Boss? I mean, complete the whole Sherlock Holmes meme."

"Yes, that is precisely what I want to do. I'm waiting for you to add fifty pounds around the gut and grow a bushy mustache. As far as one can tell from the Sidney Paget/Strand Magazine illustrations of the Canon Doyle canon, Dr. Watson was portly and greatly resembled a walrus."

"Pass."

"I hesitate to mention this, my love, but you smell. No, that is imprecise. You reek."

I did a pit check and a t-shirt sniff to verify my husband's observations.

"Jake Fuckin' Davies! Ewe! I smell like a nasty and decrepit saloon, or one or seven of its patrons all rubbing…"

I began to act out a very decadent scene.

 "There you see how you are, boyo? My Da is right when he calls you an Eye-talian Red Devil. At least, I think that is what he says."

He checked his watch.

"At this hour of the night, it is of no consequence, anyway."

I got up and went down to the bathroom below us at the garage level. It served as a cleanup space and mudroom. About 15 minutes later, I was in a towel, rocking clean and fresh, and back next to Kayne on the couch.

"Better?"

Somewhere, out beyond the Presidio, a foghorn broke the stillness of the night. Kayne kissed me and took a hit of some Premo Nick Boy.

He sounded satisfied as he said, "Quite. Much better. You have a very distinct scent, my love. Most people do — the natural pheromones and such. I find yours to be heady like a quality whisky, sporty like a new pair of cricket batting gloves, and bright like the sun on a field of wild mountain grass. Intoxicating to the point of passion's arousal, if truth be told."

My husband, the sensualist...

"Ass Pirate Jake Davies does not use deodorant, and his fans love it."

I slouched down for a lean-in.

Kayne seemed annoyed.

"Bloody hell, that's it."

He grabbed my smoochin' head from the back.

"Just how much of your virtue did you have to sacrifice to get information from the Pride of the Navy?"

"No, Kayne. I perfected the art of the dance-away with this drunken Bozo.

"Listen, Porno King Jake sexes up his marks and posts their couplings on the internet, one of those Fans Only pages. He then blackmails his conquests for more sex or for cash while his website memberships increase. He plays a dangerous game and flirts with murder in more ways than one -- his victims' and his own."

I stood up and reached for my phone to check the amateur porn sites, but Kayne stopped me, pulling me in for a cuddle-up.

"It can wait, my boy. Enough work for one day."

"And night..."

"Yes, and night."

"Your Kris?"

"Ahhh... he's still mine, eh? Well, soccer practice ended around four yesterday afternoon. He nipped home for a quick dinner and went. "Angels in America," Part Two, was last night. They are doing the marathon -- Parts One and Two in tandem, starting at 1 PM today. He mentioned that Coach McDaniel was not pleased, but these are the last performances of the run."

I cocked an eyebrow. Kayne knew the question.

"He let me know that he will not be home until this morning -- most likely late morning, if at all."

"Great."

We said nothing for a moment.

"It will be interesting to see what happens when the run of the new Ballet Purgatorio production is over, and Eglievsky moves on."

"Which reminds me, Nick, we have been invited to the opening."

"Hah. Should be a fuckin' blast."

He switched.

"Davies?"

"Crazy as shit, Boss. I thought he was behind Dr. Rockland's killing, and blackmail may be the method, but ole Jakey is not bright enough to do the technology number on her. The Quench and all of that – way too complicated. But Kayne, I got the feeling that he may be a thrill killer. You know, the psychos who get off on murder and indiscriminate death."

I rested my head against his reclining body.

Kayne said, "The Manson Family, Leopold and Loeb – they all wanted to feel what it was like to experience murder. The Zodiac Killer of the 60s wrote in letters to the police that killing people is so much fun. The abduction, rape, and murder of so many children – recreational violence. All these are premeditated or random acts of murder motivated by the sheer excitement of the action. The killers are usually young males with deep feelings of inadequacy and the need to dominate. However, women are well represented in the documented incidents."

He paused before saying, "What's missing, Nick, is the torture."

"Huh?"

"The thrill killer is most often a sadist. Before he kills, this murderer makes his prey suffer for the psychopath's gratification. In 1968, San Francisco's Zodiac killer wrote the police that his murders and his victims' torment were better than having sex. None of our victims were tortured, as far as we can tell. No sexual abuse either."

He pointed to our case map.

"Nor do these victims share any physical characteristic, which is generally the case. One who kills for pleasure frequently has an ideal victim type. They usually have similar physical characteristics, trans people, young women, children, people without housing, laborers -- that sort of thing.

Kayne now slipped out of my embrace and walked to our wall diagram. So much for leaving off work.

"What our victims *do* have in common is an odd professional link. These four were suspected leaders of illegal operations, drug lords, terrorists, etc. These three scientists had associations with a particular field, astrophysics, and their research cannot be found."

"Theft."

"Possible. We have seen this before. Competition in the race to develop new and lucrative technologies -- a bloody race for space."

"Hey, Boss. Why are we considering the thugs and the professors together? Is it the signatures?"

"Yes, the signs of the zodiac. They play out with astonishing precision. Not like a horoscope but like a cosmological link — it is the stars themselves and not the astrology that is significant here."

"Kayne, you mentioned the Zodiac Killer of fifty years ago. Are we looking at a copycat?"

"Unlikely, Nick. That appellation was based on the cryptic letters the killer sent to the police, specifically the signature he used — a circle with a dot in the center, a symbol of the sun. Our killings have a more explicit connection to the cosmos. Individual stars are actually named. The late Professor Stokes is an example.

Kayne stopped, jumped up, and turned to face me.

"Crikey! I am amazed at my inability to reason. How could I miss this? This cannot be the work of one psychopath. The killings are too close together. The timeline is most accelerated. A serial killer takes his time for fear of discovery – months, sometimes years, between his strikes.

"Nick. This is some sort of cult. The Signs of the Zodiac are the avatars of the murderers!"

"Murder as a rite of initiation?"

"Or by assignment. Contract killings."

"Hey, makes more sense, Big Man. Murder for hire, right?"

"Precisely. "

Kayne settled back, and we sat in silence for a bit, looking at the jumble of evidence on the conference room wall. It was like a window had opened. He waved a hand at the graphic and spoke softly.

"It's a club, Nick, a members-only organization of death."

Thomas Paul Severino

Chapter Thirty-Two: Helios

The Mark Hopkins, 1200 Sacramento Street, #500, San Francisco, California

By The Kris

"You have the most fantastic body. It is positively sinful, an exotic angel of light and muscle. I am absolutely entranced. You hold me captive, my boy. Ummm."

I pulled him closer and said, "Ya know, there is something about that. I just love hearing, Mr. Artem."

"That is because you are a vain and arrogant male, just like Tyoma. I like that, boy. Oh, yesss… You must never wear clothes. On you, it is a blasphemy to be clothed."

His hungry mouth moved over me as I continued, "Whatever. Training is really dope, and I have good genetics. The Sorenson side of the family looks like 'The Thunder from Down Under.' Don't know about my mother's side. I don't even know who she was, to be honest. Danish is all I got."

Tyoma came up for air, looked into my face, and said, "Your Papa never speaks of her?"

I rolled him under me and did some tasting of my own. Pulling my head up, I answered, "No. A deep family secret. He is the guardian of quite a few mysteries."

"And the two of you are estranged? Because you are gay, I am sure that is it, No?"

"For the record, no. And can we talk about something else? How about back to my smoking hot bod? You've got me going again, sexy man. Hey, tell me about this scar on your hip."

"It was five years ago, Ballet Opera de Paris at Opéra Bastille — Basilio in 'Don Quixote.' I fell executing the landing of a *sauter*. This jump requires pushing off from a *plié* to leave the floor with pointed toes and extended legs. The landing is the most challenging part, as it must be soft and quiet. It takes a tremendous amount of strength and control to master.

"I was distracted, which never happens, my Kris. But nevertheless, something had to be reattached. I was eighteen weeks in a cast and never really reached my former greatness for another year."

I traced the pencil-thin red mark with my finger from the top of his left buttock halfway down the back of his thigh.

"Great ass on you, old man, damn fine. What are you now, sixty, seventy?"

Artem rolled and grappled on top of me. He rasped, "I will teach you to respect your elders, you sassy boy. I am only six years older than your Doctor Sorenson. And I am a perfect specimen of a *danseur* in his prime. It may surprise you to know I still have many lovers."

"Not."

"I do not understand."

"I meant it would not surprise me. You have a certain vibe about you when you are interested in a man."

"Or a boy?" He said with a smile on the verge of a sneer.

Now I got him back underneath me, my jock legs holding him prisoner.

"I am no boy, my man. Hasn't been a boy who has been giving you what you need with deliberate and powerful passion, now has it? Huh? Huh?

"You are a fine braggart, my naked beauty. Does that come with taking sports dope?"

OK, stop the music… roll off…WTF?

"Wait, wait, wait. Run that by me again."

"Like the blood doping athletic scandals… you said…"

"Dude!!! I said my training was dope. 'Dope' means super cool– fantastic. No poisons in this body, hot man. The Kris is natty through and through. That means natural, no steroids."

"OK, that is Gen Z language. What is this 'Thunderstorm Down in the Underwear?' Are you speaking of your..."

"Now you are bustin' my delicious ass, Tyoma. 'Thunder From Down Under' is an Australian male stripper posse -- very fit alpha males. Yeah, even my Uncle Kick and my Uncle Mitch are prime muscled-up beauties. Nick has a theory about that... You should see them do sports. Such incredible agility, form, and endurance. But this man is better, of course."

Artem traced a design on my chest as he said, "I have not met Mr. Sechi yet. What is this theory he has about men?"

"He always says like is drawn to like. Uncle Nick says beautiful men hang out with attractive guys – hot jocks with other hot jocks... sexy-arsed dancers with their smoking hot admirers."

He moved in for a frisky kiss-up, our bodies entwined on his big bed. The covers were kicked off last night sometime during round three. I didn't know what time of the morning it was. I also didn't give a fuck.

Interesting expression, considering what was about to go down.

* * *

This whole thing came on fast, Nick. I'm not sure I know what to tell you. Really not happy where we left it. But, I can tell you this, I am in it to win it – head over ass over heels, man. You always talk about being hit by the thunderbolt – BAM, dude. I mean, seriously.

Artem Eglievski is one smooth charmer. He knows just how to get my interest, stroke my ego, and fill my mind with impossible but desirable goals... well, all the things I want – I think, anyway. I like being his... ahhh, boyfriend (what a curious word) if that is what I am.

He just says the word, and things happen that could just about never be. Doors open, people pay attention, and the fans love his ass. He can get me some incredible parts, Unk. He knows loads of people in the theater arts. Tyoma is everything I want to be right now and who I want to be with.

I don't know why we're not talking much anymore, Uncle Nick. I get the feeling you are disappointed in me, and it's all about Tyoma.

Anyway, I know you're the writer in the family, so I hope you can use this information or something.

Thomas Paul Severino

Chapter Thirty-Three: Dragon Boats Chasing Moonlight

221 Baker Street, San Francisco, California

Nick Sechi's Journal

"It's a murder club."

"I beg your pardon, Andi."

"That. That. That."

Our Administrative Assistant had almost run up the stairs and thrown her stuff on her desk like Amanda Priestley in "The Devil Wears Prada." The excited woman burst into the conference room and waved at the wall.

"So, I watched this TV show on the Court TV channel, 'The Disciples of Destruction' last night 'cause I couldn't sleep. The episode was all about Mount Vernon, New Hampshire, where two teenagers broke into this family's home. They hacked them to death with a machete. But get this – these two guys formed a club called 'The Disciples of Destruction,' and killing somebody was what someone had to do to be in the club."

"Outstanding, my girl."

Andi beamed.

Kayne unpacked the particulars.

"I am familiar with the case. It was October 4, 2009, I believe. Steven Spader, aged seventeen, and nineteen-year-old Christopher Gribble murdered Kimberly Cates and severely maimed her 11-year-old daughter, Jaimie. The killing was random and astoundingly brutal. The murderers testified that they intended to kill everyone in the home.

"Furthermore, Gribble and Spader did not know each other before the crime. The club was actually formed by Spader, who spent time recruiting members. There is evidence that there are other kill-for-pleasure groups elsewhere in the world."

Our assistant seemed very pleased with herself as she said, "They got life sentences, by the way."

Kayne continued, "Our Zodiac Murder Cult, however, is not murder for a thrill. It seems to be more of a murder-on-assignment organization. They have death contracts that create a sense of urgency. The bodies stack up due to a rush to close some macabre deal."

I watched it dawn on our Girl Friday. Her face dropped slightly as she said, "Wait a second. You guys, man. You already thought of this."

"At exactly what time was your show broadcast last evening, Ms. Rodriguez?"

"Eleven PM, why?"

Kayne pointed to himself and me.

"Three AM exactly. You got there first, Young Miss."

I joked, "In my desk somewhere, I have a junior G-man badge for you, girl. I'll add a 'wo' to the 'man,' and..."

Andi put on her glasses and exaggerated the placement of her middle finger as she adjusted them – a very seemingly innocent "fuck you."

She placed a card on the table and turned to go back to her desk.

"Too early for mail."

"Correct again, Doctor S. That was stuck in the brass plate on the carriage house. The one that says, 'Sorenson Sechi, Cracker Jack Detectives.' And I know what it means, partially anyway."

The card was slightly bigger than a business card and had two Chinese characters inscribed in black ink. Kayne scrutinized it from every angle. I made a move to pull up a program that deciphered Chinese logograms when Andi said, "Don't go to the trouble."

She tapped a blood-red, immaculately manicured fingernail on the card.

"Dragon boats chasing moonlight."

* * *

"Hey."

Kayne said, "Master Sorenson. Good to see you."

"Texted. Yeah?"

"Yes, thank you."

"It's just so convenient staying at his place."

Kayne nodded. I reviewed notes or pretended to.

"Practice. Not sure about after."

"Thank you."

Andi said, "Kris, did you talk to Matt?"

"No. Why?"

"Um… just as I was leaving last night, he popped in to say hey."

"Huh. To you, not me, then. All good. So, gonna grab my stuff and go."

Andi added, "Got the feeling I was not the reason for his drop-in."

"Huh. Dude should learn to use his phone, I guess, right?"

"Later."

He pointed at me as he left.

"Get more rest. You look old."

Thomas Paul Severino

Chapter Thirty-Four: For Fans Only
221 Baker Street, San Francisco, California

Nick Sechi's Journal

"That little... one royal pain in the ass, Kayne. I mean it. Living up to his phony-baloney titles, that's for sure."

"Easy, my love. What are you doing up here?"

I was in my gym shorts and propped up in bed with my tablet on my lap.

"We are too fuckin' lenient with him, Kayne. My parents would have busted my ass if I ever behaved like that cocky little..."

"Oh, really? So when, at the ripe old age of fourteen, you came home from sports practice and announced that you were dating a high school teammate and making *bumsen* like rabbits in heat, your mother decided to celebrate with a fresh batch of Sunday Sauce after Mass?"

"Watch it, Boss. Not *my* Dad, who took us out to the woodshed and used the strap."

"It was a tack room in the stables. And I have one word for my counter-argument."

"What's that?"

"Wooden spoon."

He pulled off his clothes and jumped under the covers.

He corrected.

"I realize that's two words, but the image of Viola Sechi charging after her sex bomb, jock son, or throwing one of her shoes and saying, 'I'll see you dead first' – well, I win this round."

He added, pulling close to me and looking at my tablet, "Having some man-time watching porn without your man? Nicola Michael, I am appalled... wait, is that who I think...."

"Yep, the Jakester. Doing a free trial. This website is gay, bi, every sort of... Bingo. Holy shit."

Like most porn, the plot was not elaborate -- cut to the sex-up and go for broke.

I pointed at the video and said, "The deflowing of one Gretchen Rockland, I will bet the ranch on it. Shit. A straight guy's fantasy – one guy and two women."

Kayne said, "Observe, my love. Domino masks, but the women are definitely the deceased chemist and the inimitable Martina Howard. From the man's build, I would agree that that is the head of Blackhawk security. He is certainly well-equipped."

"Tattoos are a dead giveaway, like a signature, Boss. Damn yeah, perhaps I was a bit hasty in turning that... whoa! Do not tickle me."

Kayne harumphed and drew back a bit.

I watched a scene between the two women.

"Ha! No personal involvement, my fine jock ass, Boss. I don't think you could be any more personally involved than that. Holy shit, wait a minute here."

The scene raced forward to its obvious conclusion. However, the story's hero was not quite finished with his adventures in Kinky Town. Next chapter: A hot naked man, also disguised, this time in a leather hood. The man was bound for the pleasure of the homegrown porn star. Now tied up, the women were forced to watch the intense man-on-man action.

The naked Davies was strangling the bound man. Kayne pointed to the captive.

"That is young LaCroix -- the inside of his bicep... there, see it?"

The tattoo was clear -- the red, green, and black of the flag of Martinique.

"Wait, Boss. This is weird. See? There are edits and unusual cuts."

I rewound and slowed the action down.

"Some of this has been... there... that looks rigged. There is the signature of some editing software that appears to have manipulated the video action. I'd say the stud might have had a functional problem."

Thomas Paul Severino

Chapter Thirty-Five: The Marina Lighthouse

The Marina District, San Francisco, California

Nick Sechi's Journal

"Hello. Hello. Permission to come aboard. Hello, can you help me, please?"

Mel Chandler put his computer into sleep mode and stood up from his desk in the Sea Star galley. He had lived on this yacht in the Marina District for about four years. The fifty-one-year-old from Carson City went up the gangway and opened the hatch. Out on the pier, a woman was calling out and rapping on the boat.

"Hello, I am your neighbor, about three boats down, and have just done the dumbest thing. I wonder if you could help me. I just need you to hold a flashlight while I recover my keys."

Chandler stepped onto the deck and said, "Sure, show me how I can help. Hold on." Returning, he went back in for a jacket and climbed onto the dock

"Gosh, thanks a lot. This won't take but a bit."

The woman, who seemed to be in her late twenties and was dressed in jeans, deck shoes, and a slicker, led the way down the pier to her boat.

"I dropped them, and they fell down through an opening into the engine hatch. I looked, but I think my keys slid under some machinery down in there."

They climbed onto the deck of a smaller, rather antique skiff.

"There is no light in the hold 'cause I think the bulb burned out. I got a spare, but I need two hands to open the unit. I have to prop open the compartment with this." She held up a wooden belaying pin used to secure the rigging

Mel took the large flashlight as the woman opened the hatch in the ship's aft. He heard a sound behind him and turned to see a large man step out of the hold with a rope. Chandler shone the light on the man's face.

"Hey, I don't get it. Why did you need me if this guy…"

The man's smile was a slice of horror in the semi-darkness.

***

"At night, with only the stars as a guide, this structure served as a lantern for ships seeking entry into the port of San Francisco by night, my love."

Kayne looked up at the retired stone lighthouse designed in the manner of an old Roman tower. Our attention turned to the police officer on the scene.

"Not much has been touched since the harbor police called it in, Doctor Sorenson. We have just verified that the individual is deceased; however, I wanted to inform you about this. Thanks a lot for coming."

"Fortunately, we were not far away. We live over in Pacific Heights, just a few blocks from here. My colleague, Chief Inspector Rosario Martell of Contra Costa County, will be joining us shortly. Tell me, Captain Simmons, why did you call us tonight?"

The Police officer muttered, "Dr. Sorenson, Mr. Sechi, whenever fucked up shit like this happens, and this is pretty fucked up, you two come to mind. And by that, I mean my department has become aware that you guys are investigating some very unusual murders in the Bay Area. I took a shot. It's only 1:30 AM anyway. You guys are just getting in from your…"

I finished his remarks, "… little homosexual sex parties. Yeah, yeah, yeah, Captain, you big 'phobe. Your problem, Marty, is you keep hanging at The Stud -- too much hoping no one will make you on the down low."

The big guy roughly clapped me about the shoulders. His trapezius squeeze was part a no-homo, straight bro-friendly grip and part "do not fuck with me, Sechi,"– the big goof.

He handed us gloves and said, "Save it, Rusty. Just tell me what you think."

The Evil League

The officers hauled the corpse out of the bay. They placed the dead man on the cobblestones surrounding the Marina District Lighthouse. The man was fully dressed, and the front of his skull had been smashed.

Kayne's hands moved over the corpse, mouth, eyes, hands, and feet. The coldness of the bay water had siphoned off all body heat. He was blue-gray.

"Dead about two hours, possibly less. The cause of death is severe trauma to the brain. The murder weapon has a curved surface area," Kayne said. "The indentation is round and has been struck as one would pound with a wooden mallet of some sort."

He raised an arm and demonstrated the attack.

"... most likely boating equipment. Please observe – fragments. The blow came from a left-handed person. Given the skull's damage, I venture that the body was placed in the water post-mortem. The rope anchoring him to the lighthouse served the purpose of securing the body and as a signal, so that the corpse might be found and not overlooked or carried out to sea. The killer is proud of her work."

"A woman, Boss?"

"She is approximately five feet, four inches in height and without substantial body mass. She is thin. With a higher center of gravity, a man of that height would have dispatched this poor man with a single blow. The murderess needed..."

He counted, "One, two, three... five shots to make the kill. Two of which were delivered while the man was on the ground."

He pointed closely to my forehead.

"The frontal bone is the hardest part of the skull. The victim was facing her when hit. One assumes he turned to her from looking another way because he had no time to deflect the blow. The last thing this man saw was the raised arm of the woman who struck him in the forehead.

"First strike high... here. His head rocks back. He is still standing. Then, she hits him twice more, lower... here and here."

Kayne now turned the victim's face.

"Once he falls, the right side of his face is down. The assassin struck the left temporal area twice more to make sure her victim was dead."

"Had she attacked him while he was looking the opposite way, she would have smashed the parietal bone here at the back of the skull, which is thinner -- fewer strikes required to kill him."

I jumped in, saying, "What do you think? Sixty? He was a member of the yacht club and a resident. See the carpet slippers with the club's crest. He was a professional -- a recent manicure. Callous on the left index finger... he writes a lot... longhand. Our man was left-handed, and he attended public school."

"Listen, Junior, you're sounding more and more like him every day with that weird crap. How'd you know he went to public school? I call BS."

I looked up at Kayne and smiled.

"Marty, you get a callous like that because you grip the pen too hard and in the wrong way. No nun in her right mind would ever teach such a weird ass penmanship grip, and they would have forced him to use his right hand as God intended. As my Mother would put it, he went to the pagan schools."

I looked at the cop and flashed my fingers, explaining, "Saint Raymond's Elementary School, the Bronx."

"Nick."

Kayne motioned to me. I reached over to the victim's inside jacket pocket and extracted the guy's wallet just as Rosie came up to us. I handed Kayne the billfold.

"Good evening, gentlemen. Do we have another?"

Kayne flipped through the wallet and announced, "Melchior Aaron Chandler, Ph.D. Professor of Nuclear Physics. UC Berkeley."

Rosie asked, "Why do I know that name?"

Kayne examined the unfortunate academic's fingertips and asked a police officer to hold the light closer.

"This man was recently on the Apple News App, an article in the San Francisco Chronicle. Dr. Chandler and his colleagues have been working on technological systems that will guide resilient engineering projects designed to offset the effects of extreme space storms – mass ejections of radiation from the sun. That sort of thing."

Whoa! Another space egghead buys the ranch.

Kayne paused.

"Nick, please hand me one of the fish."

"What fish, Boss?"

"Sweat pants pockets. Either side, there appear to be two."

I reached into each of the openings and, from each side, produced a dead fish.

"One."

"Two."

Captain Simmons cursed.

Thomas Paul Severino

Chapter Thirty-Six: Rosie

Aboard the Sea Star, The Marina District, San Francisco, California

Nick Sechi's Journal

"No computer."

"It was stolen by the murderer, Captain. When they came back for the wallet... No one goes out in their sweatpants and slippers with their billfold in their jacket pocket. He was an anomaly. Dr. Chandler was ambushed somewhere close by.

I said, "A stroll on the dock before bed, perhaps."

"How could you possibly know that they took his computer, Kayne? He may have left it at the University."

Kayne stepped to a closet off the Sea Star's galley. He opened a door and pointed to a blinking black box.

"Where there is a router, one usually finds a computer — a PC, in fact. Please observe this empty counter space and chair. There. The wood is darker in a rectangular shape, and here on the left side, the veneer is lightly scarred as if constantly irritated by a device scraping over its surface."

I volunteered, "A left-handed mouse."

Rosie said, "More than one perp. They took everything, keyboard, monitor — most likely in a hurry."

"The pads of Professor Chandler's fingers were those of a man who spent long hours on a computer. He did not use all of his ten fingers to type. Only these."

Kayne wiggled his thumbs and index fingers.

"But, as Nick observed, the man wrote in longhand — quite a bit, in fact. He reached a hand up above the desk and took down one of the books.

"Yes, the invaders were very much in a hurry... very much in a hurry... they overlooked this."

He opened a thick volume – the scientific journal of Melchior Aaron Chandler.

***

"Simple. The outline on the dead man's wet pants. The light I was using to examine his fingers caught it just right. Fish."

After promising to keep Marty Simmons in the loop, we had reconvened at La Sirenissima's, a 24-hour eatery on Jefferson, in the Marina. The three of us tucked into a booth and ordered breakfast.

Kayne was wound up. His analytic thought processes were in overdrive. So were our appetites.

"Two longshoreman breakfasts, please."

"The fish were dead when they were placed in Dr. Chandler's pockets, easy to see from their physiognomy... signature of the killer, the sign of Pisces."

"What were they, Boss?"

"Steelhead trout. They are like salmon, which spend most of their adult lives in the ocean but spawn in freshwater streams and rivers along the central California coast and in the San Francisco Bay Area."

Rosie said, "What I don't get is that no one from either of the two yacht clubs, the Golden Gate or the St. Francis, heard or saw anything. "

"If the murder occurred around midnight, most of the boat residents would be asleep. Rosie, because the deadman's journal is evidence..."

"I'm on it. I'll give you both the highlights ASAP."

Rosie flipped through her notes.

"Kayne, Nick. I spoke with the young girl in Vallejo. Her story is that she did the killing. Ann Marie Grisham is a teenage runaway from Des Moines.

Her parents are divorced, and her mother is a state representative in Iowa. The family has money but no time for their daughter. A year ago, she ended up in San Jose and caught the attention of someone who knows someone – you know, that scam.

"The girl thought she was getting a modeling contract and ended up doing sex work in a branch of Carlo D'Luca's operation. About six months ago, she became a favorite of Diana Calvert-Sans, D'luca's girlfriend and business partner. Calvert-Sans set Ann Marie up in an apartment in the Richmond District with three other girls and a house mother."

Rosie rechecked her notes.

"... goes by the name of Marsha Bevins. Ms. Grisham claims that Bevins convinced her that the only way to get out of The Life was to kill Culvert-Sans now that Carlo D'luca was dead. Grisham was shipped off to a party in Tripoli, where she saw her chance to do the kill. The family has hired the best attorneys to get the child off."

"And Bevins, Rosie?"

"Disappeared into the night, Kayne. We believe she was operating under an alias... funny."

I asked, "Something?"

"Well, yeah, Nick. The girl said that she and Bevins got pretty friendly. The poor kid probably needed a friend or a mother figure. Anyway, they would sit up and chat, doing each other's hair and girly stuff. So, Ann Marie Grisham said that this Bevins woman promised to give her a ring which she liked."

"A ring?"

"Yes, Ann Marie admired a monogram ring owned by Marsha Bevins. The way she described it, the initial M was a bit stylized. I had an extra loop that twisted. She showed me."

Kayne took a pen and drew on a napkin.

"I'd say, yeah, that could be it."

I looked at him with a puzzled expression.

Kayne said, "The symbol for the sixth astrological sign, Virgo. And kindly remember, one never rarely wears jewelry in a research lab, my love."

Rosie and I got it at precisely the same time.

"Oh, fuck me! I just realized it-- the stylized 'M ... for Marsha... and for Martina... Boss! I remember a white band on her left index finger. She takes her ring off at work."

Rosie completed the thought, "Martina Howard, Blackhawk's Director of Research, aka Marsha Bevins."

Chapter Thirty-Seven: The Autumn Moon

Chinatown, San Francisco, California

Nick Sechi's Journal

"I will have your tea ready in a few moments, Dr. Sorenson. My shop is across the street. When you have finished admiring our street art, please find your way to The Tea House of the Autumn Moon."

The man left the alley and disappeared up Grant Avenue.

I made to follow, but Kayne put a hand on my arm.

"Just a few moments, Nick."

He stalled to conceal our connection to the fleeing businessman.

He pointed to the beautiful mosaic on the wall of the small Chinatown street.

"The plaque says, 'Dragon Boats Chasing Moonlight' was created by a children's program connected to the Chinatown Community Center, just around the corner. It seems there is an ancient Chinese legend where teams compete in a race in dragon-shaped boats like these. Impressive… more than thirty thousand tiles…"

I read over his shoulder and quoted, "It goes on to say, 'The piece represents the connection between hard work and dreaming big.' So many dreams in this neighborhood, I'll bet, stretching back to the arrival of the first Chinese in San Francisco in the mid-1850s."

Kayne smiled and nodded as we walked out into the cross street.

* * *

"Gentlemen, I apologize for the mysterious way in which I have set up this meeting. Perhaps as I explain why we have turned to you for help, you will understand."

As twilight settled over the City, we entered the tea shop across from Wentworth Alley. We did not have to say a word and were escorted to a private alcove at the back of the café.

"Please allow me to make introductions, Doctor Sorenson and Mister Sechi. I believe you already know my sister, Constance Xing Zhen.

"So good to see you again, Professor Xing Zhen."

The woman smiled graciously. "I have heard from my Father of the most fortunate ending to your case in China. It seems my family is continually in your debt."

She nodded to our alley friend, "This is my brother Max Chang, the proprietor of The Autumn Moon."

Max bowed and gestured to a seated elderly gentleman.

"I have the honor to acquaint you with my wife's father, Wan Guchan."

I said, "It is an honor, Sir, to meet your family."

Kayne bowed, saying, *"Nín hǎo, wàn xiānshēng."*[9]

"Please join me for some tea, gentlemen."

We sat with the three family members as Professor Constance brewed the tea.

Max said, "My sister is preparing Wuyi Rock Tea. It is our highest-grade oolong tea. You will note that it has the scent of green tea and the sweet, mellow taste of black tea. This variety is Da Hong Pao from Fujian Province – the best. There are many essential B vitamins within it. And it contains inositol, a major curative in Chinese Medicine."

"My brother is an eternal salesman. Please pardon his marketing pitch."

"Hey, no. All good. It smells great."

Kayne addressed his question to the elder of the family.

"How may we be of service?"

---

[9] Hello Mister Wan

"Are you familiar with the San Francisco Mint, Doctor?"

"Of which one are you speaking, Mr. Wan? I believe we have three. The present and only working mint in the City stands like a fortress overlooking Buchanan and Market Streets. But we have had two earlier versions.

"The first was built in 1854 on Commercial Street, now the San Francisco Historical Society's home. During the California Gold Rush, ore discovered in the state was shipped to Philadelphia to be refined into coins. That was expensive and very dangerous. Congress decreed that San Francisco should have its own mint."

Our hosts were fascinated by my husband's command of history. Professor Xing Zhen poured more tea.

"Then, in 1859, a large vein of silver ore was discovered under the eastern slope of Mount Davidson, Nevada, the Comstock Lode. Silver and gold flooded into the city. More ore meant more coin, and that meant a larger building. In 1874, the beautiful Greek Revival building at Mission and Fifth replaced the first mint."

Mr. Wan interjected, "She is built of four-foot-thick granite blocks interlaced with two-inch iron bars to make her earthquake-proof and safe from tunnel-digging thieves. She is the Granite Lady, also under the care of the San Francisco Historical Society. I have the most auspicious job of being a night watchman, and the ghosts of my country folk surround me when I walk the corridors."

Max said, "Many Chinese immigrants worked on that building from the Griffith Quarry in Penryn, California, the source of the limestone. They hauled it to its present location, cut and sculpted what is now a landmark."

The old gentleman continued, "Sirs, there have been strange goings-on in that building late at night."

"Every night?" I asked.

"No, Mr. Sechi. It varies. Usually, once a month, I would say, in the secret vault."

"Please tell us more, Mr. Wan. You mentioned a secret vault."

"When the building was designed back in the nineteenth century, the architect created a basement chamber for the director that does not appear on any blueprints. It was intended to serve as a reserve for gold bullion or firearms in the event of an uprising in San Francisco. During the earthquake and fire of 1906, the gold and silver in the vaults on the first floor were moved into the basement. The building survived both disasters and continued to mint the coin from the ore mined in California and Nevada.

"The room has been leased by an outside group for an indeterminate period. The chamber is now empty, except for a large conference table and thirteen chairs for the group that meets there. They are on no schedule as the building is now an events facility. They always meet in the late evening and enter through a secret entrance at the rear of the building."

The elder took a sip of his tea and, with sparkling eyes, continued his tale.

"My family came here from Taishan County in the southwest of Guangdong Province. I was born right here in Chinatown. Sometimes, late at night, my grandfather would tell stories of our village in China. A group of very bad men was present, committing evil deeds. They formed a secret society and killed many people. My grandfather, his wife, and son, my father, had to leave China because of them. Dr. Sorenson. I fear that this group is much like them, evil at heart."

I asked, "Have you observed their meetings?"

"Yes, Mr. Sechi. An old walkway was made to appear as part of the old ventilation system. The first director of the Mint could observe his bullion cache from above the room on this walkway without being seen. There was always the danger of theft. It is there that I have watched the group. Alas, I cannot understand much of what is being said."

"Have you been to the police, Sir?"

The old gentleman was silent.

Max explained, "Mr. Sechi, there are things that happen here in Chinatown that are spoken of only in secret. This is one of them. My people have had a difficult history with law enforcement. The plague in Chinatown is still remembered."[10]

"Mr. Wan, I would like to see this place," Kayne said. "Do you know when this group meets again?"

"I would venture to say in one week, give or take. I will send for you when the moon is full."

Kayne said, "Then, it will be at the rising of the Autumn Moon."

---

[10] In 1900, San Francisco's Chinatown experienced a bubonic plague outbreak that led to quarantine, racial tensions, and political conflict. The epidemic, was initially denied by California's governor to protect the city's reputation and economy. This denial allowed the disease to spread, impacting both the Chinese community and the wider population.

Thomas Paul Severino

Chapter Thirty-Eight: The Last Entry
Melchior Aaron Chandler's Journal

And so the questions become, how many satellites are they willing to lose? How many spacecraft, astronauts, and expensive equipment? How many monster cyclones is the international community ready to endure before my team's recommendations and roadmaps are taken seriously – monumental loss of life, property, all of that?

Considering a solution for climate change's effects without taking into account my Project DOSPAR, our advanced observational technologies, and the Shielding Protocols is preposterous — a rejection of science and intelligent research.

The point of the whole issue is who has the money to pay for our work? Who will provide the funds to understand how the universe works around us? What are the challenges that connect the Sun to society?

NASA believes it has the research in place and under development to meet the demands of proposed government-run space exploration programs. The Russians and the Chinese haven't a clue. Well, they actually do, but their teams are going in the wrong direction. Politics, politics – let the scientists handle the truth. The politicians are out to destroy life as we know it.

Private agencies are primarily interested in securing a large profit margin. We as a planet are doomed.

The meeting with "C company" was a mess. I do not understand why a new aerospace industry based in California is reluctant to bring us on board. The key here is collaboration – interagency work to develop new or additional instrumentation. Personally, I found them to be unwilling to commit to any substantial contract.

On another note, I cannot shake the feeling that I am being watched... followed. Perhaps I am becoming paranoid.

Who could be knocking at this time of night?

Chapter Thirty-Nine: Sprints

The University of San Francisco, San Francisco, California

By The Kris

Filling in the gaps for you, Uncle Nick...

"What the hell happened to you, Sorenson? I let you start pre-season practice late cause of your 'theatrical career.' It's been almost a week, and you suck, kid. You come late for practice. Your form is way off. You spend most of your game hogging the play, and that tackle you threw at Okeyo may have put him out of the first couple of games — one of our best defenders."

Coach Austin McDaniel came at me with a pointed finger to my chest. My teammates were trying hard to look like they were not watching him spank the shit outta me.

"I took you on as a freshman, and you were good, very good. That fuck up against Gonzaga notwithstanding — a heartbreaker, but what's done is done, kid. You had a good season. I want to see a second-year man with his head in the game and not up his ass. Do you understand me? Now, I expect you put in the time, extra, in fact. I want hustle like I have never seen before. I need teamwork — that star jock character you've been rocking is over, do you hear me, Sorenson?"

"Yes, Sir. But…."

He gave me the hand.

"Save it, hotshot. Don't give me excuses. Give me results. Fifty wind sprints, right now."

He looked at the team and said, "Get your gear and go home. Tomorrow bright and early — all day."

"Coach, I got a date tonight, Sir."

"Why am I not watching your ass sprinting down this field, Sorenson? Date? He's gonna have to fuckin' wait."

"You are late. I am late. It has been quite a day, my Kristof. We can still make the party. You are in your football clothes, but that doesn't matter. We can shower and change at my condo."

The A-man was in his ballet kit with a towel around his neck. I had watched him dance with his partner, who was the dancer guy, you know, the one who also created the dance and all. Amenti, I think.

"You are a sexy jock."

We did a hug-up greeting.

"And you are a sexy Étoile."

"Artem, I want to try the second half of the piece one last time, the fast run and leaps."

"No, Bobby. You have an amazing ability to overthink and overdance at times. We have it, my boy. It will last until tomorrow. We have Ivanova's party after all."

The guy now looked me up and down. Usually, I get a smile, but I was not getting much approval from this guy, no way. I pegged him at my Uncle Nick's age, maybe younger. Dancer guys sure have great legs and asses. I had him beat with upper body, however. Mine was way better.

"Kristof, this is my choreographer, Robert Amenti. He designed this ballet and performs the title role in 'Phaethon.' He is a gifted artist who is transforming dance as we know it. A true iconoclast and artistic visionary. He makes history.

"Robert, this is Kristof Sorenson. Kris just finished a run in "Angels in America" for The Rep here in San Francisco.

Without much enthusiasm, Mr. Dance said, "Yeah, I caught that production -- some interesting moments. You just came from baseball?"

"I play soccer for USF. Forward."

"The University of San Francisco, the Jesuits?"

"Yes, I am in my second year. Hey, you guys looked real good. Congratulations. I bet you cannot wait to finish it."

Amenti kinda got edgy here. He said, "The work is complete, Mr. Sanderson."

"Sorenson."

"Yeah. We just need to make it perfect. We will be ready."

Tyoma said, "It is perfect. 'Phaethon' will be a triumph, and Robert will be its star. We must go, my Kristof. It is very late."

"It was nice to meet you, Mr. Amenti. I guess we will see you later."

"Yes, for as long as it lasts..."

He stopped in the doorway and fired the last shot.

"The party, I mean."

Thomas Paul Severino

Chapter Forty: Ensemble Piece

Alizarian Sky Condominiums, The Fillmore District, San Francisco, California

By The Kris

"Yes, my dears. So, Purgatorio is doing Tharp's 'Deuce Coupe' next. Then comes Justin Peck's 'Everywhere We Go' right after Amenti's 'Phaethon' – three exciting productions this season. This should be a year worth remembering. It is so divinely exciting."

Antonia Ivanova was holding court – all good if you throw your own party, right? Her husband was an older dude, looked like a banker or some such. He also seemed hyper-bored – ballet dancers and dance company execs all over the place. Ivanova's girl crush, Phobe Garcia-Dolan, just seemed to be a smoldering presence, all in black, her dark hair falling down her back. She remembered me from our double date – Greek food and Flex Club.

Artem and I had nipped back to his place from the Marsden Center. Got some freaky-freaky on – sweaty and tangy before showering up. *Something about an older dude... anyway...* yeah, so we dressed.

"This will look magnificent on you, my Adonis. Here. It's a silky white athletic shirt. Ah, yes. We want to show that lovely chest tonight. Oh, and this jacket. Yes. It's big on the shoulders for me, so it will fit you just right. The sequinned scorpion design on the back is superb. There is a silver slave bracelet over on the... yes, very good. We will go with a mix of flashy style, jock chic, and just a hint of the kinky, yes?"

He looked around the closet and returned, saying, "I do not have shoes for you. So we do your sports shoes, yes? Come here. We need another tear in those jeans at the knee."

"Looks very cool, Tyoma. We will be a hit."

His clothes looked very good on me – suggested some star quality and sexiness.

"This is a very critical crowd, my boy. Dancers and their entourages are incredibly glamourous. You will be examined like a bug under a microscope. And they will appear not to have even noticed you. Such is their way of the bitch critique."

Yeah, pretty fucked. I challenged, "Bring it, says me. I've been up against tougher outfits than this, my man."

I pulled him toward me and kissed him.

Let the bitches soak all this up.

***

At the party, Artem was super popular with the crowd. Everyone wanted to meet the internationally famous dancer. I got some looks, yeah, cool. And I thought sports dudes were always on the make. The dance clique had their way of perfecting the "eye fuck." Oh yeah, these men and women were high on the frisky meter.

"Call me, sexy boy. We need some time together."

"Can I get a number?"

"What are you doing later? I mean, after your sugar daddy falls asleep."

"Damn, you're fine."

"My husband really doesn't care, you know."

"Relax. It will just be the three of us."

A tall dude in leather jeans and a sleeveless t-shirt that said, "Rihanna," came up to me as I wandered out to the veranda. Broad shoulders and chest, he had a sexy face scruff and some curly but longish hair – one of those guys who knows he's hot.

Uncle Nick to The Kris: Look who's talking. Right?

"San Francisco is such a beautiful city."

"Not from here?"

The guy did a casual pose, sweeping his hand through his curly hairdo. He moved like an athlete, with a slow and measured grace.

"Naw, Fargo, North Dakota. Long story, but I like it here. Raymond."

Strong grip. Yeah, definitely a cowboy vibe.

"Kris."

"Dating Eglievesky?"

"Definitely, yeah."

"Cool. Tyoma is incredible. We are all hot for the dude. I'm a horse."

"Seriously?"

I did a look down south. Legs and ass of death in skin-tight leather. Accurate. I smiled and said, "So, brag much?"

"You are very funny. No, I dance one of the horses that pull the Chariot of the Sun in the new ballet."

"Hey, cool. How long have you been with the company?"

"Came out to California when I was seventeen, almost eighteen, so, three years. I love The City. Chance to be open and pursue my passion for dance. Growing up in rural North Dakota for a gay dancer kid was major trouble."

"Looks like you learned to scare off the bullies – nice arms, bro."

"Thanks, yeah – knock 'em down and let 'em know they can't get away with it, the fucks."

"Lotsa monsta farm chores – getting ya fit?"

"Yes, on that, but often not the right body type for the classics. Too much muscle but fuck it, I can move like a Nureyev."

He walked to the far end of the patio and crossed back to me with some spectacular spiraling moves.

"Yeah, impressive."

'Wait a minute, your name Sorenson? Yeah, I thought so, bro. As in that sexy detective guy with the smokin' hot hair, right? His husband writes the blog. Those guys rock."

"My uncles, yeah… two superheroes in the family. Make that three."

"Nice. Yeah, I read about you on there. Play soccer for USF – freshman made the team. A force to be reckoned with, men-wise. Way to go, Kris."

Fist bump.

"Hey, I am pleased you gentlemen met. Raymond Sandell, here is one of my fellow dancers. He is in the new ballet. I see a bright future for this one." Tyoma gave the tall dancer a hug.

"Thanks, Sir. Kris and I were just getting acquainted."

The three of us were interrupted. The break-in dude was swacked and swayin'.

"I'll bet you were. You listen to me, Ray Boy. You come with me to this party, and you leave with me. And in between, you don't put the moves on any other guy. You fuckin' got that?"

It was a pissed-off in the boy's face deal. I hate guys who cannot control themselves – well, with alcohol and drugs anyway.

Raymond was super embarrassed. He put his hand out to steady the newly arrived Robert Amenti. The dude was slurring, sweating, and weaving. Tyoma was just staring at him. Amenti shoved the young dancer's hand away and moved on me. Before we came chest to chest, he glared at Raymond.

"In other words, stop with the moves on this teenager. Kinda big for high school..." The dancer guy abruptly switched so that the last words were almost spat into Eglievsky's face. Then he rocked back to me...

He tapped my chest but referred to Tyoma.

"He's amazing, Sonny Boy, and that is the truth... a freakin' megastar ... no one can touch the great Eglievsky when it comes to artistry and... suh ... suh ... suh ... celebrity. Celebrity. This guy right here. Right fuckin' here."

He turned and slapped Tyoma's chest.

"... this guy... this fuckin' star, right? Up for a freaking knighthood. Did you know that... did you, pretty boy? Pretty star-fucker? Didja know? Huh? But in the sack... whoa! Yeah... that's where his performance is really..."

"Bobby. Enough. You are loud and making a scene, and you are not worthy of this shameful display. Raymond, perhaps... "

Robert Amenti staggered back as if he were touched by an electric wire.

"No! No! You take your hands off me. Only allowed to touch me on the stage... the great stage... All the world's a fuckin' stage. A stage for fucking, right, Soccer Boy? Huh? Hey, I'm talking to you, baby."

The jerk was pissing me off, and I was clenching my fists. If I tapped the boozer just right on that pretty boy's jaw, he would be out like a light. Bobby Baby looked at Tyoma with hatred.

"I was talking about your sexual ahhh... gymna... gymna... your fucking."

He swayed.

"He tell you about the sailor? Classic. The kid left the company after this one had had enough of him. Fuck yeah, so professional."

"No more, Robert. Raymond, if you could..."

This time, the big dude from Dakota took hold of the choreographer and made an effort to help him out. The other folks on the veranda watched the mess get even more cray-cray.

Amenti was pissed as shit now and shrugged off his date and colleague. His breath on my face was gross as he said, "He will throw you out, too, Superboy. When he's done, that is. Can't sustain a real hard-on for a guy for very long."

His smile was like a maniac's in a Stephen King flick. He said, "He likes new meat. Always has."

Now he continued to touch The Kris, on the chest like he was giving me a lesson or some shit— very bad idea.

"Don't take it personally, baby. Happens to many of us, and we keep crawling back to the Great Tyoma for more... more... of what-the-fuck-ever."

"Hold him up, Raymond."

Bop.

Not many saw it. It looked like the jerkwad just came in for a hug-up. Raymond closed his arms around him as Amenti's body slumped and his unconscious head tucked into my shoulder. I said to no one in particular.

"Dude is so exhausted, man. There ya go."

Big Ray Ray and I slipped Drunk Boy out and down a side exit off the veranda. There were cabs lined up on the street, and I gave the driver some cash as my new bud gave an address.

"Leave him on the fuckin' doorstep, whatever, man."

"Not going home with your man, Bro?"

Raymond Sandell put an arm around my shoulder. He had a shit eatin' grin on his face.

"Think I'd rather hang out with you guys. How'd you do that, Kris? Drop him, I mean? Very classic."

"Takes a lot of practice, man, and an asshole with a glass jaw."

* * *

"What appears to be the problem with the wunderkind of dance, Artem?"

"Our Robert has put in many hours on the work, John. We must indulge the artist and see that he gets his rest."

As Raymond and I came back up to the condo, Antonia Ivanova was up with the DJ announcing to her guests, "… and I saw him at the White Cat Cabaret over in the Haight some time ago. The boy sings like the next rock phenom. He has no idea I am doing this, but because I am a spoiled diva…"

Groans and applause.

"… well, fuck you very much. I always get what I want, and he is going to sing for me, right, Kristof?

Holy shit. I was on the spot — and loving it, to be honest. What the hell. I went for it.

I consulted with the DJ, and he hit the Latin vamp. Of course, they wanted to see male muscle, so I tossed the jacket. Not bragging, but my jock ass in motion was like a freaking heart attack, man. The smoking hot music and I were rocking out to "La Vida Loca," and the stuck-up crowd was drooling.

I took the prima ballerina's hand during the musical bridge, and we freaked danced a hot samba. Sexy AF. Both her husband and her girlfriend had resting bitch faces on as Antonia pulled off my athletic shirt and caressed my... well, it got hot.

'' ... she'll take away your pain..."

So much fucking tension, home, on the field, the bat shit crazy Amenti... and what's really up with Tyoma? I needed this cut-loose like a fuckin' drug, man. Slipping a hand to unfasten my jeans' top button, I busted moves like a pole dancer. Showoff? Oh, hell yes!

"... like a bullet to your brain...."

I howled the lyric as Antonia, coming off one of our samba rolls, caught Raymond Sandell. The ballerina threw Horse Boy into the mix. As the DJ cued up extended play, I ended up sexy dancing with the Dakota beauty to the catcalls of our fellow gay boys. Ray Ray could freak like a fuckin' wet dream. At one point, he bent in to lick my abs. It was a shit load of fun, and Antonia was in heaven.

Tyoma turned to us as Ray and I walked over to him. I managed to retrieve my shirt and jacket. Stuffed the silk into my waistband and slipped the dragon jacket on – hell, yeah, I left it open. We both know how to work it, right, Uncle Nick?

"Kris, this is John Marsden. He is Ballet Purgatorio's major patron. John, this is my protégé, Kristof Sorenson, and of course, you know my lovely Raymond."

"Hello. Tell me, are you related to Doctor Kayne Sorenson, the psycho-criminologist?"

"Yes, he is my uncle. He and his husband, Nick Sechi, are consulting detectives – pretty famous."

"Very nice to meet you, young man. Wait. Aren't you connected to the Royal family of Bulgaria?"

"Through my grandmother. Yes, Sir."

"Fascinating."

"Kris plays for USF and is a full-time student there. In addition to soccer, he has experience in the theater."

"A short while back, I caught a local production of 'Romeo and Juliet,' which was superlative. I thought you looked familiar. Quite a looker, son. Guess that's a big plus in the theater along with some sports training."

The man was a typical executive type – an expensive suit, about fifty-ish, with a swatch of white hair in his styled jet-black mane, which gave him a bit of a Dr. Strange look. His eyes, man – they were green and piercing, way darker than Uncle Nick's.

"Finding I really like acting, Sir. A lot of it is connecting up with people who can give me advice."

"If you have captured the interest of Artem Eglievsky, son, you have found yourself an excellent mentor. I am in technology, as you may know. We are currently exploring space travel, but it remains a developing interest for my company. My foundation is also interested in new artists. Mr. Amenti is a recipient of one of our fellowships. We wish him to develop some new pieces for Purgatorio as a possible new artistic director."

Atem held the man's eyes and simply nodded.

"My Kris is a boy of many talents, John, especially in the performing arts. I never do this, but I predict he will be a rising star. "

"You *always* do this, Tyoma. I surrender."

The dude looked my way and said, "Do you have representation, son, an agent?"

"No, Sir, I am new to this."

"Come and see me. I believe I can help. Tyoma will provide the contact information."

"Hey, thanks a lot."

"Your interest in this boy will pay off, John. This much I know."

"Please excuse me. I am getting the eye from our hostess. A real pleasure, gentlemen." He pointed to Ray and cut a smooth exit line, "I would say you also have a bright future, young man. I want to know you better. Walk with me."

Ray grinned like a bastard and followed the money man.

I pulled Tyoma into a corner while Raymond returned and went for drinks. The dancer was startled by my rough and energetic moves.

I spread out and pressed my body against him. I was totally up in his face, pushing one of his hands against my hard enthusiasm. I ravaged his lips with some pagan-style mouth action, wet, hard, and hot. He gasped and moved against the grip of my body.

I snarled, "You are finished calling me 'boy,' Starman. And this is proof you have a real man on your hands. You have much to make good on, I will not stop, and you will fuckin' love it. Respect the Kris and follow orders."

I don't think he knew what to say, but his body responded like it was payday – or soon to be.

I continued the make-out for a bit and then abruptly downshifted. I grinned and stepped back all nice like saying, "Aces, Mr. A. Thanks so much. Marsden is huge in the arts."

Artem tried to normalize, saying, "Perhaps, you will continue to reward me as you should." He calmed his breathing and asked, "Robert?"

Ray Boy arrived with another round in time to say, "Cab driver took him home. Dude is most likely sleeping it off. Delicate situation, Sir. He is big in the company."

"My tall friend. Eglievsky is bigger. Bigger. And Amenti behaved like a common derelict."

We enjoyed our drinks and made hot, suggestive chatter while the party guests looked over with hooded glances. It's a fantastic feeling when others want what you have. We seemed to be the epicenter of envy.

After a while, Raymond set his drink down and asked, "So, if you both are leaving, can I share a cab?"

The very sexy, tall dancer seemed to have a sparkle in his eye.

Tyoma said, "Raymond, I regret we are not going your way."

He winked at me and hugged up with both of us. Coming off a Ray-Ray kiss, the iconic star of the dance world said, "But, I assure, young Sandell, *you* are going *our* way."

I found out, as the evening continued — seriously, we both did - that the big dancer from North Dakota was appropriately cast.

Chapter Forty-One: Box Five

The Elena de Céspedes Marsden Center for the Performing Arts, San Francisco, California

From the Case Files of Kayne J. Sorenson, Ph.D.

"It is indeed a pleasure to meet you both, gentlemen. I had the pleasure the other night to meet this fine young man. You know he was a big hit with La Ivanova and her clique. He is on his way to stardom, have no doubt."

Nick, Andi, Kris, Mrs. Trasker, Rosario Martell, Raul Dos Santos, Andi's boyfriend, and I were the guests of Artem Eglievsky in his box five parterre of the Marsden Auditorium.

John Shepherd Marsden had swept in with his Ballet Purgatorio entourage from Box Six to welcome us. One could tell he was in his glory at this opening. He and I took turns making the introductions.

Nick said, "It looks like you have standing room only tonight. *Merde*, Mr. Marsden."

The members of my family in the box were shocked.

However, the billionaire laughed as he shook hands with my husband and clapped him on the back. He deferred to the Ballet's Board Chair, standing with us.

Ashraf Sah chuckled and looked around as he explained, "In the world of dance, one does not say 'break a leg.' Mr. Sechi is correct. 'Merde!' It is the French word for 'shit.'

"Long ago, when theater-goers arrived by carriages, impresarios would look to the street in front of the theater to see if the production was successful. A lot of horse manure in front of the theater meant a full house. To wish someone 'Merde" is to wish success."

Even Kris, who was pretty on edge this evening, laughed at that explanation. At home, he and Nick seemed to be continuing the Sorenson-

Sechi Cold War. Still, they were relatively cordial for the sake of the opening.

I will add here that Raul was an absolute gem of a lad. He adores Andi, and it is mutual. A keen mind and a handsome, open face suggested a genuine authenticity of character, making him a welcome addition to our family.

Regarding the Bulgarian Prince, La Ivanova and her female companion, Phoebe Garcia-Dolan, made directly for Kris and did the theater folk's sugar-slopping, as Nick calls it. I observed an icy coolness about Ms. Garcia-Dolan. Quite Interesting. I had the opportunity to let her know that I saw her perform Martha Graham's "Cave of the Heart" in Miami one season. Actually, I got a Medea-like smile… the Ancient Greek woman who kills her children, not the comic cinema character.

Antonia Ivanova turned from Kris to say, "I told you, Bee, we must demand a revival of that piece. You will triumph."

In the box, the folks let out a little cheer as a staffer brought in three buckets of champagne and began to pass out flutes of the bubbly.

Mr. Sah said, "Compliments of Mr. Marsden."

He placed a glass in Kris' hand with a "go ahead, tonight's special" expression, a *faux pas* not lost by Nick.

Everyone toasted everyone — so much chi-chi crap, as Nick would say.

Ahhh, the Theater. I would rather give birth to a dingo.

Kris asked, "How is Tyoma?"

Olivia Ortiz Leon turned from talking to Andi and Raul. She announced, "The Great Eglievsky is in conference with his choreographer-slash-co-star. I call it opening night jitters, but…"

I half-expected Kris to dash out and make his way to the star's dressing room. He stayed.

We talked and drank a bit more. Marsden invited us to the gala to follow the performance on his auditorium's stage. A few of us checked the time, and we moved to our seats.

I turned to Nick and whispered.

"Marsden. Zia Zia Carole. The third man."

Nick was gobsmacked.

As the lights began to dim, calling the audience to silence, the door behind us opened again. The six of us turned to see a naked man enter Box Five. Trasker was shocked.

Actually, he was *nearly* naked. The performer was wearing a robe and had a dancer's belt underneath. The dancer was heavily made up in blue, black, and gold accents.

"I beg your pardon."

The choreographer, Robert Amenti, approached our nephew, Kristof, and went down on one knee – quite a theatrical gesture.

"I wanted to sincerely beg your pardon, Mr. Sorenson, for my inexcusable behavior at Mademoiselle Ivanova's party. I offended you publically with accusations and inferences in the poorest of taste."

You must know, I thought that Kris would clock the brogan, so abrupt was his reaction. I saw Nick go on full alert as our lad rounded on the poor man.

Kris reached down and pulled the supplicant up carefully, using the robe so as not to smear the dancer's make-up. Our beautiful nephew almost touched the dancer's heavily made-up chin. Then Kristof carefully embraced the artiste.

I heard him say, "Stage makeup? No bruise on your jaw, bud. Cool."

Robert Amenti, the dancer/choreographer of the moment, was utterly abashed.

Pushing him slightly back, Kris said, "Hey, Dancer Boy..."

Amenti blinked with surprise.

"*Merd!*"

Thomas Paul Severino

Chapter Forty-Two: The Sun God

The Elena de Céspedes Marsden Center for the Performing Arts, San Francisco, California

Nick Sechi's Journal

The production was exceptional, and I am not a big fan. I am not sure why. Breathtaking bodies in motion... naked artistry... Lots of men... should be a Nick boner, right? Anyway...

The Great Eglievski was indeed a God of Light. His Helios seemed to fly across, around, and above Olympus' cloudy mists and mountain tops. He stretched the limits of what a human body could do, soaring and leaping with strength, skill, and beauty. More than once, the audience gasped or applauded his artistry. This was a performance not to be rivaled.

Amenti's Phaethon was, from the first note of his entrance, the quintessential problem child. The love/rage/frustration of the title character was palpable, an emotion that stretched across the footlights, into the house, and up to the farthest reaches of the balcony. He was also incredible.

Likewise, the two leads were breathtaking in their dances together. *I believe it is called a pas de deux, or something similar.* They held each other, lifted, confronted, and twisted in erotic combinations, given their costumes' minimalness. I looked over to check Trasker. It's not as if our housekeeper had not seen male ass before. She appeared to be cool.

Again, I am in unfamiliar territory, but the choreography was really crazy good. So, the story goes on, and the cocky kid with Daddy issues wants the keys to the Mustang with the Sun in the trunk, just to prove he has balls. *Kayne would say I am being a Bronx Philistine – go figure, right?*

Forgot to say that the chariot gizmo was very well done. It actually flew, pulled by four horses. Each of the horse-dudes had this prize-winning set of buns, and movements to dazzle the inhabitants of earth and sky. Tossing their braided manes and whipping thick, thrashing tails, their magnificent bodies pranced, leaped, and soared, blurring the lines between beast and human. One large equine seemed to dominate the pack, and his physical attributes …

Sorry, sorry.

So, anyway, Daddy relents, and the bastard kid sets off down the Grand Concourse of the zodiac, literally smashing up the world, burning the shit out of everything. Grandpa Zeus, whom you never see, is one pissed-off divinity.

Cocky Boy should not have skipped the gym — not enough muscle to control four studly chargers. The hotshot kid delivers some real scorched earth action, and Zeus shoots a thunderbolt at the roiling mess that Phaethon has made of the Chariot of the Sun.

Eglievsky/Helios is downstage, helpless to interfere as the production's pyrotechnics send an explosion up the kid's ass, knocking him and his ride out of the sky. Phaethon and the four horses mangle to the stage floor in a choreographed jumble.

That is when the killer struck.

The arrow nailed the star dancer in the right thigh, and he collapsed. Kayne, Rosie, and I raced out of the box. The audience was in a shocked uproar.

I yelled, "From where, Boss?"

"Above us, the Dress Circle, stage left."

I ran to catch him as the corridors and stairwells began to fill up with panicked theater-goers.

Rosie flashed her badge.

"Police. Stand back."

We went up one level and to the opposite side of the auditorium. It was impossible not to have to fight our way up the stairwell, through the corridor to the Dress Circle, and into the boxes' access.

"There. There… he ran away…"

Outside of Box 10, a hysterical woman leaning against the opposite wall pointed to the compartment's open door. Other occupants of the level were either leaving or swarming around, some on cell phones.

The boxes on the Dress Circle featured dual levels -- two seats to the rear, above and behind the four at the front. The enclosure was hung with deep blue curtains and was empty. Next to seat 6, on the floor, was a contraption unlike anything I had ever seen before. It was a conglomeration of strings, small wheels, and a scope attached to an elongated, M-shaped frame. Three metal shafts lay nearby. It was easy to see that it was a compound hunting bow with an arrow – the weapon of intended murder.

"We did not realize anyone else was in here. Until…"

"Madam, were both seats occupied during the performance?"

"No, and I thought that odd because this was a sold-out performance."

I asked, "Description? Get a good look at the guy?"

"No, actually. He arrived just after the performance began. Our attention was on the stage. You can see that that seat is in the shadows, especially when the house lights are down."

Another patron pointed and said, "I saw him run that way to the emergency exit."

Rosie sprinted away. She was on it.

Two security guards took the former occupants of the murder box out into the hall and asked for our IDs. I met their request and added our business card.

Kayne indicated the weapon and held back the nearest portion of the curtain to reveal a black equipment case with a logo for "Bay Area Video."

Andi stepped into the box ("No, I'm with them. I'm with them.") and directed our attention to the stage. We moved forward to the lower portion of the box, right against the balcony's rail.

I murmured, "A clear shot from seat 6. The dude took down Eglievsky like a hunted stag."

Andi said, "Oh, my."

Below us, Rosie Martell and Raul Dos Santos controlled the crowd on the stage and attempted to make way for the police. Robert Amenti and the company of Ballet Purgatorio were in shock, some kneeling and weeping. One of the horses had removed his head and approached the body as companions attempted to hold him back.

The house lights were up, but not the stage lights. The spotlight on Apollo had not yet been extinguished. First responders approached the circle of light as Kris, on the floor, clung in desperation to the bleeding, fallen god.

Chapter Forty-Three: Sagittarius

San Francisco General Hospital

Nick Sechi's Journal

"You have got to get all these people out of here. Anyone family?"

"I am Ashraf Sah, Chair of the... this is Robert Marsden..."

"Baby, I don't care if you are God herself, Mr. Whoever. Get your ass off my floor and go back to the waiting area where you belong. Now, you gonna do as I say, or am I gonna call my blue boys and have them Taze your ass. You see this mess in my ICU? I am not allowing this today, naa, naa, naa... not gonna happen. Go!"

The nurse swept a formidable arm in the direction of the exit. The cluster of non-essential people in the unit obeyed.

Media personnel and others were trying to gain access to the critical care station. The guards were doing their best to evacuate the curious. Kayne attempted to justify our presence to one of the security people he knew. The nurse in charge, who was taking no shit from the people, seemed to be explaining to a hospital administrator why he just threw John Shepherd Marsden out of the Marsden Critical Care Wing of San Francisco General.

Kris looked like shit, blood on his hands and face. He got the ambulance guys to let him in. Now, he just kind of staggered around. I approached him to try to help him cope with his sadness and shock. Before I could, a familiar figure in scrubs reached us, took hold of Kris, and beckoned to Kayne and me.

Matthew Crowley took us into an empty patient's room.

"Keep him here. Be careful where you touch him. I will be right back."

He looked at us and pointed.

"Doctor Sorenson and Mr. Sechi, please listen to me carefully. Wash your hands and glove up. Remove his clothes and place them in this plastic bag. There is a shower. Please clean him with that blue liquid soap, lots of it, everywhere. There is a fresh gown on the bed. I won't be but a moment."

Kayne and I did as the young nurse instructed.

Kris reacted like a sleepwalker as we got him naked, showered, and wrapped in a towel. Moments of clarity came and went. He muttered and mumbled.

"Why, Uncle Nick? Did they kill him? Stop. I need to go... Where did they take him?"

Kayne and I tried to soothe him a bit.

"Kristof, look at me, son. I need you to look me in the face. Now, some deep breaths. Kristof! Do it with me. Put all thoughts away for a bit. We will ensure that you can emerge from this physical and emotional state of shock, allowing you to be more present with Artem. Let it go, lad. Use your training. Like I taught you."

He appeared confused and disoriented but understood what Kayne was saying. His breathing went from gasping to a deep rhythm. Kris' trembling had begun to subside, and the rigidity of his body was lessening.

Matt returned with a tray on a rolling stand and a backpack. He hooked up Kris and took his vitals. An orderly with a rolling computer stepped into the room. I assisted her with the admitting procedure information.

"Hey, bud, looks like I haven't told you how sexy you look out of your underwear in a long time. There ya go. Eyes on me."

Kayne moved in next to Kris to help if he should try to resist.

Matt said, "BP and pulse need some relaxing here, but we're gonna fix it all. It will all be good. Doctor Stevens will be asked to see him later."

He took one of Kris' arms and swabbed for an injection. Kris pulled away and said, "No."

Matt pulled his head over and kissed Kris' temple. "Easy bud. Cool, so I am gonna give you something that will make you crash, OK?"

I moved in on the other side and slipped my arm around his shoulder, and held his arm for the shot. Kris looked at me like I was Judas Iscariot.

"I am not a child."

Matt carefully administered the shot and applied gauze and a bandage to the injection point. We pushed Kris back on the hospital bed.

"So, I'm gonna clear up here, Bud, and then I'll be back for a snuggle like we used… "

The boy blacked out.

Matt said, "Valium. Ya can't go wrong with the old stand-bys."

He looked at the orderly.

"He in?"

"Yes."

"Stevens?"

"Yes, it should be first in the morning."

"Thanks. Bye."

She exited as Matt took off his gloves and discarded them, along with the sharps. He picked up the backpack and opened it.

"My civies. It's a good thing we're the same size. I will take Kris' tux. We have a cleaners guy nearby who asks no questions and follows bio-safe procedures."

He looked at us and continued.

"Loverboy here will sleep until morning. Best thing for him. Stay as long as you like. Doctor Alicia Stevens will be here at about 8 AM. Do you have any questions for me?"

I said, "Yes, just one."

Matt arched a curious eyebrow.

"Matt, when are you coming back home?"

He looked at the boy asleep in the bed.

"I guess, Mister Nick. That depends on him."

He left.

***

"The assassin used the Compound Bow by Bowtech Infinite Edge Pro. It's called 'The Diamond.' The shaft pierced Artem Eglievsky's left thigh and missed shattering the femur by an eighth of an inch, but nicked the femoral artery. That is why there was so much blood. The arrow passed through and embedded into the Chariot upon which Robert Amenti was about to be fried by a bolt of lightning as part of the ballet drama."

Rosie paused.

"How's the boy?"

"As you see him. He was given a sedative at about midnight."

I said, "Sagittarius." It was not a question.

"Without a doubt, my love. But why? It does not fit the pattern. What are the possible motives for killing one of the world's greatest living artists? I admit I am quite perplexed."

Kayne tugged at his forelock, always an indication that he was without a solution to recent events.

"The weapon was brought into the theater sometime before the performance in the equipment case from the video company. We are tracking them down."

"Rosie, somebody was in the house who should not have been there, and that someone was our deadly archer. Security for the Marsden Auditorium surely has a sign-in for visitors and tradespersons during rehearsal and production times. We should look at the last five…"

"SFPD is way ahead of you, Kayne. I have asked for that list."

"And the ticket list for Dress Circle Box 10…"

The inspector said, "I will get that also."

She added, "Tyoma is expected to live despite the blood loss. Whether or not he will dance again is anyone's guess. I believe he is being moved out of the ICU later today."

Kayne walked to the window. The early dawn light was breaking into the clouds from the east. The night was on its way out.

"If this is indeed a cabal of thrill killers with the intent to promote terror in the citizenry, there is no advance warning or post-event marketing of their horrors. Have they moved on to celebrities?"

"Eglievsky is indeed a big fish. And yet, I do not believe there has been a descent into vendetta by the group. Professional jealousy? Perhaps a love affair turned deadly?"

"Word is that Amenti was not thrilled with Kris' relationship with the guy."

"No. This was an entirely cold-blooded attempt on the man's life. In cases of love gone mad, there is more passion in the crime. Amenti is jealous, but I sense that he realizes that his days and nights with Eglievsky are now limited to the professional. Furthermore, Amenti himself could have been the intended target except that that weapon in the right hands could have caught a flea on the nose of a tick – highly accurate and deadly."

Rosie said, "But he missed. Perhaps it was not intended to be a kill shot."

Kayne turned to us and said, "No. The killer was distracted. The shot was fired exactly as the percussion exploded with the accompaniment for the lightning bolt destroying the Chariot of the Sun. Our man is an expert hunter who was not familiar with the score. He missed killing the god.

"Hey, what are you doing, lad?"

"Getting dressed, Uncle Kayne. Matt left me these, I guess. It's my Manchester United t-shirt anyway."

I asked, "How are you feeling?"

"Fine."

He pulled on jeans and tennis shoes and made as if to leave the hospital room. He moved and spoke as if he had just awakened from an exhausting dream.

Kayne took our nephew's arm with fingers on his pulse spot. He said, "Kristof, it is essential that you be examined by a doctor. There will be one by in a bit."

Kris' back was to us as he hung his head and spoke. There was a bit of peevish resignation in his voice.

"I am going to find Tyoma. I will be back after."

I said, "Kris, we can... "

He turned.

"No. I want to see him alone."

He checked each of our faces and left.

Rosie said, "Brother, is that kid pissed at you."

Chapter Forty-Four: Aftermath
San Francisco General Hospital

By The Kris

"Sup?"

"He's sleeping. Lost a lot of blood. Apparently, most of it ended up on you. The doctors want him to get complete rest, so no visitors, but he will want to see you."

Artem was in a deep sleep, attached to monitors, a respirator, and an IV set up. There were beeps and drips everywhere. For some reason, I remember how white everything was, even his coloring. His hair still had a bit of the gold makeup from the night before. His right leg was held up by a sling setup and bandaged big time.

I stared at him for a long time before looking up at Robert Amenti. We were both in those blue gowns and masks. The choreographer guy responded to my unspoken question.

"No way of telling, really. His age is undoubtedly a factor. It is going to be very uncertain for a while."

"Gosh, what an awful thing to have happened. What will be the blowback to your show – the ballet, I mean?"

"After a few days, we will move the casting around. Raymond Sandell will step into Tyoma's role for the rest of the run. He definitely has the body for a starring role. Muscled Daddy Helios… I think Eglievesky will agree. He is fond of the boy."

He paused before he added softly, "As I think you know."

I felt a hand touch mine.

"Hey, bud… Dude, it looks like they shot you in that world-class ass.…"

I gently pressed Tyoma's hand to my mouth and cried like a baby -- talking snot crying. He reached over with the tubed-up hand and gently stroked my hair. We hung that way for a while. Robert Amenti stepped back a bit and bumped against Uncle Nick. I closed my eyes but could hear their quiet conversation.

"I'm Nick Sechi, Sir, and I wonder if I can ask you a few questions."

"Yes, you are Kris' Father, or…"

"I am his Uncle, and my husband and I are trying to be of assistance in finding the guy who did this," Nick nodded to the bed.

"It is like I told that policewoman. I was very absorbed in the role and, therefore, unable to give details about the shooting. It is nearly impossible to see into the audience from the stage. Suddenly, it just happened like a bomb exploding without the noise."

I pulled up a chair and sat next to the bed, holding Tyoma's hand. I wanted to hear the exchange. I could tell by his touch that he was drifting back to sleep. Over the top of his respirator mask, his eyes were starting to close.

"Mr. Amenti, is there a chance that professional jealousy is behind the attempted murder?"

"There is no one who comes near the artistry of this man. Tyoma is without peer in this profession. No one can come after him. Mister Eglievsky is one of a kind." He gestured to the bed.

He shook his head, adding, "Absolutely no one. The review in the Chronicle this morning said he actually personified the god Apollo on that stage. His dancing defied gravity and the laws of the created universe. Not since Nureyev and Baryshnikov has the dance world seen…"

Ballet Boy stopped at almost a choke before continuing.

"Let me move this forward for you, Mister Sechi, because I need to get back to the Marsden. We were lovers, but I couldn't… well, now we are not. It is that simple. Did I have him shot out of jealousy? Wouldn't it be more reasonable to do away with my rival?"

He looked at me.

The dude had a huge streak of drama queen going for him, big time. I felt the pressure of Artem's hand on my head go soft, but the monitor's rhythmic sound did not change.

"Artem, if he is conscious right now, would not be offended to hear me say he is a player. Always has been. The great Eglievsky has had many lovers over his career. He likes the young stallions with muscles, like... Raymond, like your nephew..."

"And, you. Right?"

"Yes, and I was determined to hold him, to change him, but..."

I could tell Nick was like, "How sappy is this gonna get?"

"Tell me about Raymond Sandell. Did I overhear you say he gets the role?"

"Oh, fuck. Have you met him? Body of a porn star and a dancer with a lot of potential, but dumb as a post. Nice house — nobody home. Besides, Fargo Sexy wouldn't hurt a fly. Raymond is a total bottom..."

He tried to lower his voice, but I caught it.

"Just ask your son... ahhh, nephew."

You know, there are times when, having knocked a dude on his arse, you realize you want to do it again and again. Fuck.

"I will be at the Marsden nights and days for a while if you need me. With the cast changes and some revisions to the choreography, my work will involve a total remounting."

The choreographer touched the sleeping dancer's hand quite gently and left the room.

***

"So we talking or what?"

"Look, I gotta go to practice, man."

My Uncle Kayne slipped into the room. He stood back a bit, not saying anything. Those Sorenson ice blues of his looking over the mask and under his famous shock of savage black hair... yeah, Nick's "Bossmam"... he did not miss a trick.

Nick sat in a chair by the window. A nurse has buzzed in and out, gave her patient a shot, and told us not to stay too long.

"Sorry, I've got soccer. So…"

"Sometime, you'll have to say what's on your mind, Kris."

I looked at my Tyoma. He looked frail and sad.

I turned to face my Uncle.

"You don't like him, and you do not respect me enough to let me make my own choices, Nick. That hurts. Fuck, you have never even taken the time to meet him. What was up at that Greek place?"

"Kris, you need…"

I took a step toward him.

"Do not tell me what I need. I'll tell you what I need. I need *him*. I need him to live. And…"

I choked on angry tears as I continued with, "So what? What? He's older? So's he."

I nodded to my Uncle Kayne. And took a deep breath and brought it down.

"You guys taught me to appreciate the gifts that each person brings into the mix. How has that changed?"

J'ever have the feeling you were standing outside of yourself watching what you were doing? I have no idea why I was ragging on my Uncles. I had a gut-full, that's for sure. It was just all coming out like a load of shit.

"So what, huh? He's positive. OK, the rumors are true. None of us is too stupid not to know what those biohazard symbols all over this place are, man. And anyway, he told me. Yeah, way before we started making love."

Nick did not even blink.

"So, yeah, so, he's undetectable. He's on PrEP; I'm on PrEP; you guys, even Matt. It's a PrEP world, Uncle Nick. I am old enough to be careful. And I care for this guy. I really do, yeah, and the fact that I almost lost another… but this is not about me. "

I looked at the man in the bed. Then I turned and looked at each of my uncles, but just for a second.

"Ya, know, maybe it's time I was moving on. Later for this charity case life thing."

I was gagging on my own frustration.

"Do I get to say anything, Kris?"

I shook my head and could not meet his eyes. "Man, I got to get to…"

I started out of the room.

Uncle Kayne said, "Kristof, Nick wants…"

Nick had stood up and had taken off his mask. He was bright red in the face. He pulled me into him, and I started crying again. Jesus, I am such a fuckin' baby.

"Hey, bud, you're nobody's charity case, man. This here… this thing. It's family, Kris. Family."

He stepped closer and touched my shoulder.

"Kiddo, I was wrong to have put the 'X' on someone you really care for. I was afraid for you, and I regret not being a grown-up about it. It had to do with wanting to protect you, but we cannot always do that. There is a lot of sadness out there, and we have to be on the lookout for each other without crushing each other."

I felt Kayne's hand on my head and blubbered, "Like Iron Man and Captain America."

Nick almost smiled as he said, "Kris, I promise I will do better. Give me a chance, huh?"

And that's where we left it. I kissed the forehead of my sleeping man and headed out, very unsure of just about fuckin' everything.

Thomas Paul Severino

Chapter Forty-Five: After the Aftermath
The Mission District, San Francisco, California

Nick Sechi's Journal

"Shit!"

I spit out my mouthpiece.

"Is that all you got? C'mon Kayne. You're fighting like a wuss. Man the fuck up and come at me. Do it now!"

Holy shit, was that ever a stupid thing to say.

Kayne clobbered me with moves I hadn't experienced before. Next knockdown, and I leaped back up and into him. Because we were fast, furious, and loud, with the showboating MMA moves, we had a small crowd of spectators at Hit Fit SF. The manly arts – a gay magnet... and the fans were in love/lust.

We stopped for water when a familiar guy came over.

"Nick, I hate to see this big man bust your ass. Let's take him down, bud."

Captain Michael Clarke-Mills, USN, the Director of Blackhawk, was gloved up and shirtless. He was rocking a killer smile and ready to throw down.

"Hey, no, old buddy. Think this brawler needs a daddy in this fight?"

"Not a chance. I owe him a takedown anyway. And no wedgies, bitch."

Kayne smirked and did the Aussie version of flipping the bird, followed by a two-handed "bring-it" move.

We did a fierce two-on-one, well aware that we were showing off, muscled up, and sweating. Yeah, the gym rats hung out to watch, big time.

Water brake #2. So big, Mikey says, deserting to the other side, "Kayne, I hate to see this big man bust your ass. Let's take him down."

We did another round. I fended them both off, pretty much, but took some losses. Kayne was sitting on my chest when he said, "Captain, what brings you to San Francisco? Weekend R&R?"

Big Mikey pulled Kayne up and off me.

"Tim has a meeting, and I am looking for some trouble. No rest for the wicked, I am afraid."

"Where are you guys staying?"

"Not too far from here. Parker Guest House. Church and Seventeenth."

"We know it well."

I gasped as I stood up to catch my breath.

"Dinner?"

"Thanks, but we sorta have a… well, ahh …. "

"A hookup, Dude? Shit, you *do*, dog. My, my. I am shocked. Shocked, I say."

Navy hunk pulled me in and put a hand on my ass. "Seriously, Nickster? Remember, I read the blog, Dirty Boy. You and this major hustla are fine ones to talk."

Kayne chuckled, "Raincheck, then. Dirty Boy and I will be heading out soon. Get on it, ya sex bomb, no mercy. Best to your guy."

***

"A case of misplaced anger, Nick. Most of it anyway. Kris is desperately afraid of not finding true love and of, in fact, finding it. Besides, he does not want to be left behind, a life pattern he has internalized as an obsession. You are he -- his alter ego. You represent the reservations he has regarding this affair with Artem Eglievsky and his disappointment with the course of romance as he has pursued it."

I rubbed my freshly showered body with a towel and said, "I'll tell you what, Bossman. Get that kid in gear and tag him in the ring as we did with Captain Mikey. Do his ass a world of good."

Kayne laughed and responded. "Oh, excuse me, I am looking for Nick Sechi. Yes, he is the uncle person who promised his charge that he would be more understanding and less judgmental. Not!"

He tipped his tracker.

"... two hours ago."

"Ya smug bastard. I'm only saying..."

"I'm going to blow my head. Hold that thought."

I watched my husband, in a towel, saunter off to the sinks and the blow dryer. I flashed a leering gym guy my best, "Whatchu-lookin'-at? He's taken" expression.

Kayne came back to dress, doffing the towel to the delight of his admirer. This time, I smiled.

"Andi."

I showed him the phone.

The text read, "The moon is full tonight."

Thomas Paul Severino

Chapter Forty-Six: Never Gonna Give You Up

The University of San Francisco, San Francisco, California

By The Kris

As I write this, I plan to read it over several times, make some changes, and reflect on it thoroughly. It was tough, ya know? Real difficult.

Practice blew – big time. Even I know that. I was angry. I was super sad. I made shit happen in my relationship with my family. My game showed it. I was totally out of control. I actually started a fight with the team captain, a senior, who called me on it.

"You finished, Sorenson, you fuckin' showboater? You know you were illegal with that tackle. What, what? You gonna show me how it is? Huh? Huh? You ain't shit, Pussy. Come on, tough boy, show... ooofff."

"Ya know, fuck you, Okeyo."

I had knocked him on his ass. Cussed and then, I threw myself on top of him, and we rolled around on the field. Guys were pulling us apart or trying to. I was yelling, I don't know what all.

Jesse Okeyo came up off the ground, and he was wild.

"Hold him."

They did, and Cap pulled back about to knock me out when it rained, or flooded is a better word. Coach McDaniel poured the entire contents of the Gatorade thing of sports water over my head.

I cussed again, gasped, and sputtered. My teammates, including Jesse Okeyo, laughed their asses off. Great, now McD is gonna chew me a new ass. Again.

Surprisingly, he was not pissed. He spoke calmly but sternly.

"Season opener next week, gentleman. The way you guys are looking now, Loyola will mop the field with you. Believe me, I can tell.

"Get your asses back on the field. Okeyo drills seventeen to thirty, break 'em out. And if you darlings look good, we will scrimmage before the end of practice. Otherwise..."

"Otherwise" meant wind sprints, many of them.

The team took off in many directions. Jesse called the drill formations as he shepherded the jocks onto the pitch.

"Sorenson."

I stopped and turned to look at the Coach. *Here is where he tosses me. Shit.*

He handed me the green and orange cooler.

"Fill this up."

I hustled back to the ice maker and faucet and lugged the cooler back to the bench.

"Why did they try to kill him?"

I looked at the man. There was sincere empathy there, and I had expected a firing.

The words stuck in my chest as I tried to get them out. I was determined not to cry. I shook my head.

"I dunno, Coach. I sure do not know."

The tears and snot came on, but I didn't blubber, just did a nose wipe with the edge of my uniform shirt.

There is a move in the coaching manual of every coach for every sport, I swear. It's the take-the-player-by-the-back-of-the-neck move. McDaniel did it.

"Go back to the hospital, Kris."

"But Coach, Loyola, the opening game..."

I sniffed and wiped.

Head Coach, Austin R. McDaniel, looked very hard at me and said, "I'm gonna let you in on a secret, Kris, and if you tell anyone, I will make your sorry ass miserable."

He looked at his young men and their trainers and assistant coaches on the field.

"This, what we do here, is sport. It is a game. It is a practice for life: training, teamwork, dedication, love for your teammates, determination, and hard work. But, kid, it is a shadow. By that, I mean it is not real life.

"What you have, with your guy -- *that* is life, and you need to have your head in that, all in, kid, no holding back. Otherwise, you are not worth shit on the soccer pitch. No Way."

I looked at the guy. He read my expression.

"And Sorenson, if it is not to be, at least you will never have to say that you didn't give it a full shot. At least you went for the goal. Right?"

This time, I looked at the man with the beginnings of a big kid smile.

"What? A dumb jock like me doesn't know shit about love?"

He put up a hand.

"Go away, Sorenson. You are done here."

***

"Norway? Fuck!"

Tyoma was off the ventilator. He held my hand and kissed it.

"My friend has offered to allow me to heal at his *hytte* on the Geiranger Fjord. It is his small house in the countryside. There is the tiny village of Geiranger located at the end of the fjord. A river empties into the sea nearby. The town has many good doctors. I intend to bring my own physical therapist with me. There is also one small dance studio."

"Why?"

"It is what I need to do, my Kristof. You understand?"

"I don't."

He said nothing.

"Artem, I..."

He said softly, "No, you do not. Do not say it. We have only known each other for a few weeks. It was nice, lovely, in fact… but I am not your man. No, my beautiful boy, I am… not. This is just the way things are."

Why is it that when people talk of love and breaking up and shit, they speak in incomplete sentences – a rush of words and feelings?

"I feel about you like I have never felt… damn, I just gotta make you understand."

"Kris, you and I are no strangers to love and passion. We know the rules."

Artem drew a hand near his bandaged leg.

"Not too long ago, I did something to a boy I thought I loved. I was wrong. I hurt him deeply, and this is retribution. Karma for being a shit. Payment for my sinfulness."

He looked away until the guilt slid from his face.

"Do not mistake me. I am not wallowing in self-pity. I was a satyr, as the Greeks say, a lothario. Sex without complications fuels my mind and body. You understand? My creative energies… faithfulness is not a virtue I espouse."

He struggled with this next part.

"That boy. He was a lot like you. Beautiful and so sincere. I tossed him aside with great thoughtlessness. He was heartbroken, and I didn't care. Using young men seems to be my other mastery, Kris. I am always dancing away – no attachments. I will not do that to you. You deserve better."

"Can I come? Artem, I could… we could… I want to…"

He stroked my cheek.

"What… to be with me? To change me? So many have tried. The stars are unalterable, my young friend.

"You want to spend your days in some isolated backwater tending to the needs of a failed star. No, my beautiful boy. Life holds too much greatness for you."

He put both hands on each side of my head and looked into my eyes.

"So, my boy. You have so much love here, and education, and sport, and the theater. The friends and fans recognize your stellar qualities and demand that you burn with fire for them. I have had my time in the sun. Yours is just dawning."

Artem sighed softly.

"You will grow to hate me over one cold Norwegian winter on the fjord. And besides...."

Again, he could not meet my eyes. Damn, I am so stupid.

I whispered, "Yeah, Norwegian guy... I get it."

"Yes. There is that. He..."

Tyoma could not finish, so he said, "I am who I am, my Kris. The idol of millions has feet of clay."

I pulled back and started to make my exit, kissing him and turning away. He held me back for a moment and again looked into my face.

"I wish you a long life without loneliness. May you find true love along the way."

***

"Yeah, ya got dumped, boy. Sorry."

"Do not call me that."

I pushed away from Andi.

"You have been through a lot, and you look like shit. It's after midnight. Where have you been?"

"Walking, just walking."

I swallowed hard and launched back into it.

"Worst of all. The very worst of it all..."

I clenched a fist to my forehead.

"What?"

"I blamed Nick. I fucked up my relationship with him. I knew... I knew all along... I was having these doubts about Tyoma... trophy boy... muscled up plaything... that kind of shit, ya see?"

"Yeah, I got it. You guys must have dazzled. Star dancer shows off his pretty boy."

"God, I hate that word. Anyway, I was stubborn, Andi, block-headed as shit. I wanted it to be right, and Nick was the one making it all wrong, in my mind, anyway."

Yeah. As we spoke, I finally saw the truth.

"But, he was right. Nick, I mean. Artem Eglievsky -- he just didn't feel about me..."

"The way you felt about him, right? Hey, listen, Kris, I do not want to minimize what you are going through, but I am getting one of my premonitions, dude."

I tried to finally shake off my self-pity.

"Why are you still here, Andi? That's some overtime."

"Something's up, and I want to be around."

"Nick and Kayne? Holy shit, girl."

"I need you to be part of the cavalry with me. And I definitely need this."

She took something out of her desk drawer and stuffed it into her purse before I could see what it was.

"Let's roll, Captain America."

Chapter Forty-Seven: The Chamber of the Sun

The San Francisco Historical Society at The Mint, Fifth and Mission

Nick Sechi's Journal
One hour earlier

"There is a space behind here, Nick."

Mr. Wan had given us the directions to the structure at the rear of the Mint. It was just after moonrise, so close to 11:30 PM. I used the flashlight feature on my phone to show the way.

There was a false wall at the back of the boiler room with an old wooden door. The opening could have been easily hidden with an equipment barrier. The screen could be rolled to the side. Kayne used the key given to us by the old gentleman from the tea shop. Once inside the doorway, the "mask" could be moved back into place, keeping the director of the Mint's entrance to the lower floor a secret.

A circular stairway led down to a large antechamber. Wooden lockers lined two walls. Their door panels were marked with the zodiac signs on brass plates. And ahead of us was a wooden double door with a brass plate split by the center juncture. It was carved with a large circle with a solid, smaller circle in the center-- the same symbol in the near-empty file of Gretchen Rockland. The Sun. The same sign on the paper that had been given to us by Brian LaCroix.

Behind the solar doors was a large stone vault occupied by a large, oval conference table with 13 chairs. Three electrified, formerly gas-globe chandeliers hung above the broad onyx table.

"Up this way, Boss."

A ladder took us up to a low corridor-like structure, an enclosed balcony, and a workspace tucked against the ceiling that ran the length of the vault.

"They brought the ore below up to this level, where it was lifted to wagons just above. You can see the openings, the pullies, and the rails for moving the gold and silver. This is our hideout, my love. Best we remove our shoes. The drama is about to unfold."

***

They moved into the chamber like the monks of the Inquisition in black robes and hoods. The last member of the procession was in gold. Shadows cast by the light in the vault eclipsed the faces beneath the hoods so that nothing above the chin could be seen. Each of the figures took their place at the table. There was one empty chair.

As the group was seated, a figure in black pushed open the doors and hurried to the one empty seat. Dude was totally out of character and most likely in trouble.

Someone was late to the party.

The costumes featured oversized sleeves. Each member withdrew a triangular nameplate with their zodiac sign from inside the folds and placed it on the table before them. The golden thirteenth figure was represented by a cipher that looked like the letter "U" with a serpentine stroke across it. I remembered...

"It is the controversial thirteenth sign of the zodiac, my love. The constellation Ophiuchus – the healer and the serpent. It comes between Scorpio and Sagittarius."

That was the guy in charge.

"There are eight completed and four left. These last four are critical to the plan. I congratulate the members who are present on their accomplishments. The scientific research we have gathered as a result of our Phase Two is now in the right hands."

There was no screen for the visuals. The eight murder victims' faces floated over the vault's rough stone walls in black and white. Block-lettered texts identified them to the members. The three hundred and sixty degrees of images resembled a 1950s film noir, with some of the actual death shots appearing and dissolving with an otherworldly eeriness.

"Our four new brethren..." The leader gestured to the virtual images. "Are charged with Phase Three of the Operation."

Ophiuchus continued, "At this time, I am distressed to report to you that we have had an unfortunate setback."

The sentence seemed to hang in the room. At a signal from Ophiuchus Guy, Aries pushed back his chair and walked deliberately to stand behind Sagittarius.

The assembly leader now spoke in a soft and menacing tone to the culprit.

"Without our approval, you replaced your contract. Your attempt on the dancer's life was a personal vendetta, and *de facto*, not a part of our plan. There is no room for private motives in the actions of the Star League. As you all know, such sloppy operations bring law enforcement closer into our sphere. Fully aware of your intentions, you acted without the authority of this body."

Sagittarius looked over his shoulder at the ominous presence, which seemed to grow in size as he moved closer to the frightened participant. The other members were riveted on the object of the unfolding drama.

"There are consequences for your actions."

The assassin awaited the signal from the leader of the murder cult.

Ophiuchus turned in his chair and tipped his head upward to face our enclosure. Aries lowered his hands around the neck of Sagittarius.

The group leader announced in a commanding voice, "Kindly grace us with your presence. A killing is about to occur, Doctor Sorenson."

Thomas Paul Severino

Chapter Forty-Eight: The Confederation of the Stars

The San Francisco Historical Society at The Mint, Fifth and Mission

Nick Sechi's Journal

"Leave him!"

We exited our hideout by moving down and into the vault. Kayne and I were trussed up by the wrists by the biggest of the hooded monkeys. I was forced to my knees, but Kayne took out the two who had intended to confine him. He surprised everyone in the room by leaping up onto the center of the table, jumping through the confines of his wrists, bringing them from back to front. He pulled at the ropes with his teeth and was easily free of them.

"I said, do not interfere."

Ares, the goon assigned to dispatch Sagittarius, held the unfortunate guy to his chair.

The freed captive standing on the table turned to make sure he had the attention of each member of the murderous league. Kayne put an index finger to his head and began.

"I will now unburden my mind concerning the nefarious deeds of this vile group. It is quite straightforward since each of the eight assassins signed their work, with one notable exception."

This was my hero at his incredible best.

"The maintenance woman's replacement who brought on the quench of the NMR at the Blackhawk Research Facility is a highly trained professional who has been passed over for the chance at stardom. Embittered by the systemic discrimination of her company, she decided nothing could assuage her disgust with her fellow humans but their extermination."

Kayne turned and approached one figure who was seated at the table.

"But it wasn't her ethnicity that prevented her rise. It was her cocaine addiction, by now well known to her employers."

He stooped, reached out, and gently tipped back the hood of Scorpio, saying, "Phoebe Garcia-Dolan, once an exceptional ballerina, now a drug addict and a murderer."

"My dear, the nasal traces of the evil white powder are almost impossible to hide, especially when attending the premiere of a ballet."

The woman looked at her accuser like a viper watches its trapped prey.

Kayne cautioned, "It would be wise to either give up smoking or choose another design feature for your personal cigarette case, Mademoiselle."

He made a half-turn on the table and continued, "A young man, dissatisfied with his financial attachments and running from a past involving blackmail and extortion, seeks to break free by becoming a killer for hire."

Kayne stepped closer to his second murder gamer.

"He finds that the compensation for fulfilling contracts for the Confederation is quite lucrative. Also, he has acquired a taste for it. He likes it."

He tipped the hood of Giannis Papatonis.

"You dispatched Professor Bronson, and you did not even know him."

Libra slowly stood up.

"How did you know?"

"The killer had an intimate knowledge of Greek Mythology, a need for money, and a ruthless nature. In addition, you have the iconic scales of your astrological sign tattooed on your very impressive *opísthia*."

Pretty sure that's Greek for "butt."

"One seldom forgets such a lovely body feature, *ómorfo agóri*."[11]

---

[11] beautiful boy

The Evil League

The Greek beauty grabbed the bent-over Kayne by the head and gave him a passionate Judas Kiss, marking my man for execution. He pulled a hunting knife. I struggled in my bonds, but my captor kicked me in the chest.

Ophiuchus made a hand sign, and Libra let go of his accuser and sat back down. Giannis Papatonis placed the weapon on the table. Kayne stood up and turned to my captor.

"Go a bit more comfortable with him, Capricorn. When Nick and I round out this Confederation for handing over to the authorities, you may want to plead for leniency."

I took another shot off the bastard.

Now the Boss, in theatrical style, actually quoted "Game of Thrones." He pointed at Capricorn.

"I've heard it said that poison is a woman's weapon... Yes, women, cravens, and... eunuchs. Men usually use steel..."

My wise martial arts master stepped forward on the table and turned to the side. He leaned halfway over toward the center of the table, fists held at his chest. He snapped his left leg back and forth in a roundhouse kick that was so precise and gentle it knocked the hood off the goat's member quite delicately.

"Ashraf Sah – Chair of the Board of Ballet Purgatorio. A man so eternally frustrated by sexual angst that he sought the emotional release of death and destruction by *fiat*."

The Empressario looked perplexed. Kayne made a fanning motion in front of his face. He continued his counsel.

"My researcher said that Interpol's autopsy of Esmail Faiz Haqqani showed his clothing contained considerable trace amounts of "Fucking Fabulous" by Tom Ford, an exclusive men's *Eau de Parfum* at four hundred USD per ounce. Not the dead man's but his flamboyant murder – a fact confirmed when we met Zia Zia Carole. I would have encouraged you, Sir, to consider the adage that less is most definitely more."

Now Kayne was on a roll. He instructed his audience from the center of the black table.

"Money, power, sexual release, prestige, and revenge – all with a taste... no, a *craving* for murder, a lust for blood. You are definitely an evil brood. That is indeed a certainty, but none more wicked than someone who enlists minors to do her dirty work."

He rounded on Virgo.

"The nefarious Doctor Martina Howard."

The woman held up a hand to stop Kayne's touch and pulled back her hood. She was stone-faced and ready to kill again.

"Tell us, Doctor, your sexual proclivities run the gamut of group assignations with your colleagues and their boyfriends, specifically Doctor Gretchen Rockland and her partner, to young girls. Yet your bloodthirstiness supersedes your erotic adventures to a reckless degree. Why is that?"

He did not wait for the seething Gorgon to answer. Instead, he went for two hoods this time – the first, Sagittarius.

"Petty Officer 3rd Class Brian LaCroix, our archer of death. When last we met in East Bay, you claimed your cache of hunting gear was for a friend. But the friend in question was your unfortunate prey.

"No, Lord Ochiuphus, your Sagittarius did not fumble the kill shot. He is indeed an expert marksman with the bow. The callouses on his right hand testify to his avocation."

The murderous Aries, standing behind the ex-dancer boy, lowered his face and whispered into the hood of the trapped bowman.

Kayne continued, addressing the assembly.

"The premier danseur étoile, Artem Eglievsky, has an old injury to his left hip. It is well-documented that the incident occurred during a performance of 'Don Quixote' in Paris at the Opéra Bastille. The Master actually finished the ballet before he was taken to the hospital."

Now, Kayne directed his attention directly to the young LaCroix.

"To this day, he believes he fumbled in the execution of a difficult combination, one he had done a thousand times. Immediately after that performance, you were seen mopping up the stage. A member of the *corps de ballet* assigned to maintenance duty? Quite odd, wouldn't you say?"

LaCroix stared at the table's center. The recollection was much too painful.

Kayne paused and said, "How old were you, Sir, when he sexually assaulted you?"

The answer came without expression, like a hammer striking deadwood.

"Fifteen."

Kayne was very soft with his next remark, "Despicable."

He added. "I find your case interesting. What is sometimes typical of an abused minor is seeking more humiliation to the point of self-destruction. And you did so from the demon who stands behind you with his hands on your throat. Many times, I fear. But, I digress."

Suddenly, Pisces leaped up and pointed at the miserable boy. "You seduced him! He was an honorable man, and you wanted him. The accusation was a sham. The entire junior company knew what you were up to. You were relentless in your machinations. We hated you for it."

Kayne rounded on the irate speaker.

"Enough to follow your rival into this cult of death?"

Next hood drop.

"Mr. Amenti?"

Kayne paused to allow the dramatic action to build.

"The boy dancer benefited from his association with the star. He was less talented than you, but his lover persuaded the company powers to assign him the roles that would move him from the *corps de ballet*. Principal parts... solos... LaCroix's Romeo during the 2025 season we filled with the passion and impulsivity that only a Master could impart to his pupil and bedmate. You watched with murderous envy as the star spent hours training the lad and flaunting their affair.

"Never one for faithfulness, Artem Eglievsky soon tired of his juvenile protégé. Much as he lost interest in you and your aspirations to become a choreographer of note. Ahh, *quel dommage!* Whispered promises after passionate lovemaking, perhaps. Assurances the great artist never made good on?

"Tell us, Mister Amenti, were you the snake speaking words of revenge to LaCroix, or was it the other way round? Indeed, your membership in this deadly star chamber would allow you to destroy them both.

"But this *danse macabre* has a rather unique subplot. You picked up Professor Chandler's death contract to retain your cult membership. But up to this point, you had been repulsed by murder. You needed a confederate to show you the ropes, shall we say? And your fellow in the arts was, by now, doomed to follow a libretto of revenge.

"Ms. Garcia-Dolan was just the colleague to assist – a damsel in distress. The fish in the pockets were a dramatic touch – almost as if choreographed, would you not say?"

He added, "Please allow me to counter your claim of young Brian's seduction. You know as well as anyone, Mr. Robert Amenti, that the only thing that would ever seduce Artem Eglievsky is a starring role. The man likes young boys, but his true lust is for the accolades of the stage."

 What a performance! Coreographer Boy flopped back in his seat and buried his face in his hands.

Now, Kayne went back to unfinished business. He turned around to the hulk that was Aries, who slowly applied pressure to the throat of his colleague in murder.

"You strangled the life out of the young Jasmine Elizabeth Stokes, Ph.D., and frivolously marked her with the stars in your signature constellation. You are indeed a ferocious killer who is most likely sexually inadequate. Your attempted dalliances with Doctors Rockland and Howard and the young man you are about to kill, Brian LaCroix, smack more bravado and less carnal substance. All evidence to the contrary notwithstanding, Sir. You are a CGI stallion and nothing more. These escapades recorded on your fan pages are a pitiful attempt to prove your sexual adequacy.

"Given your limitations, you do become aroused when strangling your victims, Chief Jake Davies. Your videos demonstrate your despicable technique of sexual humiliation and torture. You are indeed a monster."

Jake the Snake released his intended victim and rushed to take me out of Sah's clutches. He backed me to the wall and pressed his body against me, his meaty hands at my throat, his face a riot of rage, lust, and obsession. His mouth dripped saliva. Kayne leaped off the table.

"I will show you what a monster I am. While you watch what I will do to this pathetic bitch…"

It was almost too easy.

He could not finish because Kayne's jab to the thug's kidneys brought him to his knees, and a sidekick to the temple dropped him to the floor. Aries was out cold.

"Enough!"

The Leader of the Confederation of the Stars brought the action to a dead stop.

Kayne turned and said, "Not quite, Sir. It is time for the finale. I believe you may need to grab hold of something."

Thomas Paul Severino

Chapter Forty-Nine: Total Eclipse of the Sun

The San Francisco Historical Society at The Mint, Fifth and Mission

Nick Sechi's Journal

"But first…"

He held up an index finger.

"Gemini."

He had walked behind the man and pulled back the hood to reveal Contra Costa County's Medical Examiner, Timothy Leonard. Now, Kayne sat on the table facing the young man.

"Not a killer. A trapped victim. You were coerced into this ghastly blood cult. They needed you as a source of information, and the threat was blackmail. Neither law enforcement nor the military would hesitate to destroy your career nor that of the man you love."

Silence.

"And so, you did not dare to resist."

The young man blinked but said nothing.

"You could not have taken a meeting with the twin victims hung by the necks in that *favela* in Rio. There is no way you could have bypassed the security of two of the most well-protected drug lords on the planet, Kalisto Serian and Gantulga Nergūl. No, *you* did not kill them."

He slid up and onto the table, sitting cross-legged. He faced Ophiuchus Guy.

"But *you* could have gained entry. The heads of the drug cartels would have allowed you into a meeting. You are rich and powerful, and alliances with you would bring endless riches. Is that what you promised them, Sir? The wealth of your technology conglomerates? I think not."

Now he stood and took a step towards the megalomanic.

"It is a well-protected secret that you are investing heavily in the field of aerospace exploration – Celestia, Inc. How fortunate that the killing of these scientists has brought to your firm the research that will enable you to quickly outdistance your competitors in the race for Mars and beyond the stars. But you lack funding."

"And so, it was the bounty on Commander Eric Nathaniel Sorenson that would bring the crime families into your grip, once you delivered their 'Most Wanted' to his fate.

"You took the meeting, made the double kill, and signed it with your confederate's avatar. Tonight's meeting was not only to exterminate LaCroix. Your second victim tonight would be the reluctant co-conspiratorTimothy Leonard. How is that for inductive reasoning..."

Both his gesture and the tone of his voice were accusatory.

"Mr. John Steven Marsden."

***

Now things went into warp drive. It was "go" time.

There were four yet unnamed killers at the table, signified by Leo, Taurus, Cancer, and Aquarius. They slipped off their robes at a signal from Marsden. Two women and two men leaped up onto the table to take down Kayne in a single move.

They circled.

In the meantime, I headbutted Ashraf Sah. Did a leap through my tied arms as Tim Leonard raced over to untie me.

Marsden was in the process of saying, "Please allow me to introduce you to Ray-Lynne Hansa, Avril Dayan, Achilles Darawshi, and Jonathan Eliyahu. All former members of Israel's elite forces, the Sayeret Matkal. They are the final four of our murderous zodiac."

He pressed some buttons on his console. I jumped up to go back-to-back with Kayne against the quartet.

"But wait! Please allow me to show you the last four contracts that they will be handling."

Four face shots with names of the intended victims moved across the rough stone walls of the vault. Mitchell L. Sorenson, MD; Thomas M. Sorenson; Kayne J. Sorenson, Ph.D.; and Nicola M. Sechi.

"It would seem we could complete two of these death warrants this evening."

I yelled, "Bring it fuckers!"

Then the shit storm broke with a cosmic vengeance.

Thomas Paul Severino

Chapter Fifty: Gemini in Da Hause

The San Francisco Historical Society at The Mint, Fifth and Mission

Nick Sechi's Journal

The gunshots fired at the vault's ceiling were sudden and explosively loud, as was the voice that followed.

"Listen up, *Cabrones*. Drop what you are doing and reach for the sky. We've got you surrounded."

Andi and Kris burst through the double wooden doors. They were ready to kick ass with or without Andi's handgun.

"Girl, too many reruns of Bonanza."

She pointed to the images of light and dark. "Kris, are those your uncles?"

Kris said, "So, you guys on the table, carry on. I think we can guess the outcome. Those poor suckers will really see stars... yuck, yuck."

Kayne and I cleaned the celestial house. As each of the Israelis went down, we heaved them with kicks and shots into Amenti, Sah, Howard, and La Croix. The bodies piled up in various states of consciousness. We were fuckin' ninja warriors.

Giannis Papatonis retrieved the hunting knife and pulled up behind Kris. The nephew had been delivering a face kick to Jake Davies. The mug was coming around only to be dropped again.

Libra/Papatonis had Kris by the throat with the blade pressed against it. He commanded the attention of the tumultuous room's occupants.

"Now we are all going to chill, you folks... that's right... everybody... everybody... good. Sexy boy bleeds terrible unless you do what I say."

Kayne started to move so that he and I were boxing the killer out, outflanking him.

Papatonis hollered, "No, no, no, Doctor. I *will* kill him."

I could see that Kris was about to break the hold as we distracted Giannis. His arms were slowly moving upward. He would most likely take a slash, but not in the neck.

The doors burst open for a second time, and Rosie Martell came through with another police officer. Timothy Leonard took advantage of the confusion to bring his leg up as hard and fast as he could between the legs of the knife-wielding Greek bartender. There was a squish and a scream as he racked the guy from behind. Kris snagged the weapon from the hand of the falling murderer.

Rosie was calling for backup when I signaled to Kayne. John Marsden had disrobed and was backing up to the far end of the vault. Within the folds of the discarded costume, he had extracted a gun, his passport to escape.

There was a rear exit toward which the creep was making his getaway. I watched a thin smile make its way across his face. This was a man who was never deterred in anything he ever sought to accomplish, no matter how heinous.

At the final second, a small figure stepped out of the shadows near the vault's back corner. The Yoda-like specter seemed to be holding a broomstick. Marsden, caught by surprise, turned to face him. As the death cult leader was about to mock the intruder, the Jedi Master Adjacent made his move.

It was so fast. It was just about invisible. The old gentleman whirled around the cult leader like an insane dervish. In a split second, Marsden's gun was sliding toward me on the floor and spinning at my feet. We looked up and watched the killer of so many fall to his knees and then collapse on the chamber floor beneath the raised katana of his opponent.

John Steven Marsden, the Grand Master Ophiuchus of the Confederation of the Stars, slayer and assassin, had met his destruction at the hands of the small but mighty Wan Guchan, born in the Year of the Monkey.

Chapter Fifty-One: Family Business

221 Baker Street, San Francisco, California

Nick Sechi's Journal

"What will happen to Tim, Boss?"

"Young Leonard, it turns out, comes from an old California family. He is actually one of the last surviving members. He will be charged as an accessory to murder. Still, I suspect he will get a lighter sentence, considering he saved Kristof's life. Timothy Leonard has the resources to hire very experienced legal counsel."

"Why do you think he was even involved with the League, Uncle Kayne? He was a county ME, for gosh sake.

"My dear boy, this entire case has been a study on why people do very terrible things. Possibly to stave off the destruction of his and Captain Mill's military careers, but I confess I do not know. Something for which our friend Captain Mills may help. My sources tell me the man is sticking with the lad through this."

I addressed our assistant. "Thanks again for busting in at the right time, Andi. I think you should have that thing registered before... Good morning, Inspector."

Rosie Martell came into our offices carrying a tray of fresh coffee and a pitcher of Ashwagandha smoothies.

"Either that or I am going to have to deputize you, Ms. Rodriguez."

Andi shook her head.

"The police and I -- well, we don't exactly get along. Present company excepted."

Rosie glanced over at Kris.

"Yep, Captain Simmions gave me the skinny on the two of you and this whole gig. I just want to clue in the members of Sechi's Raiders – the dude is watching you, folks."

Kayne said, "Another blog fan, my love."

Rosie continued with, "Oh, yeah, and you buds owe me big time. I just spent twenty minutes downstairs with Mrs. Trasker."

The policewoman pointed to Kris.

"The long and the short of it is I am supposed to convince you to go back to church, something about her promising your grandmother. Better watch out, those two women are on to you, and they mean business."

"Oh, swell."

I clapped our nephew on the shoulder.

"Good luck with that one, son."

"Dudes and dudettes, I need to split. I promised Coach I would be early for practice. Uncle Nick, we're gonna train later or what?"

I looked at our lovely boy and thought, *Ahhh, to be able to bounce back so quickly from what he has been through. This is a man of action, like his Father. Yes, just like his Father. But perhaps, I'm wrong... There it was in his eyes... a sadness still to be overcome. It will take some time, my brave heart.*

I said, "You will be too tired after practice, Kris. After the game, perhaps on the weekend."

There was a hint of a smile as he shook his head and said, "Be in your gear and out by the pool at four, old man. I'm going to toughen you up big time. Later."

Kayne did an eye roll and stepped out of the exiting jock's way.

Rosie continued. "I cannot stay much longer. Gotta get back to East Bay. I just wanted to do some close out with you."

"Go."

She ticked off the specifics.

"The members of the league will be prosecuted for their killings. The evidence is pretty insurmountable. Marsden can't get out of this. When he recovers from his injuries, he'll stand trial like the rest of them. I'll bet he'll end up reading horoscopes for the San Quentin inmates for a long time.

"The feds are looking into the missing research. Celestia Inc. is over. Lawsuits out the ass. Interpol sends their best. Solving the deaths of the four syndicate leaders has helped ease their caseload."

Kayne spoke up, "But why? It is all too shabby."

Andi asked, "Meaning?"

"Marsden benefited from the deaths of the scientists. That is obvious. Artem Eglievsky? A contract for personal revenge? Seems incongruous. And what is the benefit to the Marsden's Confederacy of the Sun represented by the elimination of the heads of the four criminal organizations? There is much here that does not make sense."

Rosie lowered her voice and looked intently at Kayne.

"Marsden under interrogation revealed that he received the League's assignments, their death contracts, from an unknown source, a source who had the power to destroy Celestia and other enterprises. We are not sure if he is holding back on this one, but it seems the answers lie in that direction. A superpower of international crime who remains a shadow pulling the strings of evil – forgive me if I sound overly gothic, but I think it may be true."

Kayne looked away far beyond the reaches of San Francisco.

"Including why Marsden proposed the murders of the members of our family," I said. "There was one name missing on the kill list, Boss. You know what I am talking about."

Kayne continued with his deep stare face, looking into the void.

"Yes. My brother, Eric, Kris' father."

Kayne paused and stepped closer to the window. His remarks were toneless.

"Now I see it, my friends. Quite elementary in fact. Eric is Marsden's proposed successor to head up the Evil League. The deceased heads of four criminal organizations were in the process of bringing down the one who headed all of their hit lists. My brother. Marsden was in the process of clearing away Eric's enemies and those of us who would prevent his return to his former world."

"The two of you need to be extremely careful. Gentlemen, trust no one."

Rosie's words hung like icicles – cold and ominous.

My husband walked back and slumped in his chair. I moved over and placed my hand on his shoulder. He stared at the case map on the wall, raising his hand to touch mine.

"Yes, I believe there is a far more evil power behind this. One with a vendetta against Sorenson and Sechi because of the work we have done. A presence that sustains a grim fascination with my errant brother. They hope to prevent our continued interference in their web of crime and take Eric into their evil game."

Kayne paused and gestured to the window. The early fall day was bright and sunny as if the pall of the week's dreary weather had been lifted. It seemed that new beginnings were on their way.

He spoke as he looked out at San Francisco.

"We need to figure out a way to ensure the safety of the family, Nick. It is absolutely imperative."

Epilogue: Making Memorial

Golden Gate Park, San Francisco, California

Personal Notes by Kayne J. Sorenson, Ph.D.

"After that game, Friday night, Lad. You sure you are up to this?"

'Sure, Uncle Kayne. I sat around yesterday playing video games with Matt, so this morning's run will be great."

Nick asked, "So is Matt back in the picture?"

"Not sure, to be honest. Says we're on a break but staying close. Whatever."

We were stretching on the grass behind the house. Early fall in San Francisco often featured warm, summer-like weather, and this Sunday morning was no exception. Run time for Sorenson and Sechi Inc.

Traffic was light as we jogged our way to Divisadero Street, then south to Panhandle Park and into Golden Gate Park. We stopped for water from a vendor near the National AIDS Memorial Grove.

It is a very peaceful spot, and I believe Kris did not expect the reverence with which we approached the ten-acre sacred site. We were not the only ones in the serene place among the rhododendrons and the redwood trees. Here and there, people placed flowers, prayed, or held small group memorial services.

The dell was landscaped to perfection. Flagstone gathering areas, Sierra granite boulders, and benches were all etched with individuals' names of individuals lost to AIDS.

I broke our silence by saying, "This is obviously a place for healing, hope, and remembrance. It also serves as an important marker in the history of this dreadful disease."

Kris was amazed.

"I've never been here. Hey, are those dogwoods? They must be incredible in the spring."

I said wistfully, "Most memorials are set up after the battle is over. This particular struggle still rages on."

Nick was lost in thought, struggling in a web of intense memory. He walked away from us to a small boulder beyond the Circle of Friends near a copse of azalea bushes. The stone was etched with the name "Joshua Samuel Birch." Under the name were a few words from a poem by Shelley.

Forget the Past, his fate and fame shall be

An echo and a light unto eternity!

"Dude loved poetry, Boss. He would recite well into the night."

Nick took a flat round stone, half the size of his hand, and placed it on top of the boulder. The branches of a small white tree danced in the breeze as if to say, "Thank you for the prayer." Their green arrowhead-shaped leaves were just starting to turn to gold. Nick spoke with his back to us, concentrating on the space.

"About the time I joined the police force in Wilton Manors, Florida, I heard that Josh had died. I was pretty bowled over, you know. No one dies from AIDS anymore, or so I thought."

He put a hand to his mouth as Kris came up next to him and took the other hand.

"I planted that tree... didn't think it would grow. Guess it did. My pole vaulter... my Joshua... We sure scandalized the folks at St. Raymond's High School in the Bronx. Gay jocks who didn't give a fuck. He was a junior, and I was a freshman... he taught me many things, many manly things..."

Nick looked at us and said, "Yeah, taught me all that rab jab about getting hit by the lightning bolt. Damn."

Never letting go of Kris, Nick looked up into my eyes, touched my cheek, blinked back some moisture, and said, "And it was all true... yeah, every word of it... found out it even strikes twice, when I first met you."

Kris was silent for one incredible moment. Words were inadequate.

Nick turned to him, "And so I said to myself, Nick Man. That's it... the ultimate... fuckin' electrified..."

He looked at Kris and said, "... and then you come along... so, now going three for three."

Hug-up and then more silence.

Key change as Nick dropped Kris' hand. He sighed and looked at the young man. The sadness seemed to dissolve in the bright sunshine of the Grove.

"So, what the fuck did you think you were doing Friday night? You loused up that chest trap, and Loyola stole the damn ball. Checking out some jock arse on the other team? Head in the game, Your Hind Ass."

Kris pushed him off and resumed the run that would take us out of the Grove and further into the park. He turned so that he was running backward and facing us.

Just before Kristof turned back to face forward, he smiled wickedly and mouthed the words, "Bite me."

The End

Thomas Paul Severino

Author's Notes and Acknowledgments

Most of the characters are identified with their astrological signs of the Greek Zodiac. As Kayne tells Nick in Chapter Forty-Five, Ophiuchus is a contested constellation and the thirteenth sign of the Zodiac.

The Japanese and Chinese use an animal sign associated with one's birth year. The people of the Yoruba culture employ date-associated signs within a unique system of divine agents.

The Chamber of the Sun in the San Francisco Mint is my fictional creation. The landmark building is not.

***

With much sincerity and affection, I thank my dear friend Keith Hickman for his excellent and generous work as the copy editor for this and other Kayne Sorenson Mysteries. You help me be a better writer, my friend, and I am very grateful. I highly value your friendship, laughter, and keen insight into the world's doings, both real and imaginary.

I continue to be inspired by my husband, Tony Walner. His intellect, authenticity, humor, and love sustain me and call me to become a better person and author. He is truly a gift for which I am thankful. The sound of Tony's laughter is music to my soul.

Thomas Paul Severino

Afterword:

Thank you for reading <u>The Kayne Sorenson Mysteries: The Evil League.</u> I hope you enjoyed the tale. Nick and Kayne will be back soon. In the meantime, please investigate <u>The Amazing Adventures of Rebecca Quinto: The Last Maya.</u>

An excerpt from this, her latest adventure, follows.

Thomas Paul Severino

The Last Maya

The Amazing Adventures of Rebecca Quinto

Thomas Paul Severino

Thomas Paul Severino

Prologue: Jack

Huehuetenango, República de Guatemala

"Do not delay after school. We have many visitors, and I need all the help you can give me. Hand me the maize flour in the big container, Jacinto."

While Rosalina Ochoa De Leon instructed her sister, Carmencita, on the dinner menu, Jack's mother began preparing one of the dishes. Usually, the inn's cook handled the kitchen responsibilities. Still, over the weekend, the cook got married, and her employers at Casa De Flores Tikal made adjustments. Carmen Varela-Garcia had offered to help her sister. She checked on her baby in the woven baby wrap. The newborn was asleep.

Jacinto Davide De Leon stuffed the last of his eggs-in-a-corn-tortilla roll-up in his mouth, placed his mini tablet on the table, and went for the plastic flour container for his mother.

"Mom, the WiFi is out again."

At eleven, the boy was a savant at navigating the web, social media, and internet information sources, far ahead of his parents, aunts, and uncles.

"Thank you. Finish your mosh, *mi hijo*. Tia Carmen made that porridge herself, just for you."

His Auntie pointed to his bowl and plate. She made her point, saying, "Jack, the most important meal of the day for Guatemalans – *desayuno tipico*. We tell the gringos a 'typical breakfast,' hearty and delicious."

"Ay, do not call him that, Hermana. It sounds so American. That should be enough chilies. Remember, you're not cooking for our family. They are gringos and have delicate stomachs."

He preferred the nickname Jack. His Auntie was cool.

"I need to see to housekeeping. Jacinto, drink your orange juice, and do not forget your lunch. Make sure you eat all of it. Do not give my food to that dog either. Cauli has not finished what is in her bowl. Is everyone in this family wasting food?"

The excited hotelier made the sign of the cross. She pressed her hands together as she said, "There are countless poor children in this city who have nothing to eat. It is a sin to waste food, my son. I put in some of the *pepián* from last night's dinner, your favorite."

"Thank you, Mamá."

The boy gathered up his backpack and kissed his mother and aunt goodbye. His little three-legged dog looked up at him, expecting just one more secret morsel. Jack shrugged, petted his best friend, and said, "See you later, girl. School."

The family pet headed over to her basket in the corner. This was Cauli's favorite spot for watching her humans. From her comfy dog bed, the pet's eyes carefully scanned the comings and goings of the hotel's kitchen. She sighed. *Her boy would be home to play in no time.*

Jack stopped at the kitchen door.

"Mom, don't forget…"

The woman was taking off her apron. She said, "Yes, yes, little one, I will call the WiFi guy."

She raised her eyes to heaven and said, "Americans without internet access… heaven forbid."

***

The Academy of San Cristobal was only three blocks away, behind the big, crumbling church. On the street, Jack De Leon hooked up with his besties, Carlos and Rafaela Maria. They discussed the upcoming math exam and the exciting upcoming civic soccer match.

Rafaela turned around as they walked. She kept moving but backward. Lagging just a bit, she returned to catch up and walk between her companions.

"Are those buzzards following us, you guys?"

"Where?"

"The blue van down the street."

"You are creeping me out, Rae."

"Carlos, it's OK," Jack said. "We'll report it to Ms. Fernanda when we get to school. No one will get in trouble. They are always telling us to say something if we spot trouble."

In the excitement of beginning a new school day at San Cristobal's, the children forgot all about the men in the dark blue van.